The New and Improved
Vivien Leigh Reid

Also by Yvonne Collins and Sandy Rideout

Introducing Vivien Leigh Reid:
Daughter of the Diva
Now Starring Vivien Leigh Reid:
Diva in Training

The New and Improved Vivien Leigh Reid

Diva in Control

Yvonne Collins and Sandy Rideout

St. Martin's Griffin ✠ New York

This is a work of fiction. All of the characters, organizations, and events portrayed in this novel are either products of the author's imagination or are used fictitiously.

THE NEW AND IMPROVED VIVIEN LEIGH REID. Copyright © 2007 by Yvonne Collins and Sandy Rideout. All rights reserved. Printed in the United States of America. No part of this book may be used or reproduced in any manner whatsoever without written permission except in the case of brief quotations embodied in critical articles or reviews. For information, address St. Martin's Press, 175 Fifth Avenue, New York, N.Y. 10010.

www.stmartins.com

ISBN-13: 978-0-312-35828-0
ISBN-10: 0-312-35828-8

First Edition: February 2007

10 9 8 7 6 5 4 3 2 1

The New and Improved Vivien Leigh Reid

one

I scan the crowd around the arrivals gate for one of my mother's conspicuous disguises. With her vast collection of wigs, hats, scarves, and sunglasses, the possibilities are nearly endless but something always blows her cover.

Mom isn't an inept CIA operative; she's an actress, and the disguises are meant to keep her fans at bay. As far as I can tell, the Annika Anderson filmography takes care of that on its own. She has made over twenty films, most of which are simply forgettable, but a few—the ones my Dad likes to watch again and again—are downright awful. So bad, in fact, that Annika was stuck in the B-movie category for years. All that changed three months ago with the release of *Danny Boy,* an A-list movie that has garnered great reviews. Even so, the odds of her being mobbed are pretty remote, especially in Los Angeles, where everyone's a star.

A hand rises from a nearby knot of people and snaps fingers in my general direction. Unless Mom has shrunk, or less likely still, opted for flats, the hand can't be hers. "Annika?" I call uncertainly.

"Don't *ever* call me that," the owner of the hand says, folding every finger but one.

The knot of people parts to reveal Sasha Cohen, my former costar on a soap opera called *Diamond Heights.* As always, she is dressed in white from head to toe. Even the tiny dog under her arm is wearing a white scarf.

As the throng of admirers closes around her again, she says, "Get over here. I can't wait all day."

"Nice to see you too," I grumble, nudging her fans aside. "What are you doing here, anyway?"

She signs another autograph without looking up. "Daddy made me come."

My mother and Sasha's father have been dating for nearly four months, and that fact probably hasn't made Sasha any happier than it's made me. Jake seems like a nice enough guy, but with Sasha coming as part of the Cohen package, I'd rather reconstitute a family somewhere else.

A girl takes her autograph book from Sasha and offers it to me. "I think I've seen you before. You're somebody, right?"

Sasha reaches over and snaps the autograph book closed. "She's nobody. Don't waste your paper." Directing me with her pen, she adds, "I could get through this faster if you'd turn around and stoop."

I let her use my back to sign another dozen autographs. I even hold her purse and her dog without complaint because Dad's last words as he put me on the plane were, "Be nice." It's obviously going to be tougher than I had expected. While I knew I couldn't escape the Cohens entirely during Thanksgiving weekend, I didn't plan on spending a second alone with Sasha.

I assumed that Mom would make that easy by monopolizing my time. After all, I'm only here for four days and we hardly ever see each other. I live with my father in Seattle because Annika abandoned me for Hollywood when I was only three years old.

By "abandoned," I don't mean she left me in a Dumpster. Rather she divorced my father, gave him full custody, and more or less disappeared for twelve years. She claims that Dad didn't want her around me and he claims she didn't try very hard. The only thing they agree on is that she paid regular child support. For a long time, the nicest thing my father could say about Annika was, "At least she's not a deadbeat."

Our family of two (three, counting Grandma Reid) managed

just fine until I hit puberty and my newfound preoccupation with boys and makeup caused Dad to arrange a reunion with my mother. Faster than I could say "no frigging way," I was on a plane to Ireland where Annika was shooting *Danny Boy.*

Mom and I didn't hit it off right away. In fact, we still spend nearly as much time fighting as we do getting along. I guess you can't build a bridge across a twelve-year rift overnight. Our relationship evolves at the pace of a Mardi Gras parade—two steps forward, one step back—but at least it's moving in the right direction.

It helps that we've discovered some common interests, the most important being acting. Mom was initially reluctant to let me take a small role in *Danny Boy,* but when that worked out okay, she became very supportive. At her suggestion, I spent the past summer in L.A. taking an acting course at an elite school. She also encouraged me to audition for *Diamond Heights* and I won the role of Willow Volume over ninety-three other hopefuls.

On the show, Sasha and I both played rich, nasty divas. For her, it was typecasting, although with Jake as producer she didn't have to audition. For me, sadly, it became a matter of life imitating art. Within a matter of weeks, I got so caught up in my role that I started to behave like a diva both on and off the set. By the time the producers created a spin-off show for Willow, my head had become too big for the studio and the role went to Sasha's character instead. Worse, they killed off Willow and I got fired. As in sacked. Terminated. Dismissed. Booted.

It was the most humiliating experience of my entire life and I'm still not over it. There's no mystery about where my diva gene came from, but you'd think that with Dad's sensible accountant genes to offset it, I'd have more self-control.

I've been punished for my behavior by seeing Sasha prosper in the role created for me. She's not the best actress in town—even her father admits that—but she must be doing something right because *Between a Rock and a Hard Place* is doing well. If my inner diva weren't in recovery, I'd give the credit to her surgically enhanced bustline, but the new and improved Leigh Reid is a good sport.

Sasha isn't burdened by the same need to be a gracious. "Stand still," she says, jabbing me in the shoulder with her pen. "And stop squishing Olivier."

I reposition my right hand on my knee and hoist the dog a little higher with my left, silently repeating a yoga mantra: *From the unreal lead me to the real. From darkness lead me to the light.*

After the *Diamond Heights* debacle, I realized I needed something to keep me sane and grounded, and yoga fit the bill. To my surprise, I actually enjoy it. I don't know if yoga is making me a better person, but it's definitely making me a calmer one. If I decide to pursue acting again some day, I'll have the tools to keep my perspective.

Signing her last autograph with a flourish, Sasha starts off down the corridor, leaving me to follow with dog, purse, and my suitcase. When I catch up, she flicks her dark mane over her shoulders and eyes my jeans, pink zip-up yoga jacket, and sneakers. "I see you still haven't found your style. No one's going to give you a part if you look like that."

"I'm not trying to get parts," I say. "I'm just here for a quiet weekend with my mother."

Ignoring this, she heads out to her white Mini Cooper, which is illegally parked in the passenger pick-up area. The airport security guard hovering beside it accepts the fifty-dollar bill she offers him and rushes to open the driver's door. Sasha takes the dog and slides behind the wheel, chitchatting to the guard while I flip down one of the back seats and squeeze my suitcase into the Mini. When I'm done, I open the front door to find the dog carrier strapped to the passenger seat.

"Olivier gets car sick if he isn't up front," Sasha explains. She gets out and holds the seat forward so that I can climb in behind her. "Don't sit on my cover."

There's a copy of *Soap Opera Digest* on the back seat featuring her sultry image.

Before she can grab it, I quickly lower my butt onto her photogenic face.

★　★　★

I hear the muffled sounds of Pink's *Trouble* and retrieve my cell phone from my knapsack. "Mom, where are you?"

"Didn't Sasha tell you? Jake needed my help with the turkey."

"You don't cook," I point out.

"True enough," she agrees. "But I'm a great cheerleader, right, sweetie?" The sweetie in question appears to be Jake because the kissing sounds emanating from my phone are loud enough to make Sasha shudder in the front seat.

"You said we were going out."

"Change of plans, darling. We're having our Thanksgiving tonight because Ursela isn't free on Monday."

Ursela is Sasha's older sister. She doesn't live with Jake, so I don't see why our plans have to revolve around hers. "Can't we just have a quiet night at your place?"

My question comes too late. She is already distracted by clanging pots and pans. "See you soon, darling," she says, and hangs up.

Sasha watches me through the rearview mirror. "When's the last time you spoke to your mother?" she asks.

"A few days ago. Why?"

Her eyes crinkle. "Just curious."

Determined not to play into her mind games, I fish my makeup bag out of my purse. Sasha waits until I'm applying mascara before hitting the brakes to avoid an invisible hazard, thereby causing me to jam the wand into my temple.

"Quiet," she says, over my squeal of pain. "You're scaring Olivier."

I reach for the uneaten tuna sandwich Dad packed for me this morning and consider hiding it under Sasha's seat to rot in the

California heat. The words of my yoga instructor fill my head: *Anger is one of the six poisons that surround the spiritual heart.* Sighing, I put the sandwich back in my bag. Sasha is lucky I've become an enlightened human being.

After a few moments of peace, her cell phone rings. "Hi Gorgeous," she says, her voice soaring up a few octaves into boyfriend range. "I'd be better if you were here with me."

She glances into the mirror again to make sure I'm taking it in. If she's trying to make me jealous, she'll have to work harder because I am on a guy hiatus. Granted, the hiatus wasn't my choice, but after losing two guys this summer, it's actually a relief.

I blew it first with Rory Quinn, the guy I met in Ireland. Rory is cute, kind, and smart, and our long distance relationship lasted an entire year. By the time he visited me in L.A., however, I'd succumbed to diva fever. Under its influence, I'd fallen for someone from my acting class. Gray Cowley has Hollywood roots a mile long and I couldn't understand why he'd be interested in a girl like me. Then I found out he was only interested in what a girl like me could do for his career. Specifically, he wanted to use my connection to Jake Cohen to get a job. By the time I realized Gray was slime, my relationship with Rory had disintegrated.

Losing Gray hurt my pride but losing Rory broke my heart. The only good thing I can say about the experience was that, unlike my firing, the breakup wasn't televised.

Rory went back to Ireland to hate me from afar, and I returned to Seattle to hate Gray from afar. I kept that up until I started yoga class and learned that hatred is the enemy of enlightenment. I can't squander my energy on hating Gray anymore, but that doesn't mean I want to run into him this weekend. Fortunately, L.A. is a big city.

Sasha steers the car onto the Pacific Coast Highway with one hand while continuing to hold her cell to her ear with the other. "As bad as ever," she says, lowering her voice. "She's a loser, just like her mother. It's going to take a week to get the smell out of my car."

It's going to take a lot longer than that. I pull the tuna sandwich out of my bag again and slide it under her seat.

The road to enlightenment is long and I have plenty of time to get there.

★   ★   ★

The Cohen's palm-lined driveway is crowded with cars when we pull in. Sasha parks between a pumpkin patch and a pen containing a large, ugly turkey pecking idly at fake yellow and red leaves. I seriously hope this isn't the bird Annika is helping Jake prepare for dinner.

I look up at the stone beach house, with its wide windows and breathtaking view of the sea. On the wraparound deck, people are watching the sun set with cocktail glasses in their hands.

"Welcome back, beautiful," a male voice says. I press my face to the car window to see Gray Cowley standing beside the Mini. With his messy, sun-bleached hair, unbuttoned white shirt, and faded jeans, he is so hot that I almost forget how despicable he is. "I've missed you so much," he says, offering a brilliant smile.

He has? The last time I saw Gray, he was making fun of my final performance for acting class. Maybe my role in *Danny Boy* made him realize what he lost. Or maybe he had a drug problem last summer that he's managed to kick. That kind of thing happens in Hollywood all the time.

Sasha opens the driver's door and steps out into Gray's arms, saying, "I was only gone an hour."

He fastens his lips to hers. Either he still has the drug problem or Gray has realized that Sasha can do more for his career than I could.

They block my exit from the car until I finally clear my throat. Sasha releases him and turns to me. "Leigh, this is my boyfriend, Gray Cowley."

"We've met," I say, unfolding myself from the Mini. These cars weren't built for anyone over five foot ten. Not that I ever admit to being that tall.

Gray slides his hand down to Sasha's butt and grins at me. "Howya doing, Leigh?"

"Oh, right, I forgot," Sasha says, grinning up at him. "You broke Leigh's heart, didn't you, baby?"

"I liked him for about a minute," I admit. "But that was before he flunked out of acting class."

Gray's smile falters but before he can comment, Jake appears on the deck. He is dressed as a pilgrim in black knee-length pants, long white socks, and shoes with big buckles. Beside him is a tall, thin woman in a fringed, buckskin dress and moccasin-style boots. Her face is streaked with bands of red and yellow makeup, and her long black braids are topped by a single white feather. I hope that isn't who I think it is.

A small white dog in a pilgrim hat jumps into the woman's arms and my heart sinks like a stone.

"Osiyo, Vivien!" my mother calls, coming down to greet me. A blond curl has escaped her wig and encircled one of the braids. "That's Cherokee for 'hello'."

"What's Cherokee for 'politically incorrect'?" Sasha asks Gray.

My mother hugs me with one arm and Brando tries to lick my face. I take him and untie the pilgrim hat. "Annika, when I let you keep my dog, I didn't say you could dress him up like one of your Madame Alexander dolls," I say.

"Oh Vivien, try to get into the Thanksgiving spirit," she says.

"It's Leigh," I remind her. My mother named me after her idol, actress Vivien Leigh. I've always gone by my middle name but she can't get the hang of using it. Similarly, I can't get the hang of using "Mom."

Annika tries to pout but her lips are too freshly pumped with collagen to purse properly. "Jakey," she says, "my daughter could use a dose of your charm."

Handsome, silver-haired Jake gives me a smile that probably works on most women but doesn't on me. That's because most women haven't been fired by him. At least, he let the director of *Diamond Heights* fire me and it amounts to the same thing.

"Leigh," he says, kissing my cheek. "You're even lovelier than your mother."

Neither Annika nor Sasha looks pleased to hear this.

He motions to Gray. "How about taking your arm off my daughter and unloading Leigh's suitcase?"

Gray lunges for the car and Jake leads the procession up the stairs, saying, "Once you're settled in your room, Leigh, come back down and join the party."

I tug on my mother's arm until she slows down. "What does he mean, *my room?*"

"He means you don't have to share a room with Sasha," she says. "Yours is in the east wing, just down the hall from our room."

I stop in my tracks. "*Our* room?" It comes out so loud that Sasha immediately turns to watch.

Annika greets some guests at the top of the stairs as an excuse not to answer.

I wait until she turns back before asking, "Are you living here?"

"Well, most of the time," she says, still not meeting my eyes.

Sasha clears everything up for me. "She moved in last week-end."

★   ★   ★

I flop onto the low, platform bed and stare up at the metal beams that cut across the white ceiling. The sleek, minimalist décor and flat-screen TV are an improvement over the fairy princess bedroom my mother created for me at her place, but it doesn't make up for the fact that it's in Jake's house. I can't believe Annika moved in after only dating him three months. She didn't even ask me how I felt about it. Hell, she didn't even tell me she'd done it. Our relationship is less evolved than I thought: two steps forward, two steps back.

There's a knock at my door but I ignore it. Annika can beg if she wants but I am not joining the party. "Don't you have a peace pipe to smoke?" I call.

"Make me a more interesting offer." The door opens to reveal red dreadlocks that belong to my friend Karis Tate. I run over to give her a hug.

I met Karis in acting class too. Like Gray, she is descended from Hollywood royalty. Her father is a director and her mother, Diana Russell, is an Academy Award–winning actor. Unlike Gray, however, Karis doesn't brag about her connections.

I'm happy to see that she is wearing the little soybean charm I gave her. Our friendship was nearly a casualty of my ego, but I managed to pull out of the dive before it was too late. "It's so good to see a friendly face," I tell her. "I'm surprised my Mom was thoughtful enough to invite you."

"She invited my mother too," Karis says, grinning. "I think Annika wanted to tell her in person that she beat her out for a role."

That sounds like Annika. She is so intimidated by the Oscar attached to Diana Russell's name that she gets all loud and awkward in front of her. Being a diva herself, Diana always let my mother know her place in the pecking order; the fact that she is here at all confirms that Mom's status has improved because of *Danny Boy*. Annika has one stiletto planted on the A list at last.

"Did she mention that she moved in here?" I ask, throwing myself onto the bed again. "It's not like I hate Jake or anything, but—"

"He did fire you," she supplies.

"Exactly. Plus he spawned Satan."

"And gave a role to the guy who used you."

I stare at her. "He did?"

"Yup. Sasha just told me that Gray starts on her show next month."

"This just gets worse by the minute."

She sits cross-legged on the bed. "Gray and Sasha deserve each other. You were way too good for that creep."

"I wasn't at the time," I point out.

Karis laughs. "How is Rory, anyway?"

"Cold. It took him two months to answer my letter of apology. Then he didn't really say much in his e-mail."

"But he's opened the door. Maybe there's hope yet."

I wish that were true but I sense Rory will never really forgive me. After all, he flew all the way from Dublin to spend time with me and I behaved horribly.

Karis stands and pulls me to my feet. "Enough moping. There's a party going on downstairs with some cute guys—and a bartender that doesn't ask for ID."

"I didn't bring anything to wear," I say, examining the meager contents of my suitcase. "I'd planned on borrowing Annika's clothes but I can't just walk into Jake's room and start going through the closet."

"You look fine," Karis assures me. A surfer girl to the core, Karis's standards aren't that high. She has dressed up for the occasion in a T-shirt without holes and baggy cargo pants. "Lose the jacket, though," she says, pushing me toward the door. "There are pen marks all over your back."

★   ★   ★

Annika hovers encouragingly over Karis and me as we troll the overflowing buffet table. My mother is always pushing everyone else to strap on the feedbag without letting a morsel of food touch her own lips.

Gesturing to someone in the front hall, Jake asks, "Is that who I think it is?"

"It's Roger Knelman," I say, following his gaze. Roger was our director on *Danny Boy* but he is also Mom's former boyfriend. The term "boy" is misleading, as Roger is pretty old. "Is that his daughter?" I ask of the twenty-something blonde beside him.

Mom flashes me a look. "That's his wife."

The woman he left Annika for, I suppose. Whatever his shortcomings as a boyfriend, however, Roger is a fine director who managed to bring out Mom's best performance ever.

Jake's eyes have narrowed. Obviously, I'm not the only one

who's aware of their history. "What's he doing here?" he asks my mother.

"I invited him," Annika says. "He's your daughter's director and it would have been rude not to. You can't possibly be jealous, darling." She nuzzles his neck until there's war paint on his chin. "You know you're the only pilgrim for me."

Mollified, Jake trails after Annika to greet Roger.

"What does Dad see in that has-been?"

Karis and I turn to see a slightly older version of Sasha. The hair is a shade lighter and the eyes a shade paler, but otherwise they could pass for twins. Their personalities must be similar too if she's insulting my mother. It's not even true: Annika wasn't anyone before now.

I grope around mentally for my Zen before introducing myself. "I'm Leigh Reid, Annika's daughter."

"I know who you are," Ursela says. "You're the one who got fired from *Diamond Heights*. I suppose you came here expecting Dad to find you another job."

Karis jumps in before I can. "She doesn't need your Dad's help. Some of us win our own parts, you know."

Ursela's eyes widen as the shot hits home. Sasha isn't the only Cohen who has benefited from parental connections. Jake's first wife is a former Broadway star who got Ursela several stage roles. I've heard rumors about why Ursela has since dropped out of acting, but Annika will only confirm that she's taking a break to study stage design.

Running her eyes over Karis, Ursela says, "You don't take after Diana at all."

I'm still trying to figure out how to defend Karis without dissing her mother when a waiter offers us champagne flutes. "For the toast," he says.

The music dies and Jake, now standing before a marble fireplace big enough to roast a bison, calls for everyone's attention. "I'd like to thank all of you for joining Nika and me for our first annual Thanksgiving party," he begins. "I have so much to be thankful for this year, but I must say, this beautiful, talented, classy lady beside me makes the top of the list.

"Classy?" Ursela hisses behind me. "Please."

Karis grabs my sleeve to stop me from responding.

"Nika has brought me so much joy," Jake continues, wrapping his arm around my tittering mother, "that I can barely remember life without her in it. And I never want to experience life without her in it again."

Suddenly, the party around me fades and I feel like I'm watching my own life on the big screen.

Scene 1: Leigh Has a Very Bad Feeling

INTERIOR BEACH HOUSE, NIGHT

Jake stands before a crowd at his tacky Thanksgiving bash and gushes over Annika in her Pocahontas outfit. She gazes up at him, her eyes filled with desperate hope. As Jake reaches for something on the mantel-piece, the camera scans the crowd and zooms in on Leigh's expression of dread. The room goes quiet.

The camera swings back to the fireplace. In slow motion, Jake drops to one knee.

                    JAKE
        Annika, would you do me the honor of be-
        coming my wife?

He holds up a massive diamond ring and then slips it onto Annika's finger. It's a perfect fit.

Tears stream down Annika's face and she turns to-ward her daughter. To the rest of the world, Leigh Reid might look surprisingly calm but Annika knows better. In fact, she realizes instantly that she must put her own dreams on hold for the sake of her daughter.

> ANNIKA
> I adore you with all my heart Jake but I can't marry you—at least not now. I'm still getting to know my wonderful daughter and she needs my undivided attention. I neglected my responsibilities as a mother too long and now I must repair the damage I've caused. I know you'll understand because your own daughters are damaged—so damaged that I can't ask my Leigh to become their stepsister. If you can get them into counseling, we'll talk about marriage later. In the meantime, it would be best for all concerned if Leigh and I moved out tonight.

Annika starts to slip the ring off her finger but thinks better of it. After all, a rock like this may never come along again.

> JAKE
> I'll wait for you, dearest. Seeing you sacrifice so much for your daughter only makes me love you more. I promise to get my daughters the help they need.

A cheer rises from the crowd and the camera zooms in for a close up of Leigh's smiling face.

Karis's voice brings me back to reality. "You're taking this awfully well."

The smile freezes on my face. Instead of turning away from Jake, Annika is clinging to him like a fly on pest strip.

"Yes!" she screams. "A thousand times, yes!" It's a line from the movie version of her favorite Jane Austen novel.

Jake turns in our direction and beckons. "Girls, come on up here. I want to get a photo of my new family!"

I chug the rest of my champagne and chase it with Karis's. Then I make my way to the fireplace.

Sasha follows with her sister, saying, "This is the worst Thanksgiving of all time."

For once, I actually agree with her.

two

I sit at the top of the stairs listening to the clatter of dishes and muted voices in the kitchen below. With last night's party still fresh in my mind, I haven't been able to bring myself to face everyone at our first "family" breakfast. All the yoga in the world can't help me adjust to sharing my life with Sasha Cohen.

The voices suddenly get much louder and Jake's angry bass rumbles up the stairs: "You lied to me!"

My mother says, "Jake, calm down."

"How can I calm down?"

I get to my feet and run down the stairs. If they're breaking off the engagement already, I want to be there to witness it.

Clad in a navy silk dressing gown, Jake is pacing angrily beside the long granite counter when I enter the kitchen. Annika trails behind him in her powder blue, feathered negligee wringing her hands. Brando trails behind Annika in his matching blue collar. Sasha and Ursela sit at the polished oak table watching the parade.

Although it's only eight A.M., Annika is coiffed and fully made up. She must have risen before dawn to get a jump on it. I wonder if Jake has even seen her without makeup before. If not, he'd better stick a viewing clause into her pre-nup. The man has a right to know exactly what he's getting.

Not that Mom isn't attractive. She is. In fact, with her golden curls cascading artlessly, as they are today, she looks angelic. But it isn't artless. It takes a lot of time and a lot of money—more every year—to pull it off.

"What's wrong?" I ask, bending to scoop up Brando just as Olivier snaps at him. His teeth graze my hand instead and Sasha smiles.

"Nothing's wrong," Annika says, her voice higher than normal. Whatever Jake thinks she's done, she sounds guilty of it. A secret affair, perhaps, or undisclosed debts. Maybe there's another abandoned child she just remembered.

"Like hell it isn't," Jake says.

Sasha gets up from the table and walks over to the coffee pot. "Dad, you're totally overreacting."

Something isn't right here. Sasha can't be defending Annika. "About what?" I press.

Jake turns to me with an expression I recognize, even though his eyes are blue and my father's are a muddy hazel. "About my daughter getting arrested for drunk driving—and lying about it."

Sasha heaves an exaggerated sigh as she tops up her coffee. "I didn't think it was a big deal. Everyone in this town has had a DUI."

"Not my daughter—my *underage* daughter!"

Ursela weighs in from the kitchen table. "Come on, Dad, Sasha barely blew over. And it's her first offence."

"That's supposed to make me feel better?" he asks, pacing again.

Annika wraps an arm around his waist and bats several coats of mascara at him until he slows down. "It's partly our fault, Jake," she says. "We offered the champagne and we didn't take her car keys."

"She used to have better judgment," he says.

"It's probably Gray's influence," I suggest helpfully. I reach for the Cheerios and Sasha deliberately slops hot coffee onto my hand.

Jake turns on Sasha again. "Is that boy behind this? I'll fire him, Sasha, don't think I won't. And I'm grounding you until you get your license back."

Sasha rolls her eyes at Ursela. Something tells me that their father doesn't follow through on many of his threats.

Missing this silent exchange, Annika bravely steps in to support Sasha. "She's been punished enough, Jake. Losing her license for a year is a high price to pay." She turns to Sasha. "You've learned your lesson, haven't you, honey?"

I don't believe this. If I got caught driving under the influence, Annika would have the cops drive me straight to a rehab facility. She's desperate to ingratiate herself with Jake's kids.

Turning beseeching eyes on her father, Sasha says, "I've learned my lesson, Daddy. Really. It was a stupid mistake and I promise it will never happen again."

She squeezes out a single tear that melts Jake's heart instantly. "Alright, enough said, kiddo. Just as long as you understand this is serious."

"I feel terrible," she says, dabbing at the tear.

I'm impressed by the improvement in her acting skills. On *Diamond Heights,* Sasha wasn't able to cry on command. "Bravo," I say. "Nice performance."

She scowls at me for a moment. "You're wearing a white shirt."

"Very good! Now what color are my jeans?" I shouldn't be goading her, but I figure my mother's surprise engagement earns me a day off the enlightenment track.

"White is my signature color," she says.

"The stores didn't get your memo: They're still selling it to other people."

Annika floats over and hugs me. "I haven't said a proper good morning to my maid of honor."

I slip out of her grasp and walk to the fridge. "Isn't it customary to ask if I want that role?"

She giggles nervously. "Of course you do. Every girl dreams of being her mother's maid of honor."

I grab the soy milk and turn to face her. "There's something fundamentally wrong with that sentence."

"Well . . ." She hesitates. "I suppose most girls would prefer their parents to stay married to each other—"

"You got that right," Ursela interrupts.

"But life doesn't always work out that way," Annika continues smoothly. "Your father and I divorced a long time ago, Vivien, and now I have a second chance at wedded bliss. I want the most important person in my life to be a part of that."

If I were the most important person in her life, she probably would have remembered to tell me she'd moved in here. The truth is, Annika is the most important person in Annika's life.

"We've already set the date: Valentine's Day. Isn't that romantic?"

I snort. "And so original."

"Darling, you're becoming as cynical as your grandmother."

I don't bother defending Grandma Reid because she takes plenty of shots at Annika too. According to Dad, Grandma didn't think much of my mother even before she abandoned Dad and me, and she certainly hated her afterward. She wasn't too thrilled when Dad sent me to Ireland, especially when I took an interest in acting. I guess that's because I was showing signs of being Annika's daughter.

Prior to that, my mother and I had nothing in common but the so-called beauty mark on our left cheeks. I have Dad's hazel eyes, mousey brown hair, and bone structure. Specifically, I've been described as having a muscular build, although I don't see how that's possible when I never worked out prior to discovering yoga. As for personality, I would have said that Annika and I were complete opposites until I went off the rails during *Diamond Heights*. Grandma was right to be concerned.

"You've spent far too much time with that old . . . woman," Annika continues. "It's just as well you're going to stay here until the wedding."

"What do you mean, *stay here?*" I glance at Sasha, who appears to be equally shocked. "I can't stay in L.A."

"Why not?" Mom asks. "You were all for it three months ago."

"A lot has changed since then."

"Like she got fired," Ursela offers.

"And dumped by Gray," Sasha adds.

I ignore the demonic chorus. "I'm in the middle of a school term, Annika."

"And you hate your school," she says. Turning to Jake she adds, "She calls it the Turd Academy."

"The *Nerd* Academy," I correct, as the sisters guffaw. "It's for gifted students."

"I've already spoken to your father and he's going to arrange for you to study by correspondence," Annika says. "You can stay as long as you like!"

If Dad gave in so easily, it can only mean that he is resigned to seeing Annika move on with her life. He used to be so angry that he would only refer to her as "the actress." I thought he might still love her under all that venom, but this fall he's been dating more. Not that he admits to it, but he started "working late" more often on Thursday and Friday nights. Naturally he always gets home before midnight to set an example for me. Dad is hyperconscious of being a good role model.

"Leigh, be reasonable," Mom says, pleading now.

"For God's sake, Annika, let her go home," Sasha says, so urgently that Olivier fires off a volley of barks at nothing.

I glare at Sasha. "Isn't there somewhere you have to be? It's a beautiful day for a drive."

"Dad!" she protests.

Jake has been staying out of it, but I can tell he's uncomfortable because he's picked up the same piece of toast several times and put it back down without taking a bite. "You provoked her, Sasha," he says. Turning to me, he says, "Leigh, we're counting on you to help plan the wedding. It would mean the world to both of us."

Obviously, Jake isn't above sucking up to the future step kid either. "I can't," I say. "I have a life back in Seattle."

That's overstating the case. I don't actually have many friends at the Nerd Academy, and I already dated—and got dumped by— the only cute guy in the whole school. Now even Dad wants to off- load me. The only reason to hurry home would be Grandma and that's pretty sad.

"I guess I'll need to sweeten the deal," Jake says. "And I know just the thing: There's an opening on my new show that you'd be perfect for."

"On the catering truck?" Ursela asks.

He shakes his head at her. "Leigh is a good actress. *Diamond Heights* may not have worked out but this show is quite different."

Freak Force, he explains, is an action-adventure series. The pilot has already been shot and tested on viewers and the audience complained that it's too male dominated. Jake has asked the writer to create a role for a female lead.

"Leigh can't play a superhero," Sasha scoffs. "She could barely play herself on *Diamond Heights*."

Freak Force doesn't sound like my kind of show and I'm not that interested in acting again—at least not yet. Still, I find myself saying, "I can chase bad guys, Sasha."

Jake looks at Annika and says, "You don't even need to audition, Leigh. You'd be doing me a favor."

I recognize a shameless bribe when I see one. Well, Leigh Reid's affections cannot be bought. "That's a nice offer, Jake, but I prefer to *earn* my roles—unlike some people."

"My, what high principles you have," Sasha says. "You can tell your friends at the Turd Academy all about them when you blow back to Kansas."

"Seattle," I yell over my shoulder as Annika herds me out of the kitchen.

In the hall, she says, "You are being very rude, young lady. Jake just made you a very generous offer."

"*Generous* maybe, but not gen*uine*. He only did it because he knows you want me to stay. Didn't you tell him I don't want to act anymore? And even if I did, I'd rather prove my worth."

Annika fixes me with icy blue eyes. "How are you going to manage that if no one will put you in front of a camera? Hollywood is a small town with a big memory, Vivien. People won't forget what happened on *Diamond Heights*."

"They can't write me off because of one show," I protest. "Especially when I had good reviews."

She shakes her head impatiently. "With a hundred hopefuls lined up for every part, producers don't need to take chances on someone who has a rep for being hard to work with."

A rep? I have a rep? I sink down on a bench and stare at the marble floor. If only I could rewind that whole experience and play it over. I'd trap the diva genie in her bottle and bury it.

Noting her advantage, Annika says, "I'm not pressuring you to make a career of acting, but if you're at all serious about it, you should take this job. You'll need to prove your worth to keep it."

"I can't," I say.

She taps one feathered mule. "Why on earth not?"

I have a dozen reasons but the flimsiest one pops out. "Because it's action-adventure. That's not real acting."

"Tell it to Jennifer Garner," she says. "I know you're scared, Vivien, but don't let it hold you back from a good opportunity."

"Scared? I am not scared! *Freak Force* just sounds lame."

"It's going to be a hit, I'm sure of it. The male leads are dreamy."

"*Dreamy?* You can't say things like that anymore."

"I'm engaged, darling, not dead." Sensing the battle is won, she extends her left hand to admire her ring. "Shall I tell Jake you've changed your mind?"

"I'm thinking about it." What I'm thinking is that doing this show could banish my firing from Hollywood's collective memory. It will clean the slate.

"Don't think too long," she says, gliding back into the kitchen. "Or Ursela may decide to give acting another try."

★   ★   ★

"What choice did I have?" I ask Karis. "She threw my 'rep' in my face."

We're sitting outside a changing room in Wedding Belles Bridal Shop. Annika hijacked our plan to spend the afternoon hiking in Topanga Canyon and dragged us shopping instead. She claimed she wanted help choosing a theme for the wedding, but what she really wants is to orchestrate a détente between the Cohen girls and me.

"I'll still have to prove my worth once we start shooting," I continue, doodling on a magazine to avoid meeting Karis's eyes. "But I feel like a total hypocrite."

"Don't," she says. "If my mom got me a role on a show, I'd take it in a second."

"You would?" I ask, relieved. Because Karis's parents don't support her acting ambitions, she's been trying to get parts the hard way, through cattle call auditions. She's already won two guest appearances on sitcoms, so it's just a matter of time before she gets something big. Still, I feel guilty about having an opportunity handed to me on silver platter.

"You'd be so much better than I am for this show, Karis. It's action-adventure and you know I prefer mental workouts to physical ones."

"I can help you train if you want. It'll be good for me too." She taps the magazine I'm holding and adds, "Nice job."

Sasha dropped her purse and a copy of *Soap Opera Digest* on the coffee table to leave both hands free to browse the racks with Ursela. I've adorned her photograph with horns and a bushy mustache. With Karis's input, I draw a thought bubble over Sasha's head and write something obscene in it.

Jake showed me the *Freak Force* pilot earlier so I describe the storyline to Karis. It's about college students who gain superpowers after stumbling onto a secret nuclear-testing site during an African safari. A sudden explosion causes their DNA to merge with animal DNA, and when they regain consciousness, the government recruits them to fight the forces of evil.

"Cool," Karis says when I'm done. "Are the guys as hot as your mother says?"

"I didn't notice. I'm only doing this to clean the slate, Karis. It makes no difference to me what my costars look like."

Karis blackens some of Sasha's teeth on the magazine cover. "Of course not. But how hot are they?"

I take the magazine and fan myself with it. "Explosive."

Karis laughs. "What role do you play?"

"The girlfriend of one of the guys. She was given up for lost after the nuclear disaster but reappears in the second episode. The guys play a panther, a gazelle, and a cheetah, so maybe I'll be a lion. Or a zebra."

Karis takes the magazine out of my hand and defaces it further. "You sound excited."

I nod sheepishly. "I didn't expect to be but I am. I just want to prove myself again, Karis. I swear I am going to work my butt off until no one in this city remembers what happened on *Diamond Heights*."

The door to a changing room opens and Annika's blond curls appear atop a vast cone of white ruffles and tulle. A salesclerk gathers up the train and steers Mom onto a pedestal before a three-way mirror. As she twirls, the skirt sways like Scarlett's hoop skirt in *Gone with the Wind*.

"What do you think?" she asks, breathlessly.

"I think your corset is too tight, Scarlett."

"Ignore her," Annika tells the frowning clerk. "That's my daughter's idea of humor. *I* think this dress is stunning."

"Stunning is right," I say, as Karis struggles to keep a straight face. "It looks like a bomb went off in a toilet paper factory."

Annika admires her reflection. "I'm a bride, darling, and I want to look like one."

I flush with embarrassment for her. "But you're forty-fo—"

"Vivien," she says, puffing with indignation as she always does when her age is mentioned. "There is no law saying you have to be twenty to wear white. And no bride is a virgin these days anyway."

"I'm glad you're so progressive, Mom. It means I can explore my options while I'm here. Dad's so uptight about the whole sex thing."

She smiles at me in the mirror. "I have double standards for you, darling."

"I've noticed."

Sasha steps out of another changing room wearing a sleek, revealing white dress that showcases her toned body. She walks over to the pedestal and says, "Do you mind, Annika?" Annika gathers her crinoline and steps down so that Sasha can admire herself from every angle. "Isn't it gorgeous?" Sasha asks.

If Mom is annoyed by Sasha's efforts to upstage her, she hides it well. "You and Gray must be pretty serious if you're trying on wedding gowns," she says, smiling.

"We are," Sasha declares. "And I knew this one would be perfect for me."

"Everything is perfect when you're sixteen," Annika says, her smile fading.

Sasha turns to look at her. "Well, you look nice too, Annika. It's a lot of layers but you can carry it off."

Ursela says, "Absolutely. Dad will love you in that."

Mom cranes around Sasha to look in the mirror. "Do you really think so?" She sounds doubtful now. "I just want this to be a very special day."

Karis comes over to reassure her. "It will be. Don't worry."

Annika beams at Karis and straightens her shoulders. "My first wedding was a disaster, you know." She catches my eye and backpedals. "Well, 'disaster' isn't the word. It was more like a non-event. Leigh's father doesn't believe in wasting money on fuss and bother."

That sounds like my father alright. If it weren't for Grandma, my birthday might pass unnoticed.

Annika keeps talking. "I wanted to wear a beautiful dress on my wedding day, but Dennis had decided we should invest our savings in a condo. So I wore a suit I already owned. We got married at City Hall and celebrated with a small luncheon afterward. It was low-key, to say the least."

She sighs, still disappointed over my father's romantic shortcomings all these years later. No wonder their marriage didn't work out. Dad married a butterfly when he should have settled for a moth.

"That's a sad story," Ursela says, smirking.

"But my happy ending is still to come," Annika says, brightening as the sun hits her diamond ring and casts spangled light onto Sasha's dress.

"You'll have to do it up right this time," Sasha says. She steps off her pedestal to select a glittering rhinestone tiara for Annika. "Try this."

"A tiara?" Annika asks. "Isn't it too much?"

She has to ask? If there's one thing I can say for Annika, she's usually pretty sharp. Her desperate need to win over the Cohen girls is dulling her edge.

"Mom . . ." I begin.

Ursela speaks over me. "It's perfect. You look like a princess."

"I can't wait to see Dad's face when he sees you in it," Sasha says. "Buy the dress now before someone else does."

I can't just stand by and let them make a fool of my mother. That's my job and right now she's too easy a mark. "Mom, this is the first dress you've tried on. Let's check out a few more stores before you make any decisions."

Annika seems relieved to have an out. "Well, if you think so, darling. Trying on dresses is half the fun, after all."

Sasha glares at me before stomping back into her changing room. I bend over and slide her purse and *Soap Opera Digest* under the door before beckoning Karis and making a run for it.

★　★　★

Annika is alone when she tracks us down at the closest Starbucks' patio. "I figured I'd find you here," she says, sitting across from us wearily. Even Brando is drooping over her arm, exhausted from the wedding frenzy.

"How'd you manage to shake the witches?" I ask.

"Vivien," she says, "you're not making this any easier."

"Mom, the sooner you accept that your future stepdaughters are evil, the sooner you can call in expert help."

Annika turns to Karis. "Can't you do something with her?"

Karis shakes her head. "She's right about the Cohen girls. At my school, people still talk about how sadistic Ursela was. Now Sasha is following in her footsteps."

"I know they can be . . . difficult," Annika concedes, "but I have to win them over—for Jake's sake."

"Mom, they make fun of you."

"I'm getting used to that," she says, raising her eyebrows at me.

"Yeah, but I'm your flesh and blood," I point out. "Plus, I don't make fun of Jake."

"We'll have to make the best of it, darling," she says, before leading us out to the parking lot.

We climb into Annika's new BMW sedan—a "moving in" gift from Jake. The license plate says HERS, and the car is custom painted claret, just like Mom's vintage Volkswagen Beetle.

"Hey, Mom," I say. "Since you've upgraded, can I drive your Beetle while I'm here?"

She turns the key in the ignition. "I'm afraid not. It wouldn't be right to let you drive when Sasha can't."

"But that's not fair! I'm a responsible driver and I shouldn't be punished for Sasha's mistakes."

"It would only cause more tension, darling. We have to start thinking about what's good for the entire family."

"If I promised to try to get along with the Cohen Coven would you let me drive the Beetle?"

She shakes her head. "We'll carpool to the studio. It will give you and Sasha a chance to get to know each other better."

I cast a despairing look at Karis in the backseat. "Can you hook me up with a hit man?"

three

It's the bodysuits I notice first. Any girl would. In fact, it's tough to notice anything else. There must be strategic padding in there, because no human male could look *that* good without help.

Mind you, these aren't human males, but human*oids*—a blend of wild animal and college freshman. And they're my costars on *Freak Force*.

I just arrived at the studio for the first time and I'm waiting in the shadows for the director to surface. The rest of the cast is in the middle of shooting a scene in which they're stalking an armed man in a technology laboratory.

There's nothing for me to do at the moment but admire the scenery and marvel over the wardrobe department's genius in creating the sleek and futuristic costumes. It's *Matrix* meets the savannah. The Gazelle is wearing a taupe bodysuit with two black stripes running down the sides and a headpiece with horns. The Cheetah's bodysuit is gold and black and the actor has amber-hued contact lenses. And the Panther—the hottest of the three—is wearing a shiny black bodysuit, a hood, and a skinny visor over his eyes. All the actors' faces are slightly enhanced by prosthetics, which makes them appear almost like mythical creatures: part human, part god.

I think I've found a new religion.

The Panther advances slowly across the set toward the villain and crouches behind him. Sensing a threat, the villain spins, sees the Freak Force, and bolts. The Cheetah bounds across the set, tackles the villain, and pins him to the floor. The Panther circles menacingly. Meanwhile, the villain's sidekick appears in the doorway, and the Gazelle crosses the room in a single leap to kick the gun out of his hands.

I watch, mesmerized, as the actors perform a series of martial arts moves. It's almost like a dance. They lunge and leap and kick in a controlled, graceful way. There are thuds and grunts and scraping noises that I assume will be overdubbed later with suspenseful music to heighten the drama.

It's so different from *Diamond Heights,* in which the characters mostly shopped, hung out at clubs, and dissed each other. The only stunt I got to perform was my character's death scene, and then all I had to do was flail around and fall off a stage.

Dad teased me later that it wasn't acting—it was just taking my natural clumsiness to new levels. But I don't think I'm *that* clumsy. Sure, I've been known to walk into stationary objects or fall off curbs, but only because I don't always pay attention to what's going on around me. Grandma is probably closer to the truth in saying I have a "busy brain." I can focus when I need to focus. Still, learning the superhero choreography is probably going to be a stretch for me.

Abby, my best friend, seems to think so. I was so excited about landing the part that I called her in New York. I should have stuck to a text message because then I wouldn't have had to hear her laughing insanely at the thought of me doing martial arts. I expect that sort of honest response from Karis, but Abby is usually more tactful. She doesn't fully understand how sensitive the aspiring thespian can be.

I'm the first to admit I'm not athletic. The Nerd Academy's emphasis on cerebral pursuits has left me free to enjoy an inactive lifestyle. It's a sad waste of what our high school nurse calls my "healthy Body Mass Index." My recent discovery of yoga has made me stronger and more flexible, but I sense it's going to take more than that to fly across the room on a guide wire.

Hopefully my character is one of the less adventurous savannah dwellers. A zebra, for example. As far as I can tell, all they do is graze and maybe make a run for it when the lions are hungry. Even I can run. Plus, black-and-white stripes would be perfect to distract viewers' eyes from the skintight bodysuit. Knowing how television works, however, I won't get off that easily. I'm the only woman in the cast and they're probably going to want to put me in some sexed-up Elektra-style costume. I'd prefer to be known for my acting skills rather than my physique, but the stiletto boots would be fun. I can see myself now, twirling through the air, looking chic while high-kicking the crap out of the bad guys. . . .

"CUT!" The shout brings me back to reality. It's obviously the director, but he must be watching the action from monitors behind the set because I can't see him. "Let's do another take," he says. "Rudy, I need you to hold your head up when you do the leap. I want to see that pretty face."

Pretty face? That's an odd thing for a director to tell a male lead. Come to think of it, that whiny petulant voice sounds familiar. And not in a good way.

"My horns get stuck in the guide wire if I raise my head," says Rudy, the gazelle.

"YP, not MP," the director says.

Uh-oh. The expression means "Your Problem, Not My Problem" and there's only one person I've met who's rude enough to use it: Chaz, the director's assistant from *Diamond Heights*. For some reason, Chaz loathed me on sight, and when my character ultimately got the axe, he did a dance of joy.

If Chaz is my new director, choreography is going to be the least of my worries.

★　★　★

Chaz's tie arrives on set before he does. It's extremely wide and covered in pink dollar signs, but what's really odd is that it's been hacked off mid-chest. I can tell by his swagger that this isn't the result of a chance encounter with a chainsaw, but a deliberate style statement. He's also wearing sunglasses in a darkened studio.

How is it that some divas prosper in Hollywood and others die horribly? Where's the justice? He even manages to get away with using only one name, like Madonna.

I wait until he's finished speaking to the actors before offering a tentative, "Chaz?"

His nose wrinkles as if he smells something foul and he turns his shades in my direction. "Yes?"

"It's me. Leigh Reid. I'm here for my wardrobe fitting and makeup test."

Without so much as acknowledging me, he walks away. I follow, dodging between equipment carts, until he reaches the craft services table. He pours a cup of coffee and sips it before raising his shades to look me over. Snapping the shades back into position, he bellows, "LEX."

Before I have time to wonder if that's even a word, a mini-Chaz appears, complete with sawed-off tie and eyeliner. His shades are resting in a bleached blond mop of hair with roots as dark as Chaz's. The guy flips up the headset of his walkie-talkie and asks, "Yes, sir?"

"Coffee? Bitter?" Chaz says. "Hello!"

Lex isn't fazed by the sarcastic shorthand. He swings his headset into position and depresses the switch clipped to his vest. "Craft services, we've got a Code Red at the table! Repeat, Code Red!" To Chaz he adds, "Fresh pot on the way, sir."

Chaz beckons. "Come."

I'm not sure if he means both of us but I tag along anyway.

"I'm not happy about this," Chaz says, dropping into his director's chair.

"Stale coffee is inexcusable, sir," Lex says. "I'm sorry."

"Not that—*her*." Chaz jerks his head toward me. "I didn't write a part for a girl on this show."

"You're the writer?" I ask.

He acknowledges me for the first time. "Don't sound so surprised, Scarlett." That's a reference to Scarlett O'Hara, the character Vivien Leigh played in *Gone with the Wind*. When I auditioned for *Diamond Heights,* I used a scene from the movie and Chaz apparently hasn't gotten over it. "I wrote a fabulous pilot and I refused to sell it until a studio agreed to let me direct."

"That's great, Chaz," I say. "Congratulations." My progress toward enlightenment has made saying this almost painless. "Thanks for deciding to let a girl join the cast. I promise I won't let you down."

"The mere fact that you're here is a letdown," he says. "I didn't 'decide' to let a girl join the cast, the studio did. And I can't believe Jake Cohen made me hire you knowing that you got fired from *Diamond Heights* for bad behavior." He leans forward to stare at me, forgetting that the impact will be diminished by the shades. "I'm warning you, Scarlett, there is no room on my set for a diva."

Before I can answer, a guy from craft services arrives and presents Chaz with fresh coffee. Chaz turns the shades on him and says, "Cup? Hello!"

Lex jumps in to translate. "He prefers china."

So, what Chaz really means is, there's no room on his set for *another* diva.

★   ★   ★

A thirty-something bald guy in a vintage Rolling Stones T-shirt lets me into the hair and makeup trailer and says, "Effluvia?"

Maybe there's a secret password no one's told me. "Pardon me?"

"Effluvia," he repeats. "That's your character."

Effluvia . . . I like the sound of that. It's strong yet feminine—just what a superhero should be.

"Didn't Alex tell you?" he asks.

"You mean 'Lex'?"

He nods. "He left your script for you but it's NMJ—that's

Chaz-speak for 'Not My Job'—to brief you on your character." I pick up the script from the couch but he takes it from me. "Rule number one in my trailer is no reading during makeup. I need a blank canvas to work my magic."

"No problem," I say. In my experience, makeup people can be temperamental artists but they do work magic. In half an hour, they can hide my mole, make my nose look smaller, and transform me from an average teenager into a glamorous woman. "What's rule number two?"

Ushering me to a chair, he spins it away from the mirror and says, "No one sees my creations until they're complete."

"I can live with that . . . ?"

"Drake," he supplies, smiling at last. "And rule number three: no chitchat while I'm working." He plugs an iPod into speakers and mystical lounge music fills the trailer. "This is going to take a while. You might want to use the time to meditate."

I close my eyes. "Feel free to hide my mole."

Drake is already clattering his products. "Trust me, when I'm done, you won't recognize yourself."

My transformation into Effluvia actually began an hour ago when a dresser from the wardrobe department helped me into a dark gray bodysuit. It's similar to the ones the guys are wearing, except that mine is iridescent and covered with sparse little hairs. Although it's skintight, I don't feel nearly as exposed as I used to in Willow Volume's bikinis on *Diamond Heights*.

Effluvia obviously isn't a zebra, but the dresser got called away before giving me any clues about her role in the Freak Force. While Drake pats product onto my face with a sponge, I ponder the options. An elephant is the obvious choice but Chaz wouldn't go there. Ditto a hippopotamus. There's nothing cool about pachyderms, and as much as Chaz hates me, he's not going to ruin the look of his show. He takes himself too seriously for that. Maybe Effluvia is a human crossed with an exotic bird . . .

Scene 2: Leigh Takes Off

INTERIOR STUDIO, DAY

Leigh Reid peers nervously over the edge of the plat-form as the dresser attaches silver wings and talons to her costume. On the set far below, the other actors have taken their marks.

CHAZ
Scarlett, we can't wait all day.

The grips strap Leigh to the guide wire. Below, the faces of the Panther, the Cheetah, the Gazelle, and the villain are turned up to watch.

CHAZ
And...action!

The grips lower Leigh from the edge of the platform and give her a gentle push. She soars out over the set, feeling weightless and free. Angling her wings, she spirals downward gracefully before snatching the villain with her talons and arcing back up to the platform.

CHAZ
Cut! Leigh, that was perfect. You nailed it in one take. You are Effluvia.

The rest of the cast gathers as Leigh climbs down to join them.

PANTHER
Welcome to the cast. You're amazing.

"Stop smiling," Drake says, shaking my shoulder. "A blank canvas, remember?"

"Sorry," I say. I'm actually glad he interrupted because I was letting my imagination get carried away. There's no point fooling myself that this is going to be easy. It won't be, and the sooner I start being realistic, the better.

Scene 3: Leigh Gets Real

INTERIOR STUDIO, DAY

The grips shove Leigh Reid off the platform and she sails out on the guide wire, screaming. It's so much higher than she expected and the wire doesn't feel sturdy enough to support someone with her healthy BMI. Arms pinwheeling, she flails until one wing snags the wire. Leigh plummets to the floor and takes the villain down with her. He curses, although that's not in the script. There's an audible snap as Leigh's ankle breaks.

CHAZ

Cut! You ruined another take, you idiot.

PANTHER

[helping Leigh to her feet]

Lighten up, dude! Can't you see her ankle
is broken?

LEIGH

[hobbling toward the ladder]

Let's go again, Chaz. I'll get it right
this time, I promise.

"I said, stop smiling," Drake says. "You don't want to be here forever, do you?"

It already feels like forever. I expected prosthetics after seeing the rest of the Freak Force, but I had no idea it would take so long to apply them. If I'm going to have to spend so much time in this chair every day, I'd better start using it wisely.

Meditation is a great idea, especially with all the stress in my life right now. I could use the help to stay focused on set. Plus, it will keep me from telling Chaz exactly what I think of him.

★ ★ ★

Drake is still at work when I wake up. I must have been out for a while because my whole face feels different. It's tight and compressed, as if someone stuck my head into a china vase.

"Keep your eyes shut," he says, "I'm almost done." He spins my chair to face the mirror. "Open!"

I open my eyes and blink into the bright lights.

"What do you think?" he prods.

I want to scream but my voice has turned to dust.

Horns. I have horns.

"Am I a . . . *a rhino?*" I rasp.

"A rhino! How could you say that? A rhino has one large horn." He takes a paintbrush and counts out my horns. "One, two, three, four. What animal has four small horns?"

I shake my head and my long, narrow nose wags from side to side. "I don't know."

This isn't a test I'd normally fail. Animals have been my lifelong passion, and until I tried acting, I'd planned to become a vet one day. The prosthetics seem to be affecting my brain.

Reaching up, I poke the wrinkly gray bump at the end of my nose with one finger. It's rubbery and lifelike. "A wild boar?" I suggest.

"Close. A warthog." He fumbles around on his tray until he finds an odd-looking contraption with white crescents. "Your tusks, Effluvia."

I clench my jaws. "I am not wearing those. No way."

Drake shakes his shaved head. "Just once I'd like to meet an actor who puts her craft before her vanity."

He offers the tusks again and this time, I open wide.

★ ★ ★

The only way I can tell that Lex is amused when he arrives to collect me is that his eyebrows shoot up over his shades. I don't let on that I'm fazed by the costume because a professional takes such things in stride.

The prosthetics are reasonably light, but the nose is so long that I feel like I'm tipping forward. As if my own nose weren't big enough! I turn to say good-bye to Drake and my snout hits the doorframe.

"Careful," he calls after me. "That's my handiwork."

I turn to Lex and ask, "Ho con Eshlusia's coshume ore colicated than eddyone elshes?"

Lex stops walking to stare at me. "Excuse me? I don't speak warthog."

I take the tusks out of my mouth. "I said how come Effluvia's costume is more complicated than everyone else's?"

"Because she was closer to the nuclear explosion and the damage to her DNA was more severe," he says. "She's the least human member of the Force."

Of course she is. Chaz, the creator, made sure of that. He probably thinks I'll throw a diva tantrum and quit, but he's going to have to work a lot harder than that to scare off Leigh Reid. I see his challenge and I accept it. I will act my butt off to show viewers the humanity that remains within poor, deformed Effluvia's heart.

Lex escorts me back to the wardrobe trailer and the dresser does a double take when he sees me.

"Wow," he says. "Wow. Wow." Then he collects himself. "Drake is a master, isn't he?"

"Sure," I agree, because I know Lex is going to report anything I say to Chaz. "The bodysuit is nice too."

"Wait till you see the rest of your costume," the dresser says, reaching for two gray sacks, each dotted with bristles. He hooks one onto the front of my suit and the other onto the back, creating a paunch balanced by a bulbous backside. Working *this* butt off might be hard.

I waddle around the trailer in the costume. It feels as if the Earth's gravity has gotten stronger. "Could these be made from something lighter?" I ask.

"They need to be heavy to move like the real thing," the dresser explains.

Lex frowns. "I hope you're not making diva demands already. Chaz won't like it."

"It was just a question," I say. "Anyway, I'm sure I'll get used to them."

The dresser points to my hind quarters. "It's the best part."

I crane my neck and see a scrawny string attached to my new bottom that has a tuft of black hair on the end of it.

He hands me a small remote control device. I press the red button and my tail jerks upright.

Lex gives up his serious act and laughs so hard his shades slide down his nose and his eyeliner runs.

"Warthogs hold their tails in the air when they run," the dresser explains, struggling to keep a straight face.

I examine myself in the mirror. Inside, vanity and professionalism are fighting a desperate battle, but the force of good is winning. That's mainly because I can see the upside to the situation. Specifically, this costume hides every last trace of Leigh Reid, and that means I can either succeed or fail on *Freak Force* without anyone even recognizing me.

"I'm so glad Chaz ditched the zebra idea," Lex sputters. "The warthog is inspired."

I turn my snout in his direction. "He was going to make Effluvia a zebra?"

Lex nods. "Changed his mind at the last minute."

The minute *after* Jake told him he'd cast me in the role.

★   ★   ★

Lex leaves me to find my own way to set, which I manage with only one mishap. When passing the craft services table, I sweep a fruit tray to the ground with my backside and when I turn to inspect the damage, I take out the pastries as well.

A woman in track pants hurries over to help me. "Don't worry," she says, "you'll get used to your new body in a couple of days."

"How long to get used to the face?" I ask.

"It could be worse," she says. "You could be playing a baboon. Or a hyena."

I'm not sure a warthog ranks any higher in the savannah hierarchy, but she seems nice so I don't argue. "You're the first woman I've seen on set today."

"We're a rare breed here," she says. "Chaz apparently works better with plenty of guys around. He calls it 'menergy'."

"Isn't gender discrimination illegal?"

She laughs. "Hollywood is above the law."

Before I can introduce myself properly, Chaz calls across the studio, "Is that you, Scarlett? Get over here. The guys gave up their lunch to do your makeup test."

I join them on the set and everyone falls silent, staring. Chaz is the only one grinning.

The Cheetah finds his voice first. "You've got to be kidding."

"That is ug-ly," the Panther says.

Rudy, the Gazelle, leans a little closer. "What is it?"

Chaz actually claps his hands with glee before announcing, "It's a warthog!"

The Panther stares at my chest. "Isn't it supposed to be female?"

"Now, Julian," Chaz says. "This is your former girlfriend."

"Thank god I got out while I could," Julian says.

Rudy gives him a high five. "Dodged a bullet, man."

Julian turns to Chaz. "We already established that the girlfriend dies in the explosion. Why couldn't we leave her that way?"

"Ratings are going to tank," the Cheetah says.

Beauty really is only skin deep. Beneath those sexy bodysuits are jerks, not one of whom has the courtesy to say hello to me. It's like they've forgotten there's a real person inside the costume. A person with feelings. A person who isn't hideous.

"My hands are tied," Chaz says. "The studio wants girl power on the show, and this," he gestures toward me, "is Jake Cohen's future stepdaughter."

"You mean she didn't even have to audition?" Julian says. He lifts his visor to stare at me and his eyes are a clear, spooky green similar to a panther's. I guess the visor is supposed to add an air of mystery.

"She's probably just the comic relief," Rudy says. "No talent required."

"Yeah, but I had four callbacks to get this gig," Julian persists. "And she just walks right into the role? It's nepotism."

"Excuse me," I say. "I didn't *ask* for this job, Jake offered it to me based on my previous acting experience."

"She was fired from her last job," Chaz says. He lowers his voice conspiratorially to add, "Ego trouble."

"Chaz," I say, exasperated. "Do you have to mention that every five minutes?"

Julian answers for him. "Did someone just say 'hormones'?"

I clench my fists in anger and accidentally hit the button on the remote control, sending my tail straight into the air. The guys laugh so hard they have to support each other, and Chaz flings himself into his director's chair, well pleased. "Let's get the test done and break for lunch."

Someone snaps a slate in front of my face. "Effluvia test, take one!"

"Cut!" Chaz says. "Tusks! Where are they, Effluvia? You can't look fierce without your tusks."

I hold out the tusks. They gleam as if covered in saliva and the guys groan. "Could I speak to you privately?" I ask Chaz.

Chaz rolls his eyes at the guys. "Stand by for a tantrum."

Ignoring this, I approach his chair. "I'm all for looking fierce, but I assume you're giving me lines and with these in my mouth it's hard to enunciate."

Chaz turns to the guys. "She doesn't like the tusks, boys."

Julian shakes his head in disgust. "Diva."

It's like he punched me in my cushioned belly, but I have a valid point and I'm not giving up. "Chaz, I could just *act* fierce."

"If you're not up to it, Scarlett—"

"I'm sure there are other stepdaughters Jake could cast in the role," Julian finishes.

I stuff the tusks back in my mouth. One day I will use them to gore the Panther, whether it's in the script or not.

four

Annika flips through the catalogue and points to a wedding invitation. "This one has a bride and groom playing tennis," she says. "Jake and I played tennis on our first date, you know." She raises the book for closer inspection and adds, "Look, it says TWO LOVE at the bottom!"

I flick my eyes at the invitation. "Cute."

"Vivien, you barely glanced at it."

"That's because one of us needs to glance at the road."

Annika is behind the wheel, but she never lets driving get in the way of other activities. It's quite common to find her applying makeup or reading scripts while pelting down the Hollywood Freeway. Wedding planning is simply expanding her horizons.

Debris spills out the back of the pickup truck in front of us. I put my right hand on the dashboard and raise my left so that it's poised to grab the wheel if necessary. It's a position I got used to last summer. I thought Annika might lighten up on the pedal when driving the BMW, but if anything, she's worse. "Mom, be careful!"

Annika peers at the road over the catalogue and deftly skirts the debris. Slipping the car into third gear, she takes a sip of her coffee and blasts straight across four lanes of traffic to the off ramp. "Darling, *you* be careful—or you'll turn into your grandmother."

There's a snicker from the backseat. "What kind of superhero freaks out on the freeway?" Sasha asks.

"The kind who wants to live to fight again," I say.

If Sasha were as brave as she sounds, she wouldn't have voluntarily taken a backseat to me. "Heads up," she says, bracing herself on my headrest and snagging my ponytail in the process.

Ahead there's a yellow sign warning that the lane ends in fifty yards. Annika is too busy groping around in the glove compartment to notice. "Mom, construction!"

Locating a tube of her signature Chanel Glazed Poppy lipstick, she applies it while cruising onto the shoulder and passing a long line of drivers who are politely waiting to merge. There's a clunk as she takes out a pylon.

She's humming happily as she careens into the *Diamond Heights* studio lot to offload Sasha.

The security guard leans into the window. "Nice to see you, Ms. Reid. I hope this means you're back onboard?"

Sasha answers for me. "They're exhuming Willow's corpse today. Hold your nose."

I tell the guard about *Freak Force* and he leans in to shake my hand. "Prime time! Congratulations. What animal are you playing?"

Annika, who spent some time consoling me about Effluvia's physical shortcomings last night, steps in to save me now. "It's still a state secret."

"You might as well tell me," Sasha says. "If you don't Daddy will."

Annika pretends she doesn't hear this and guns it across the lot to the *Rock and a Hard Place* studio. Opening the door, she swings her legs out of the car.

"I'd know those stems anywhere," Roger Knelman says. "Best set in Hollywood."

Mom stands and smoothes her very short skirt. "Oh Roger, don't be silly." Her voice has taken on the special lilt she always uses for her favorite sport, namely fishing for compliments. However, her first catch of the day is nowhere big enough, so she tosses it right back. "I'm sure you see much nicer legs than mine these days."

In the right mood, Roger enjoys the sport too. "Annie, I've yet to meet the ingenue who can hold a candle to you."

Convinced that the sea holds still more, Mom waggles her fishing pole again. "I don't believe that for a minute."

Roger clears the decks for Moby Dick. "I'm quite serious. Your beauty has ripened to perfection."

I can only see Annika from the waist down but I know she's eating it up because she assumes the red carpet pose, with one foot slightly ahead of the other. Her hand moves automatically to one hip.

"Hey, Roger," I call, "ripe is only one step from rotten."

He leans down to peer at me through thick glasses. "Shut it, Verna."

I'm pretty sure Roger gets my name wrong all the time because he thinks it's funny, but it's possible that he is going senile. After all, he's at least sixty. I know he's a good director, but otherwise I really don't know what Mom sees—make that *saw*—in him. He looks like Gollum from *Lord of the Rings*.

Sidling his rumpled butt up alongside Annika's skirt, he leans against the Beemer and asks, "When do you start rehearsals for *The Farm?*"

"Today," she answers. "I'm a bit nervous."

"Don't be," he says. "You're going to be great."

He takes a package of cigarettes out of his pocket and offers it to Annika. She lifts her hand and then lets it drop to her side. "I can't."

I lean across the driver's seat and stick my head out the door. "You can't?"

Mom looks down at me. "Don't tell me you haven't noticed I stopped smoking, Vivien. You usually keep track of every cigarette."

She's right, I'm slipping. "I've had a lot on my mind."

"I heard about *Freak Force,* Viola," Roger says. "Trying to expunge your record?"

I start to protest but my voice trails off. "Yeah."

"Good girl," he says, looking back at my mother. "Annie, have a smoke. I know you want one."

Annika's hand twitches toward the cigarette but before she can take it, Sasha slides over to Mom's side and pushes the seat forward, crushing me against the steering wheel. "She can't, Roger. Daddy doesn't like it."

"I wanted to quit anyway," Annika says, stepping aside so that Sasha can climb out. "It's not good for my skin."

"How do you like the car, Roger?" Sasha asks. "Daddy bought it for Annika. Did you know they're engaged?"

"Of course," Roger says, laughing. "Witnessed the proposal myself."

Judging from Mom's pout, someone just put a kink in her fishing pole.

★　★　★

I was kind of looking forward to my first stunt rehearsal until Lex told me I had to attend in full warthog glory. His story is that the stunt coordinator needs to see how I move in costume, but it's probably some sort of hazing ritual. It was perfectly obvious yesterday that the *Freak Force* is an exclusive boys' club.

Despite being in the makeup chair for two hours, I am the first to arrive in the studio's gym. I'm surprised to see a makeshift living room set up alongside the cardio and weight equipment. There's a couch, a coffee table, and an old bookshelf full of paperbacks. I guess it's meant to simulate a real set environment.

I decide to warm up my muscles by doing my yoga routine and quickly discover that Downward Dog doesn't translate to Downward Warthog. With my huge paunch, I can't even get my upper hooves on the ground. The Tree pose is a little easier. It requires lifting my left hoof off the ground and tucking it in at my right knee while raising my arms over my head and bringing my upper hooves together so that they point at the ceiling. I take a deep breath and close my eyes, silently repeating my mantra: *From the unreal lead me to the real. From darkness lead me to the light.*

It sounds a little woo-woo but it actually fits the situation. With *Freak Force,* I have an opportunity and a challenge. Effluvia may be a warthog, but I want her to be the best damn warthog TV audiences have ever seen. After all, she has special powers. The script describes her heightened sense of hearing and smell, but hopefully Chaz will come up with something more exciting. For example, my Google research indicates that warthogs are renowned for their ferocity. Those tusks aren't just for show.

A voice interrupts my meditation. "Excellent balance. That will help you a lot."

I open my eyes to see the woman I encountered on set yesterday walking toward me carrying several crowbars. When one of them starts to slide out of her grasp, I leap forward to grab it so that it doesn't hit her foot. I needn't have bothered because it is as light as a loaf of French bread. It's not a crowbar at all, but a chunk of high-density foam shaped and painted to resemble the real thing.

The woman laughs at my expression and tosses me the other crowbars one by one. "Prop guns are heavier," she says. "Just like the real thing."

"But safer, right?" Not that I'm worried or anything.

"Definitely. We're using the electric version and all they do is give off a flash."

I hand the crowbars to her again and she continues, "These props are actually harder to work with because you have to make something so light *look* heavy and dangerous. Some actors take years to get the hang of it but you won't."

"I won't?" I ask. I was already prepared to like her just because she's the only other person around here without a Y chromosome, but now I'm her biggest fan.

"You're agile and your reflexes are good even in that getup. You'll be fine."

Encouraged, I ask, "Do you work with Fred, the stunt coordinator?"

"I *am* Fred, the stunt coordinator," she says, extending her hand with a grin. "It's Fredericka to my mother, Freddy to everyone else."

I try to hide my amazement. Freddy is pretty, slim, and petite—the exact opposite of what I expected in a stunt coordinator. If she can do stunts, maybe I can too. After all, I've got at least eight inches on her and a healthy BMI to boot.

"The guys will be here any minute," Freddy says. "Why don't you pop your tusks in and we'll get started." I start to complain but Freddy shakes her head. "You need to get used to every physical nuance so that there are no surprises on set. Chaz hates surprises." Although she doesn't say it, something in her tone suggests that she sees our director for the pain in the butt he is. "If it helps," she continues, "consider the tusks the final touch that transforms you from Leigh the actor into Effluvia the superhero."

I pop in the tusks and say, "I em Effuria." It comes out garbled but Freddy doesn't laugh.

"Atta girl," she says. "You are Effluvia and you are fierce. Say it."

"I am Effuvia and I am ferce."

"That's not fierce," she says. "Let me hear you."

I take it up a notch. "I am Effuvia and I am ferce!"

"Louder!"

I repeat the words at her command until I feel inspired to add a fearsome growl.

"Is someone strangling a pig in here?"

Freddy and I turn to find the guys standing behind us; they're not in costume but regular gym gear. Julian and Jed, the Cheetah, are so tall and muscular that Rudy seems like the runt of the litter beside them. Julian is definitely the best looking but his defective personality shows on his face. First, I don't like his grin. There's something nasty about it. Second, he has very dark hair and eyebrows, and there isn't nearly enough of a forehead in between. In fact, if he hopes to build a female fan base, he'd be wise to get Drake to do some strategic plucking.

"Julian," Freddy chides him. "Let's start off on the right foot."

"I'm just saying pigs don't growl, they grunt."

I rest one front hoof indignantly on a padded hip and say, "I em nut a fig."

Rudy pokes Julian and says, "Hairpins are flying in the barnyard."

Concentrating, I try again. "I am a warthog."

Jed puts his hand on his hip to mimic me. "You go, girl."

"Enough," Freddy says, herding us into an area covered in mats. "You're all on the same team and you might as well make the best of it."

In the scene we're rehearsing, the Freak Force takes on a mutant beast whose bite can cause a victim to become feral and savage his own comrades. Using her keen sense of smell, Effluvia tracks the beast to an abandoned house. As they enter, the Panther takes the lead because of his excellent night vision. They corner the beast in the basement, where it attacks and bites the Panther. Instantly infected, the Panther turns on Effluvia, his former love.

Holding up a crowbar, Freddy says, "Julian, you're going to grab this and lunge at Leigh. Leigh, you raise your right arm to block the blow. Then you step back three paces, spin, jump, and kick Julian in the chest." She draws an imaginary X across Julian's breastbone. "Right here."

Julian fixes me with his green eyes, which are less spooky in the bright light of the gym, and says, "Break a rib and you're dead. For real."

"As if," I say. Can he really believe I have that kind of power? He is seriously overestimating my BMI.

Freddy intervenes. "You barely need to touch him, Leigh. A gentle tap is perfect. The action always gets bigger when the camera rolls and the adrenaline flows."

A gentle tap. Got it.

She beckons Julian with both hands and he comes at her with the crowbar. Raising one arm, she demonstrates the block and then signals him to lunge for me. When he does, I raise my arm, slapping the crowbar out of his hands.

"Not bad, Leigh," Freddy says. "But no cringing. You're fierce, remember?"

"At least she isn't crying," Julian says.

Crying! Who does this guy think he is? I don't have to take his crap. Glaring at him through my piggy eyeholes, I mumble some profanity.

That he understands. "Did you just swear at me?"

I offer a noncommittal oink, which annoys him more.

This time when he comes at me I don't cringe.

"Good," Freddy says. "Let's move on to the kick. I'll demonstrate it for you at quarter speed, half speed, and then at full speed."

She goes through it three times, each faster than the last, until her final kick is almost a blur. At precisely the right moment, Julian falls backward onto the mat as if she has made contact.

Even at quarter speed, it looks complicated, but I comfort myself that Freddy thinks I have what it takes. What I lack in technique, I can make up for with soul.

Scene 4: Leigh Reid Proves Herself

INTERIOR ABANDONED HOUSE, NIGHT

Leigh Reid deftly blocks the crowbar before spinning, jumping, and extending her leg. Yes! It's a direct hit. Julian feels the light touch on his sternum and falls back onto the mat. Standing over him, Leigh sees the surprise and reluctant admiration in his eyes.

FREDDY
[helping Julian to his feet]
Bravo, Leigh! Not bad for a stunt rookie.

LEIGH
I think the kick landed left of the
mark.

                        JULIAN
                     [grudgingly]
              No, it was right on target.

Jed and Rudy nod, clearly disappointed.

                        FREDDY
             You were fierce. Definitely fierce.

                      ★   ★   ★

Julian is lying on his back on the mat underneath a pile of paper-backs. "I can't work like this."

"What happened?" I ask.

"Your big butt knocked over the bookshelf, that's what happened."

Jed and I lean over to help Julian up at the same time, and my butt attachment hits Jed in the face.

Clambering to his feet, Julian turns to Freddy. "This is a frig-ging joke. We've been at this for two hours and she's knocked over everything *but* me."

Unfortunately, he's not exaggerating. The stunt is so much harder than I expected. The spin I conquered after a few attempts, but the jump-and-kick sequence seems nearly impossible. If I get off the ground, I forget to extend my leg. If I extend my leg, it comes nowhere near the invisible X on Julian's chest. I've lost my balance and fallen over more times than I can count, although Rudy says I'm up to nineteen. And this is just the first stage of the fight.

"Be patient," Freddy tells the guys. "She's still getting used to the suit."

"We didn't have to adjust to our costumes," Rudy says.

Freddy points to a torn mat. "That's where you got your horns stuck on the first day."

"Once I blew it," Rudy says. "Not fifty times."

"She's carrying a lot of extra weight," Fred says.

"You can say that again," Jed says.

"Teamwork," Freddy reminds them. "This show will be more successful if you support each other."

The guys exchange hushed comments featuring the words "princess" and "diva." It makes blood pound in my ears but Freddy is right. I have to win these guys over or our bad chemistry could doom the show.

While the guys move to their starting positions, I take a moment to center myself. I can do this. I just need to become one with the costume. *I am Effluvia and I am fierce!*

Freddy calls action and Julian charges at me with the crowbar, aiming not for my head, but my diaphragm; I miss the block and he runs into me. I hit the mat, winded.

"Julian," Freddy barks. "What the hell was that? You're not supposed to throw your whole weight into it."

He shrugs. "Sorry, my aim was off. But if the warthog can't take it, maybe she's not up to an action show."

She walks over to Julian, stares up at him menacingly, and jabs a finger into his chest. "I'm trying to give you the benefit of the doubt, here. Maybe this is some sort of method acting and you're trying to get Leigh pissed off enough to really go for it, but I'm telling you to stop fooling around."

Julian, a foot taller than his coach, looks down at her, cowed. "Okay, Freddy."

She turns to me. "Focus, Leigh."

Although her tone softened, I can tell she's losing faith in me and if she does, she might tell Chaz I'm unfit for stunts. What if I'm the first actor ever to get fired from a job before I utter one line on camera? If I'm fired again, I might as well give up on acting forever and consider a future as Sasha's driver.

I have to nail this kick.

Taking a deep breath to steady my nerves, I visualize my foot hitting Julian's chest in exactly the right place.

When Freddy calls action, I spin once, jump, and extend my leg. And *wham!* My foot connects with Julian—a little harder than I wanted but not too hard. He drops like a stone onto the mats and I raise my arms in triumph.

Freddy darts past me and falls to her knees beside Julian. Confused, I turn to Jed and Rudy, who are doubled over in apparent commiseration.

I look back to find Julian writhing around on the mat, both hands covering his crotch.

★　★　★

While we wait for Julian to arrive on set, I try to decide which incident is more damaging to my rep, the *Diamond Heights* firing or the *Freak Force* crotch kicking. Although the former is technically more serious, I suspect the latter could have more staying power. Who wouldn't want to hear the story about the warthog who destroyed a guy's manhood?

Not that Julian is entirely emasculated. After all, he was too manly to let Freddy call a doctor. He simply limped off to his trailer with a little help from Rudy and Jed.

By the time he shows up in costume, you can hardly tell he's been injured, except for a slight hunch and a pinched expression on his face.

Rudy and Jed are standing guard over him in case the crazed pig attacks again. Surely they know I didn't kick him in the groin on purpose. I mean, *ew*. Even warthogs have standards.

I plan on apologizing as soon as the guys break rank, but I have no idea what to say. "I hope you can still have kids" probably isn't going to cut it. Maybe there's a card for this. There's a card for everything.

Chaz and Lex flutter around Julian for a while, throwing glares my way. Eventually they decide to shoot the first stage of the stunt. To ease Julian's concerns, Chaz enlists Freddy to take me through the kick a few more times in front of everyone. We've been working on it together for a long time, but I'm still flustered. By paying attention only to Freddy, however, I manage to stay focused and prove I've mastered it.

At last Julian takes his mark. I take mine and execute the kick perfectly again and again. Each time, Julian flinches before my foot gets anywhere near him.

Chaz retreats to his director's chair complaining about "broken trust." After a short sulk, he demands a fresh tie and cuts it off with a flourish. We start again.

Two hours later, Rudy and Jed give up on solidarity and start teasing Julian about losing his nerve. Julian turns red and hurls his visor at the wall. That's when Chaz pulls the plug on the stunt for today, and we move on to another scene.

By the time we wrap, we're five hours behind schedule and Chaz is beside himself. He doesn't even try to keep his voice down when he starts complaining to Lex about me. "I knew she'd be a disaster. But if I fire her, Jake will think it's personal. Getting Freddy to tell Jake she's hopeless is the only way."

Lex shakes his head. "Freddy still thinks Leigh has potential. She said 'accidents happen'."

"Accidents are already happening to Jake's budget. I'm going to have to steal time out of next week's schedule to shoot the kick we missed today," Chaz says. "Talent obviously doesn't mean anything to him, but overtime costs might."

Slightly reassured by Freddy's support, I set off for my trailer. It's a tiny heap of rust wedged between two distant Dumpsters—not the kind of accommodation a lead actor usually gets, but marginally better than my *Diamond Heights'* cubbyhole on the honey wagon (the truck with the washrooms). Tonight it will be a welcome refuge.

Halfway there, I hear the click of heels behind me and turn to see Sasha with Olivier. Ducking between a couple of trailers, I skulk in the shadows. The last thing I need right now is for Sasha to see me in costume.

Footsteps approach from the other direction and Sasha calls, "Excuse me, do you know where I can find Chaz?"

I peek out and see that she is speaking to Julian, who is already in his street clothes. He walks over to her and his hunch immediately disappears. "I'll take you to his trailer," he says. "Cute dog."

They start walking but Sasha stops abruptly and clutches Julian's arm with a little squeal. "What's *that?*"

His pinched expression returns when he sees me cowering beside the trailer. "A character from our show." I see he hasn't troubled himself to learn my real name.

Sasha ponders this for a moment before calling, "Is that you, Leigh Reid?"

I nod my long nose and her laughter peals out.

"Oh my god, you're hideous," she says. "I can't believe Daddy did this to you."

This time I wag my head and say, "Chaz."

"Brilliant," she says, laughing so hard that she drops Olivier's leash. She pulls her cell phone out of her purse and snaps my picture. "Wait till Ursela sees this."

Julian leans over to pick up the leash. "Sasha Cohen, right? I thought I recognized you. You're great on *Between a Rock and a Hard Place.*"

I'm amazed at how quickly he's adjusted to the whole nepotism thing. I guess it's only a problem when the beneficiary looks like a warthog.

Sasha flashes a row of perfect teeth at him. "I saw your pilot and you were the best thing in it."

He directs some teeth back at her and I notice his smile can be nice enough when he wants it to be. "Should I take you to Chaz or do you want to stay here?"

"Chaz is waiting for me," Sasha says. "We have dinner reservations." Waving gaily at me, she calls, "You've got to do something about those warts."

Julian laughs. "She's got bigger problems to worry about."

"Don't I know it," Sasha agrees.

She clicks off and Julian follows, still holding Olivier's white, rhinestone-encrusted leash. If you ask me, that's even more emasculating than a kick in the crotch.

five

I arrive on set Monday morning to find a cardboard tube from Abby waiting in my trailer. Her text message says it's something to inspire me before my second run at the stunt scene today.

It's more encouragement than my mother offered. She barely paid attention when I told her the crotch-kicking story and simply offered to drive Karis and me shopping to "take my mind off it." I jumped at the chance. My recent advances in enlightenment mean I don't care about material things as much as I used to, but a girl has to wear something.

As it turns out, there was no risk of my succumbing to crass consumerism, because Annika hijacked the mission and dragged us to a wedding trade show. While she flitted from booth to booth in search of the perfect theme, Karis and I followed in her wake mocking everything until she finally snapped: "You do not understand the pressure I'm under, Vivien. I am an A-lister now and I have to stay ahead of the trends. It's not enough to have a nice wedding, I have to have the best damn wedding this town has ever seen."

Fortunately, Karis understands the pressure *I'm* under dealing with a fringe A-lister, so I didn't need to be embarrassed by the tantrum.

Leaving Annika to explore the ancient Greece theme in a fake Parthenon, Karis and I went in search of free food and makeup samples. By the time we found Mom two hours later, she'd joined a belly-dancing demonstration in the Sultan's tent. There was a veil pinned to her baseball hat "disguise" and a few more tucked into her waistband. I have to admit, she was pretty good for a novice. She got the steps down perfectly, but her undulating would have been more impressive if she actually had hips.

Until a few years ago, Mom was the opposite of athletic. She didn't work out and she didn't dance. Other than stepping outside to smoke, her only regular exercise was driving erratically. When she turned forty, however, she realized that it was all downhill from there and decided to hire a personal trainer. She took up cardio workouts, but also joined Pilates and yoga classes. More recently, she's taken several types of dance lessons, probably to be prepared if things really go south with her career and she ends up doing a "Dancing with the D-list" reality show.

What amazes me is that Annika is good at all of it. She can dance, run stairs, and play tennis well enough to give Jake a run for his money. I inherited none of this natural athletic ability. I am more like Dad, who is dexterous only with a remote control. Sure, he watches a lot of sports, but in real life his only exertion is walking our dog.

How is it that I got the wrong traits from each parent? If I could just reshuffle the genetic deck and deal myself a fresh hand, life would be so much easier. For starters, I'd take Mom's looks, Dad's emotional stability, Mom's athleticism, and Dad's reliability.

One thing I wouldn't change is my friendship with Abby. Despite seeing so little of each other, we've managed to remain close since she moved to New York nearly two years ago. That's why I'm not surprised she sent something to cheer me up today.

I open the tube to find a poster from the *Charlie's Angels* movie, only she's doctored it so that my face appears over the bodies of all three leads, each in a fighting stance. Across the bottom it reads, *"She's Fierce. She's Fabulous. She's Vivien Leigh Reid."*

Peeling off some of the tape that's holding my kitchenette cupboards together, I stick the poster on the wall over the sofa and smile. Abby hasn't lost her talent for reminding me not to take myself too seriously.

★ ★ ★

INTERIOR A RAMSHACKLE HOUSE IN NORTHERN
ALASKA, NIGHT

Effluvia uses her keen sense of smell to lead the Freak Force through the darkened kitchen toward the basement stairwell. She notices a box of donuts on the counter and pauses. While the rest of the team waits impatiently, Effluvia eats two donuts. Then she wipes her mouth with her hoof and continues down the stairs into the basement.

"Cut!" Chaz hollers. He walks onto the set, his yellow cut-off tie practically glowing in the dim light. It must be a navigational tool to help him see with sunglasses. "Scarlett, Lex dropped the new script pages at your house for a reason. Did you bother to look at them?"

I pull a sticky piece of cruller off my tusk and nod.

"Then explain why you took a single bite of one cruller before moving toward the stairs." He snaps his fingers until Lex appears with a script. Chaz raises his shades and makes a show of consulting it. "Just as I thought: *'Effluvia eats two donuts.'* Two." He holds up a hand and counts off two fingers. "What I saw was Effluvia taking a single bite of one donut, which didn't even give the guys a chance to roll their eyes."

"But Effluvia ate two bagels and drank a hot chocolate in the previous scene," I say. "And she'll be grabbing a couple of tacos in the next one."

I'm impressed that I managed to make my point so succinctly. The hours I spent rehearsing while wearing my tusks yesterday really paid off.

Chaz crosses his arms. "And your point is?"

"That no one can spend that much time eating and still fight crime."

"Effluvia is a warthog," Chaz explains, as if that fact might have escaped me. "Warthogs graze."

"Maybe so but if I keep grazing like Effluvia, you won't need padding on my costume."

"YP, not MP." He turns to the guys. "Would any of you complain if I asked you to eat donuts?"

"Bring 'em on," Rudy says.

"You're not worried about your figures?" Chaz persists.

"Actually," Jed says, checking himself out, "I think this costume makes me look fat. What do you think, Rudy?"

Rudy smirks. "Chicks dig love handles."

"I don't have love handles," Jed protests in a shrill voice. "Do I, Julian?"

Julian raises his unibrow. "Do not ask me to check out your bod, man."

Chaz shakes his head, now sorry he started this. "My point is Effluvia's constant eating will humanize her. Don't you want to bring your character to life, Scarlett?"

"I can bring her to life with one cruller," I say. "Or I can take a bite of two different donuts to sell the idea that she's constantly grazing." Chaz opens his mouth but I plunge ahead. "Better yet, if you include an insert shot of the empty box the audience will understand that Effluvia has eaten *all* the donuts."

"So, now you're editing the show too?" Chaz asks. "Wow, I'm so lucky to have a generalist in the cast who can weigh in on all aspects of filmmaking. That worked out great for you on *Diamond Heights*."

What's a Monday morning without an unspoken threat? Apparently, having a rep means I can't even make a constructive suggestion without looking like an unreasonable diva.

Chaz leans in and tweaks my snout. "You'd better work on your attitude, Pork Chop, unless you want Effluvia to come to an untimely end."

Make that a spoken threat.

We roll another take and this time I eat two full donuts. Chaz cuts the camera and says, "Faster, Scarlett. I need to see you grinding through those crullers. This is no time to be ladylike." He comes over to share a nugget of directorial wisdom with me. "You see, Effluvia is an opportunist. She's all for fighting crime, but sees no reason to go hungry while doing it."

I sense that Chaz and I are often going to differ on character motivation but I am a pro, and a pro doesn't argue with her director.

The next take, I grind through the first cruller so fast that crumbs fly through the air. By the end of the second, I can barely breathe through the plaster mask and let out a sound that's a combination between a snuffle and a snort.

The guys dissolve into unscripted laughter and I stop eating.

"Cut!" Chaz says. "You were doing fine, Scarlett. Why'd you stop?"

"Because they laughed," I say, outraged. "It ruined the take."

"It was in character," Chaz insists. "Let me be the judge of what's working."

"Did you see her go?" Jed asks the other guys. "It was like a wood chipper."

We do the take again and I give the director exactly what he wants. As I open my mouth to shove in the last chunk of cruller, a belch escapes.

"Cut! Print!" Chaz calls, this time *before* the guys crack up. "Maybe I underestimated you, Scarlett. You're really getting Effluvia."

★   ★   ★

I hope Chaz continues to think he underestimated me because we're about to revisit the aborted fight sequence from last week. I doubt a stomach full of donuts is going to help my performance, but a professional does not hide behind excuses. After all, it could have been worse: This could have come after the tacos.

Freddy gives me a quick refresher on choreography and I visualize my foot connecting with Julian's chest. Foot—chest, foot—chest. Basically, it's all in the jump. As long as I get enough height, Julian's manhood is safe.

I am Effluvia, I chant silently. *Fierce and fabulous.*

Puffing, I bend over to stretch out my hamstrings.

"Whoa!" Rudy says. "Watch where you're swinging that bootie, Katrina."

The guys have taken to calling me Katrina, after the hurricane that destroyed everything in its path. I tell myself that nicknames, however unflattering, mean they're accepting me as one of the team. Maybe it was the belch that won them over.

Jed turns to Julian and says, "I hope you're wearing your armored boxers today."

Rudy snickers. "His agent added a new clause to his contract this weekend. If Katrina turns him into a soprano, at least he can sue."

Everyone chuckles but I don't even react. A professional thespian cannot allow herself to be distracted by the inane ramblings of small minds.

Chaz calls action and the Panther's eyes begin to glow beneath his visor.

I deliver my scripted line: "Panther, no! It's me, Effluvia!"

Excellent delivery if I do say so myself. Just the right level of terror without going over the top.

Julian lunges toward me with the crowbar. I block it, spin, and leap.

Suddenly, time seems to slow down, allowing me to analyze my jump as if I were a commentator at the Olympics. *It looks like Leigh Reid has all the height she needs. Her form is good—left leg tucked, right leg coming up . . . up . . . The trajectory appears to be spot on. But wait, her right foot is still climbing . . . Now it's in line with her opponent's visor. She's overshot, people and it's going to cost her marks. There's still a second to pull the kick. Can she do it? I'm afraid she has too much speed. Uh-oh.*

My foot connects with Julian's temple and he hits the floor with a sickening thud.

I land on top of him, like a cushioned steam roller. Several pairs of hands grab me and throw me to the side. People drop to their knees beside Julian on the mat.

Freddy's voice breaks the stunned silence. "Medic!"

★　★　★

Julian's eyes flutter open. "What happened?"

The medic moves away to speak to Chaz and I take his place beside Julian. "I'm really, really sorry."

Jed leans over him to explain. "Katrina struck again. Show him, Rudy."

Rudy performs a series of spastic kicks and Jed crumbles to the mat beside Julian.

"Once again, the mighty Panther goes down like a girl," Jed concludes.

Julian rubs his head and groans.

"It's on film," Rudy tells Julian. "You gotta see it for yourself."

Propping himself on one elbow, Julian looks up at me and says, "Could you do me a favor?"

"Anything," I reply. "What do you need? Water? Aspirin?"

"I need you to stop trying to kill me."

"It was an accident," I say.

Freddy pulls me to my feet and leads me away. "Don't worry, he'll be fine."

"I thought I had it, Freddy. I'm sorry."

She smiles sympathetically. "Last week you hit too low, this week too high. Next time you'll be just right."

Chaz comes up behind us. "She won't have that chance. I want you to bring in a stunt double."

"Come on, Chaz," I say. "I can do this."

He continues as if I haven't spoken. "In the meantime, Effluvia is about to discover her new superpower."

I know this isn't going to be good but I ask anyway. "What is it?"

This time he answers me. "The power of invisibility. And if I pray hard enough, maybe it will come true."

★ ★ ★

My mother is standing at the marble-topped island in the kitchen examining china plates and linen swatches when the cab drops me off. When she said she was too busy to pick me up after work tonight, I assumed she was rehearsing, not choosing place settings.

"Where's Jake?" I ask. Chaz probably sent a news alert that I knocked out one of his headliners, but if Annika knows she doesn't let on.

"He's working late and Sasha is out with Gray," she says. "It's just the two of us tonight, darling, so I thought you could help me make some big decisions."

"I'm not in the mood for wedding planning," I say. "I had a really bad day."

She keeps her eyes on her china. "All I want you to do is sample appetizers."

"Mom, did you hear me?"

"Yes, you had a bad day."

"A *really* bad day. I'm quitting the show."

"Come over and sit down," she says. Finally, a little maternal concern. I perch on a stool across from her and she passes her hand over the place settings like the assistant on a game show. "Which one says A list?"

I stare at her incredulously. "I just said I'm quitting *Freak Force* and you're not even taking me seriously."

"You've never quit anything in your life. Do you like the round plates or the square?"

"I've quit lots of things," I say, searching my mental archives for something to prove her wrong.

"While you're trying to come up with an example, cast your vote," she says.

I run my eyes over the place settings and choose one. "I quit gymnastics."

Her brow furrows. "Are you sure, darling?"

"Yes, I'm sure. I was there—and you weren't."

She shakes her head. "I meant are you sure about the place setting? You barely looked at them. As for gymnastics, you didn't quit. You finished the course but didn't go back for level two. Same for piano lessons. And ballet."

"How do you know that?" I grumble. "Did Dad send out a newsletter?"

"He didn't need to. I grilled him every Sunday night for twelve years."

I struggle to digest this new information. "You spoke to Dad every week?"

"Just about. I missed a few when I was on location. That must have been when you quit things."

I see what she's doing. She's trying to throw me off track so I won't rock the boat with talk of quitting when Jake gets home. Well, it won't work. "There's a first time for everything."

Annika takes several boxes out of the fridge and arranges hors d'oeuvres on a platter. "I'm surprised you'd give up so easily."

"Easily? You have no idea. The show is a nightmare."

She pushes the platter toward me. "But you like acting."

I push the platter back. "Acting, yes. But I've only said two lines on camera. The rest is all stupid stunts."

She pushes the platter toward me again. "Try something, darling."

"I can't," I say. "I ate seven donuts today."

"Seven!" she asks, instantly on high alert. "You can't eat all that fried food. That's over fifty grams of fat, forty of sugar, and at least eighteen hundred calories!"

Mom is better informed than Wikipedia when it comes to nutritional values.

I list off the foods Chaz made me eat today, knowing it will horrify her. "He's really working the pig angle. He wouldn't even let me use a spit bucket."

"That's unacceptable. Didn't he see *Super Size Me?*"

"He's not thinking about my health, Annika."

"But if this keeps up, you'll never fit into a bridesmaid dress."

And we're back to the wedding already. "Mom, I'm trying to tell you, I've got bigger problems."

"Vivien, you're not the first actor to knock someone out during a stunt," she says. Smiling at my reaction, she adds, "You didn't think Chaz would keep news like that to himself, did you?"

I shake my head and sigh. "What did Jake say?"

"Not much." She nudges the platter toward me again hopefully.

Giving up, I take an egg roll and bite into it. She picks up a pencil to record my impressions. I offer a rating of seven and she leans across the island to pop a cheese puff into my mouth.

"Jake knows stunts go wrong sometimes," she says. "How's the puff?"

"Soggy. Cheese puffs are dated anyway."

"Not dated—*old school,*" she corrects. "Old school is good."

I watch her take notes for a moment. "Will Jake be mad if I quit?"

"It's not about Jake," she says. "It's about the fact that no other studio will hire you if you quit."

"Why? Just because I don't want to do stunts doesn't mean I don't want to act."

"Quitting is career suicide," she says. "Far better to get fired."

"Well, I should be able to manage that." I've already done it once; I'm practically an expert.

She selects a salmon roll and nibbles at it. "No one's going to fire you after one bad kick."

"Two. And this time Julian has a concussion. The studio had to hire a nurse to keep an eye on him overnight."

"Freddy told me he's fine," she says, pressing another appetizer on me.

"You spoke to Fred?"

"Of course, darling. I needed to make sure you hadn't hurt yourself kicking that boy. Fred said you're doing well considering you have thirty extra pounds of warthog to haul around."

"She did?"

Annika nods. "And Jake was impressed you could kick that high."

Feeling a little better, I take another appetizer. "I hope Julian doesn't have brain damage. But if he does, it might actually help his personality."

"Vivien," Mom says. "That's terrible."

"You wouldn't say that if you saw how mean he is to me. All the guys are. They make fun of Effluvia." I reach across with chopsticks to pick up the rest of her salmon roll. "It's not her fault she's butt ugly."

Mom laughs. "It sounds like you're warming to your character."

"Just put yourself in her place for a second: You're on a nice safari, there's an explosion, and you wake up to find you've become a warthog. Suddenly you're fat and deformed and your boyfriend—who is somehow hotter than ever—dumps you because he finds you totally repulsive."

Mom twists her hair into a casual bun and anchors it with a single chopstick. "I can't imagine it," she says, sounding genuinely sympathetic. "Poor Effluvia."

"At least she has a pretty name," I say.

Annika uses the other chopstick to spear a dumpling and offers it to me. "I think you're on the right track here, Vivien. You've realized that Effluvia is an empty vessel you need to fill."

"She's got a lot going for her. I just wish the guys would look past the warts."

"The costume will give you a chance to isolate and hone your voice and body skills." She stands and carries the dishes over to the dishwasher. "You know, darling, I wouldn't be surprised if this role ends up being a terrific career booster for you."

I stare after her, realizing that she's manipulated me into keeping the role in less than fifteen minutes. No wonder Jake proposed so soon.

"No one will know who I am in that costume," I point out. "Chaz says he's not even listing me in the credits because a mystery will be good for ratings."

Annika bristles at this. "That vengeful little man. I'd like to take one of his silly ties and . . . But never mind. I promised Jake I wouldn't interfere."

She collects a bottle of sparkling water from the fridge and pours it into champagne flutes. "Consider yourself lucky that people won't know your name. You have no idea what a burden it is to be recognized wherever you go."

Neither does she but since she is being nice, I don't say so. Instead I point to a series of appetizers with my chopstick. "Those are A list."

She looks elated at my endorsement. It doesn't take that much to make her happy these days. It's almost as if Jake is making her stable.

"Let me tell you a story," she says. "Do you remember *She Devil?*" How could I forget? It garnered Annika her first and only award: a Golden Raspberry for Worst Actress. To be fair, it couldn't have been easy to fight a zombie while wearing red leather short-shorts and silver stilettos. "In the final scene, I took on the zombie using a long pole. And I knocked two of his teeth out."

"Did you get in trouble?"

She shakes her head. "But only because the zombie wasn't an actor but a stuntman. I went to his trailer to apologize and he gave me some good advice. 'Just put it behind you,' he said. 'Focusing on what went wrong is the surest way to fail again.'"

I wish Chaz and the guys had been as generous today. "I don't see how I'm going to face everyone tomorrow. I'm so embarrassed."

"Act like you don't give a damn what they think," she suggests.

I can tell from her expression that she's thinking about the time in Ireland when I gave her similar advice.

The phone rings and she checks caller ID before picking up. "Hi sweetie. Yes, you can come home now. I'm all done here."

★　★　★

I'm e-mailing Abby on the kitchen laptop when Sasha comes home.

"Hey, loser," she says.

With no parents around, she's really opening up. "Back at you."

"Hear you decked your costar—after destroying his manhood."

My stomach clenches but I keep it light. "All in a day's work."

"Gray hasn't been able to stand up straight since I told him."

"Gray hasn't been able to stand up straight since he left his cave." I'm supposed to be too enlightened for this, but I deserve a break after what I've been through.

She slides into the bench across from me and props her chin on her hands. "You're so harsh. No wonder you can't get a boyfriend." She waits for me to toss a barb back, but when I don't she moves on. "Chaz gave me a copy of your script. Hope you don't mind."

"Not at all. It's nice you two have stayed so close since *Diamond Heights*."

"He's hysterical. I loved what he did with your character's name."

I lift my eyes from the screen and see she's toying with me. "Don't you have potions to brew?"

She gets up. "No, but I do have a boyfriend to call. Unlike you."

I wait until she leaves the kitchen before logging onto an online dictionary.

Effluvia

1. An invisible emanation, as of vapor or gas.
2. The odorous fumes given off by waste or decaying matter.

Odorous fumes? Does that mean what I think it does?

Sasha instantly reappears in the doorway to confirm it. "How does it feel to be named for a fart?"

six

When I was about six years old, I had a secret dream that my father would marry Abby's mother. It didn't stay a secret for long, because I decided to propose to her on his behalf. Anyone could see she was perfect for him. She was pretty in an outdoorsy way, she was so kind that she didn't even laugh during the proposal, and she was more fun than all the mothers in the neighborhood combined.

In other words, she was the opposite of his first wife. Annika never baked cinnamon buns or painted a mermaid mural on my bedroom wall or threw parties to celebrate my half-birthday (or my real birthday, for that matter). Abby's mother did all of these things for her daughter. And once, when Abby won a public-speaking contest, her mother had a party with fireworks. Fireworks! But the thing that I liked most about Abby's mother is that when she picked us up from school, she'd hug Abby, then me, and finally Ryan, Abby's little brother. It was like I outranked her own son.

Dad never denied liking Abby's mother. In fact, he brightened every time she called to give him advice on Halloween costumes, bake sales, or school uniforms. The problem, he said, was that Abby's mother was still married to Abby's father, and from all indications, happily so. When I proposed a duel with Mr. MacKenzie, Dad said that unless it was a battle of the calculators, he'd probably lose. With such a pessimistic attitude, it's no wonder he's still single.

I didn't give up right away. I asked Grandma to buy me bunk

beds so that Abby and I could share a room when they moved in. And I asked my first grade teacher to marry Mr. MacKenzie after the breakup so that he wouldn't have to raise Ryan alone. I even left flowers on Mrs. MacKenzie's porch and forged my father's signature on a card. That's when Dad sat me down and convinced me to let Abby's mother come around on her own.

Ten years later, we're still waiting. The MacKenzies moved to New York, where Abby's mother continues to excel at parenting. If there is something—anything—to celebrate in Abby's life, she buys tickets to a Broadway show. Abby pretends it's embarrassing to get so much support, but she already appreciates the traditions they share.

Annika and I do not have traditions. For that, we'd need a history. It may be true that she called Dad every week to check in on me, but that doesn't make up for the fact that she wasn't there. Her rare visits were a blur of red lipstick, hair tossing, and loud, uncomfortable laughter. It was painful for both of us—so painful that I once removed the heads from all the Madame Alexander dolls she'd given me and strung them into a voodoo necklace. Annika screamed when she saw it—a genuine, bloodcurdling scream. If she'd screamed like that on film, maybe Roger would have cast her in a quality production sooner.

Since Dad forced us together last year, Annika has made a real effort to have a relationship with me. It's probably too late for cinnamon buns and fireworks, but the Broadway shows are still an option. Over time, we may develop traditions of our own.

Mom seems to have been thinking along the same lines because she arrives at my bedroom door on Friday night ablaze with an idea. "Darling, let's dress up and go to the Beverly Hills Hotel—just the two of us."

"You mean like the Fire Drill?" I ask. After I got fired from *Diamond Heights* in August, Annika took me out on the town to console me. She bought me a cool purse, lent me a designer dress, and let me drink champagne in the hotel's Polo Lounge. It was a pleasant end to what had been the worst day of my life.

"Exactly," she says. "Only without the firing."

That's a relief. I was afraid that Jake had asked her to break the news that I've been kicked off *Freak Force*. After all, Effluvia hasn't had any scenes all week. That's not uncommon for a show with so many leads, but under the circumstances it's making me nervous.

I end up wearing the same black-and-white Narciso Rodriguez sundress as last time because it made me look so sophisticated that no one asked me for ID. Plus, I like that the halter-style top reveals my back, which I consider one of my best features. Mom lends me a purse, but I have to wear my own ballerina flats because my feet are a size (she says two) larger than hers.

Annika follows my lead and wears the same Carolina Herrera dress she wore last time and chooses a couple of wraps to protect us from the late-November breeze.

Leading me out to the garage, Mom dashes my hopes of driving the Beetle for old time's sake by insisting we take the BMW.

For Annika, sentiment is all well and good, but not if it gets in the way of making a better entrance.

★ ★ ★

Stepping inside the Beverly Hills Hotel is like going back to a grander Hollywood era. I half expect the real Vivien Leigh to stroll past on the arm of a handsome man.

"Shall we eat poolside?" Annika asks. "The Cabana Club is a little more relaxed than the Polo Lounge."

"As long as they serve champagne, I'm good," I say.

"There will be no drinking for you tonight, young lady. Special occasions only."

"Coming here is a special occasion. Besides, don't you want to do a taste test for the wedding?"

"Jake is handling the bar and I'm happy to leave it in his capable hands," she says, leading me downstairs to the patio entrance.

There's a sign at the door saying the Cabana Club is closed for a private function. Annika ignores it and walks outside. "Let's just take a look, darling. I want you to see how pretty it is."

I grab her arm and put on the brakes. "We can't."

She wobbles on her stilettos but keeps going. "Vivien, you're being silly. Look at all these people. No one will even notice us."

She might be right. There must be over two hundred guests mingling on the patio.

"Isn't it gorgeous?" she asks, pausing to admire the décor.

It is. There are garlands of puffy white flowers, white silk box lanterns hanging from the trees, and large urns filled with white tulips and trailing vines. Floating candles and white rose petals cover the surface of the pool.

Closer to the bar, people are dancing. One woman is wearing a white strapless gown—and a veil.

"It's a wedding," I say, grabbing Annika's arm again and shifting into reverse.

She cranes to get a good look at the bride and frowns. "It's Leslie Nelligan."

Until recently, Leslie was always a little higher in the B-list pecking order than Annika. In fact, Annika had a small role on Leslie's movie, *Love Slayer,* long ago.

"I read she was getting married in Hawaii," I say. "It must have been a PR stunt to fool the paparazzi."

Annika pulls a heart-shaped notebook and a pen out of her purse and passes them to me. "Let's take some notes. Number One: Get the name of Leslie's floral designer. Number Two: Leak the news that we're holding *our* wedding in Paris.

"The gossip columns haven't even mentioned your engagement," I say. "The paparazzi aren't going to be a problem."

"Number Three: Call *People* and announce our engagement."

I counter, "Number Four: Call your pharmacist to up your meds."

"Number Five: Warn daughter not to be so rude."

She strolls away and I follow anxiously. "Mom, come on, we're not guests."

"We could be guests."

"But we're not. We're crashers."

"We're *researchers*," she says. "Let's just scope out the buffet table and leave."

"Why would you want to copy Leslie Nelligan's wedding anyway?"

"I don't want to copy it, I want to surpass it. Leslie's never made it off the B list and she's marrying a mid-ranking cinematographer. I can do better than this. I have to, for the sake of Jake's reputation."

"For the sake of Jake's reputation, let's not get thrown out of here," I say.

"Would you relax? It's not like we're stealing anything, except ideas." She turns and takes a flute from a passing waiter. "And one glass of champagne. Leslie owes me that: She pretended not to know me at the Screen Actors Guild Awards last year."

"She probably *didn't* know you. You played a hooker with one line in *Love Slayer.* All it showed was your legs."

"I had the same legs at the awards ceremony," Annika points out, before downing the champagne in two gulps.

At the buffet table, she opens her purse and starts stuffing personalized wedding trinkets into it: napkins, a matchbook, a picture frame, and a candle holder.

"Annika!" I say, scandalized. Next she'll filch the porcelain bride and groom off the wedding cake.

"Annika!" someone echoes.

I turn, expecting to see an angry groom flanked by hotel security, but it's actually Roger Knelman.

"Roger, what a surprise!" Annika says, more bubbly than one glass of champagne should make her.

Roger is wearing a nice suit and he looks almost handsome in this dim lighting. He is also so pleased to see Annika that I become suspicious. Did they plan this little rendezvous in advance? I should have known Mom and I couldn't enjoy a tradition of our own. Annika always has an agenda and it usually involves men.

Roger takes Annika's hand and kisses it. "Dance with me, Annie."

"Don't you dare leave me here alone," I say. I snatch at her arm and end up with a handful of satin wrap as she heads toward the dance floor.

"You won't be alone for long, Virginia," Roger assures me.

Annika calls back, "Find someone to teach you the merengue."

"Why would you want to learn the merengue?" a male voice asks, behind me.

Great. Some loser is already hitting on me. I refuse to turn around and encourage him.

The owner of the voice steps around me to reveal a tall, dark guy with spooky green eyes: Julian. I haven't seen him since I clocked him.

"I don't want to learn the merengue," I say. "I don't even know what it is."

He laughs. It sounds like a genuine laugh, not the snickering that usually comes out of his mouth. I notice that his teeth are nice—straight and white without the artificial Hollywood glare. But I am not fooled by the friendly facade. I know that he hates me, which means he'll call security as soon as he figures out we're not on the guest list.

"Would you believe me if I said the merengue is a defensive move designed to kill an opponent instantly?" he asks.

It must be a trap. He probably wants to demonstrate the move on me. "Sure, I'd believe you," I say. "But I wouldn't want to learn it."

"You don't need to," he says. "That dress is already a killer."

If I didn't know better, I'd think he meant that. Why is he being so nice? Maybe it's a guy thing: You leave your fight behind on the basketball court (or the movie set) and pretend it never happened until the game resumes. It's a good philosophy but not the way I usually operate; I fully intended to hate him off set as well as on it. But if he wants to rise above it and engage in clever banter, I'll give it a try.

"Thank you," I say. "It's only set to stun."

He laughs again. "Lucky for me."

I wonder briefly if I've slipped into an alternate reality, but when I glance over at Annika I see that she is shimmying around Roger and laughing louder than the sixteen-piece band. In other words, Situation Normal, Annika Flirting Unacceptably.

Julian looks out at the dance floor too and points to an elegant couple. "That," he says, "is the real merengue."

"Wow," I say. "They're really good."

"They should be, considering how much they practice." He rolls his eyes and adds, "My parents."

"Are they professional dancers?"

He shakes his head. "It's just an embarrassing hobby. My father is a film editor and my mother a wardrobe designer."

That explains why he looks so sharp in his dark gray suit, mauve shirt, and purple tie. Plus, I think Drake had a go at his eyebrows; they look positively tame tonight.

"That's quite a Hollywood pedigree," I say.

"You wouldn't know it from my résumé. I've been acting for three years and I only have a handful of credits. My parents refuse to open any doors."

Recognizing dangerous territory, I toss out a joke. "They'd rather you dance?"

He smiles. "Something more stable. The more boring the better."

Now I see why he was so pissed off about my walking into a role on *Freak Force*. His parents are like Karis's—addicted to a precarious business themselves, but preferring something saner for their kids. Annika had a moment like that in Ireland when I first started to act, but she's been supportive ever since. Maybe acting is her idea of a family tradition we can share.

Julian flags a waiter and takes a couple of glasses of champagne. I accept the flute he offers but sip it slowly, knowing that I have to stay on my toes. Julian's nice-guy act is pretty convincing, but he does make a living pretending to be something he's not.

I can't figure out his game but I have a few theories: a) He's working on character motivation by examining the Panther's feelings for Effluvia; b) He feels bad about how he's treated me on set and wants to make amends; c) He's battling one of those Hollywood drug problems; or d) The dress really is a killer.

At the moment, I'm going with choice d. Julian wouldn't be the first guy to discover his good side when there's female flesh on display.

I have to admit, I like the way he's looking at me. No one has looked at me like that since Rory and that was *months* ago.

"Tell me something about yourself," he says. "All I know is that you're a dangerous weapon."

Fearing that this is a veiled reference to my incompetence in the stunt department, I redirect the conversation again. "I can't say more. I'm undercover tonight."

"As a friend of the bride or the groom?"

I consider lying but he must know one of them well enough to ask. "Neither. My mother and I are just passing through."

He studies me for a second. "You mean you're crashing?"

"Not exactly. I mean, not intentionally. Mom wanted to show me the Cabana Club and ignored the sign." I point to her, now dancing cheek to cheek with Roger. "She gets carried away."

"Well, since you're here, you might as well enjoy it," he says, turning to the buffet table. "Try the lobster. They had it flown in from Maine."

"I can't eat their food," I say. "It's for invited guests."

"And the booze is for crashers?" he asks, glancing at my drink.

I grin at him. "Just trying to blend in."

He piles food onto plates and leads me to a table. "You can relax. I RSVP'd that I was bringing a date—and I didn't. So from now on, consider yourself my guest. It's an honor to be seen with someone wearing Narciso Rodriguez."

"It's my mother's," I say, lest he think I'm the type to swan around in designer dresses all the time. The new and improved Leigh Reid doesn't need labels. "What happened to your date?"

"She couldn't make it."

"Dumper or dumpee?" I ask.

"No comment." He lifts his glass to mine. "But it all worked out."

It certainly did. If this is the way guys operate with each other, I'm all for it. I can separate business from pleasure. I will have a great time with Julian tonight and go back to hating him on Monday morning. It makes perfect sense.

As we finishing eating, the band takes a break and a deejay cues up Gwen Stefani.

"Finally," Julian says. "Music we can dance to." He drapes his jacket over the chair and leads me to the dance floor.

Scene 5: Leigh in the House

EXTERIOR CABANA CLUB, NIGHT

Leigh Reid moves to the music with such contagious enthusiasm that a crowd begins to gather. Julian tries to follow along, but Leigh is so hot there are scorch marks on the dance floor. When the song ends, the crowd applauds spontaneously.

A slow song comes on and Julian pulls Leigh close. She rests her head on his shoulder, realizing that if this works out, she'll be able to start wearing heels again.

> JULIAN
> I'm sorry I've been such a jerk to you on
> set.

> LEIGH
> And I'm sorry I knocked you out.

> JULIAN
> It's okay. I'll help you rehearse if
> you're willing to put in some long hours.

Leigh nods, staring into Julian's exotic eyes. He leans down and kisses her. The music gets faster, but they continue to sway in their own little world.

JULIAN

Why don't you move into my trailer on Monday? That tin can Chaz assigned you is a wreck.

LEIGH

Isn't it kind of soon to be moving in together?

JULIAN

When it's right, it's right.

LEIGH

Julian, I want to but set romances usually end in disaster. As long as we're both on this show, I think we should just be friends.

JULIAN

I can't just be friends. It would kill me. Either we're together or...we're not.

LEIGH

[eyes filling with tears]
Please, don't make me do this, Julian.

Someone gives my shoulder a little shake. "I said, what are you thinking about?"

I look up at Julian, stunned. Progressing from zero to breakup in the course of two dances has to be a record even for my active imagination. "Work," I say. "I'm just wishing Monday wouldn't come." That's when Cinderella's prince loses his charm.

Before I can say more, Annika arrives beside us on the dance floor. "Darling, we have to go. I heard the floral designer is in the kitchen."

"So?"

Annika pries my fingers off Julian's shoulder one by one. "This woman is the Wolfgang Puck of floral arranging, and someone needs to take notes while I interview her." She offers Julian a smile and a toss of her ringlets. "Please excuse us."

"Mom, this isn't a good time," I protest, replacing my hand on Julian's shoulder.

Annika leans in and sniffs. "Do I smell alcohol? Because if I do, young lady . . ."

Realizing that lingering is only going to cause further embarrassment, I tell Julian I'll be back and follow my mother off the dance floor.

"I've heard it takes months to get an appointment with this designer, and I don't have months," Annika says. "Besides, judging by his expression, your cutie will wait for you anyway."

"Do you think so?" I ask.

"I have seen that look before, darling. Who is he?"

"Julian Gerrard. He's on *Freak Force*."

She smiles. "Then it's a good thing you decided not to quit, isn't it?"

Annika raises one hand to silence me as we enter the kitchen. With the other, she seizes the arm of a young woman who's adorning the dessert trays with pink roses.

The tray tips and the woman steadies it. "Are you trying to get me fired?"

"On the contrary," Annika says. "I'm here to offer you another job."

The woman looks at us and shakes her head. "Sorry, I can't do your daughter's wedding. I'm booked every weekend till 2009."

Annika waves her rock under the woman's nose. "I am the

bride. And as it happens, it's a weekday ceremony: February four-teenth."

The florist snorts. "If you're thinking 2012, I have an open-ing."

Annika deflates. "Surely you can squeeze us in? My fiancé is an influential producer and you know who I am."

The woman shakes her head. "I don't but it wouldn't matter."

A woman wearing a headset and clutching a clipboard flies into the kitchen, calling, "Dessert trays! Two minutes, Nina."

"Nearly finished," the florist says, glaring at Annika. "I've been distracted."

Ms. Headset examines Annika closely. "I recognize you."

Mom stands a little taller. "You do?"

"Mom," I caution her.

She ignores me. "I'm Annika Anderson—from *Danny Boy.*"

The woman checks the A's on her clipboard. "No Anderson here." Her eyes narrow. "Is *Danny Boy* a publication? Are you pa-parazzi?"

Before Annika can protest, Headset confiscates Annika's purse and empties it onto the counter. When she sees Mom's stash of wedding favors, she grabs each of us by the arm and escorts us out of the kitchen. "I don't know what you're up to, but if you don't leave now, I'm calling the police."

"Can't I say good-bye to my friend?" I ask.

The woman scowls at me. "Only if you want to say hello to the LAPD."

Julian catches up to us as we near the exit. "Where are you going? You're supposed to be my date."

"Darling you heard the Headset," Annika says. "We have to go."

"I'll meet you outside, Mom."

★　★　★

Julian smiles as Annika slips out the door. "Busted?"

"Busted. I've got to run but thanks for everything. I'll see you Monday."

"Monday?" he asks. "Sure, that'll work but it'll have to be late. Give me your number."

That's sweet. He could just look me up on the cast list, but he wants to make it personal. I scrawl my cell number on the heart-shaped paper and hand it to him.

He kisses my cheek as he accepts it. Then he glances at the piece of paper and says, "You're going to have to give me your name now."

"Very funny," I reply. "If you ask for Effluvia, I'm hanging up."

His smile vanishes and he is silent for a long moment before saying, "You're not that . . . that hog?"

Uh-oh. "I thought you knew."

"How would I know that?" he asks. "I've never seen you without your prosthetics."

"But you've heard my voice," I say. "And my photo is on the wall with yours in the production office."

This doesn't slow him down. "You tricked me. So that's what you meant by undercover."

"That was just a joke," I insist. "You're being stupid."

His face flushes. "If you tell anyone on set that I asked you out, I'll—"

"You didn't," I interrupt. "I asked *you*." It's not exactly true but it might calm him down.

"Well, don't say anything."

He's ashamed of being interested in me. How flattering. "Like I'd want to."

Lifting his hand, he crumples the heart with my phone number and drops it on the floor. "Unless there's a camera rolling," he says, "don't ever speak to me again."

seven

Roger leans into the BMW and says, "Did I mention you looked sensational at the Cabana Club the other night?"

"Thank you," I say. "Tell Annie to let me keep the dress."

Roger laughs but Annika raises her shades to give me the eye. "I believe he was speaking to me, darling."

I know that but Roger is spending too much time fanning the flames of Annika's vanity. He quit that job years ago. Still, he tosses her another compliment about her dancing before doing a salsa step back into the studio, singing, *"Feeling hot, hot, hot."*

Sasha punches the back of my headrest to signal that she's ready to be released from the backseat. "Isn't there a law about old people dancing?"

Annika ignores worse comments from Sasha every day, but this time she reacts because it's about age. "Watch it, Sasha. Or you'll be paying cab fare for the rest of the week."

Sasha climbs out of the car. "You couldn't stay away from Roger that long."

"Roger and I are just old—er, *longtime*—friends. Nothing more." She looks to me for support. "Right, darling?"

The dirty dancing episode at the Cabana Lounge suggested otherwise, but I don't intend to share my suspicions with Sasha. "They're just old friends," I confirm. "It's probably hard for you to relate to since you don't have any, Sasha."

"I have loads of friends," Sasha retorts.

"No, I mean *real* friends. Not people who hang out with you because your Dad can get them jobs."

Sasha swings her purse and the buckle connects with my funny bone. I get back into the car, rubbing my elbow.

"Feel better?" Annika asks.

Actually, I do. I'd been on edge about returning to set today but now I feel quite calm. Antagonizing Sasha seems to be more effective than yoga.

★   ★   ★

Forty-six minutes and counting. That's how long I've been on the elliptical machine and I feel like throwing up. Sure, I've read the articles that recommend easing into an exercise routine but I don't have that kind of time. There's a panther around these parts who needs his butt kicked, and I intend to turn this feeble body into a machine capable of doing it.

The lights in the gym begin to flash on and off, and for a second I wonder if I'm having a heart attack. It would be uncommon in someone my age, but I have a lot of stress in my life at the moment.

I slow down to a comfortable pace and the lights stop flashing.

"Are you trying to kill yourself?"

Pulling my headphones out of my ears, I look toward the gym door to see Freddy standing with her hand on the light switch. "Just trying—to get into—shape," I puff.

She walks toward me. "Too much too soon causes injuries. Off you get."

I resist. "Freddy, Chaz is going to—fire me—if I don't do better. Or make me—invisible—which is probably worse."

"I admire your determination, but at this rate you'll take yourself out of the game. How long have you been here?"

"Half an hour," I lie.

"Don't make me pull the plug, Leigh."

I let the machine slow before jumping off and collapsing onto a mat. "When does it get easier?"

"Not for a while. Did you eat breakfast?"

I shake my head. "Effluvia will be binging on junk all day."

"Look, I'll make you a deal," Freddy says. "I'll help you train if you follow my advice to the letter. That includes eating healthy meals. If you agree, I'll talk to Chaz today about letting you use a spit bucket."

I lift my head off the mat. "You'd do that?"

She smiles. "If I don't your mother will."

I clamber to my feet and make a move to hug her, but she backs away. "Only my own sweat, thanks."

Freddy leads me to the free weights and does a set of squats while holding a barbell across her shoulders. She's like a mighty ant that can lift twenty times its actual body weight. When she's done, she removes more than half the weight and helps me do a set. My legs are shaking after ten repetitions.

"Strength is the real key to doing stunts well," Fred explains. "But it's not about bulging muscles because you'll be faking the hits anyway. The strength is for putting height into your jumps, distance into your leaps, and control into your spins."

She illustrates her point with a series of martial arts moves, alternately kicking and dodging out of the way of a large punching bag that hangs from the ceiling.

"You're ahead of the curve as far as flexibility goes," she continues. "But you're behind it on strength. Drop and give me ten."

"Push-ups?" I ask, stalling.

When she nods, I lower myself to the dirty gym floor and, with difficulty, put a few inches of air between my chest and the hardwood. There I stick, unable to go up, unwilling to crash down.

Freddy sighs. "I see we have some work ahead of us."

★　★　★

Most people would consider gentle stretches a light warm-up, but for Freddy it means a hundred crunches, fifty squats, thirty lunges, and ten (ladies') push-ups. I'm worn out before we even start working on a stunt. If I'd known training would be this hard, I'd have let Chaz fire me.

Today's stunt sequence is fairly straightforward, but I'm still nervous because our guest villain is Sir Nigel Wanley, the well-respected British actor. I was surprised Chaz could land a star of Sir Nigel's magnitude, and as it turns out, he didn't. According to Drake, Sir Nigel actually *asked* to be on the show after seeing the pilot. He has a soft spot for science fiction, having begun his career playing a robot on a popular TV show. Back then he was just Nigel Wanley, but nearly thirty years—and dozens of major action roles—later, he was knighted for his contributions to cinema.

Sir Nigel's résumé may intimidate me but his title doesn't. After all, I've hung out with people who outrank him. Okay, one person but it was an actual Irish lord, with noble bloodlines. Lord Tracy of the famous brewing family invited the *Danny Boy* cast and crew for cocktails after we filmed on his estate. I chatted with Lord T. over a glass of sherry, and once you've hobnobbed with real nobles, knights are no big deal.

Still, with my rep already in tatters, I don't want to become the girl who kicked a knight in the groin, or anywhere else for that matter. There's plenty of room for error in today's sequence. Effluvia is to begin with hand-to-hand combat with Sir Nigel, then charge and knock him to the ground. He pulls her to the ground in turn and she finishes the job by chewing off his trigger finger.

Freddy takes me through the sequence a few times with the punching bag standing in for the villain.

"Let's see more energy," she says after my fourth try. "The bag hardly moved when you charged."

"I'm trying to be gentle. Sir Nigel is pretty old."

"Excuse me? He's only fifty-two and he's been doing his own stunts since before you were born. If you come at him like that, you'll embarrass yourself."

She tells me to picture someone else's face on the punching
bag and it isn't hard to think of a worthy villain.

Scene 6: Leigh Teaches Julian a Lesson

INTERIOR STUDIO, DAY

*Chaz calls action. Leigh Reid immediately springs
and plants a kick on Julian's chest.*

JULIAN
[staggering backward]
What the hell was that?

LEIGH
Payback. For the way you treated me
Friday night.

JULIAN
Me?! You tricked me, you sneaky—

*Leigh delivers a wicked punch to Julian's diaphragm
before he can finish.*

LEIGH
Warthog. That's my role and I'm not
ashamed of it. If you weren't such a con-
ceited jerk, you'd be able to recognize
your own costars.

*Leigh winds up and swings again. Julian tries to
block the blow, but he's not fast enough. He reels back
from the combination punch to his jaw.*

JULIAN

Chaz! Cut! She's out of control!

LEIGH

Sure, cry to Daddy, you whiner.

JULIAN

What is wrong with you?

LEIGH

I'm tired of putting up with your crap.

JULIAN

You mean you're tired of hitting on me
and getting burned.

*Leigh grabs a two-by-four that turns out to be the
real thing and swings it at Julian's thigh.*

LEIGH

How's that for hitting on you?

JULIAN

You're deranged. That's what lust will do
to you.

Leigh drops the two-by-four and charges.

Freddy examines the broken chain from which the punching
bag once hung. "I guess that's a wrap on the training session."

I examine the chain for myself. "Did I do that?"

"You did. I want you to cut that energy by half, okay? If Sir
Nigel ends up in the hospital, you're not the only one who'll get
fired."

As I turn to go, she adds, "And skip the war whoop. You sounded deranged."

★ ★ ★

We're shooting at a grocery store today and, as usual, my rusty old tin can is parked furthest from set. Even to get to the cast pick-up point at craft services is a ten-minute walk.

I stop dead when I get close enough to the idling cast van to see that Rudy and Jed are already inside. If I could skip the ride, I would but it's the last pickup and I'd be late for call. Besides, it's starting to rain and I'm already in costume.

I decide to be positive. Today is a new day and a fresh opportunity to prove to the guys that I'm part of their team.

Jed sees me coming and says something to Rudy that involves a rude hand gesture. Rudy laughs so hard he slumps into the seat and disappears from view. Clearly the Maturity Fairy didn't visit this weekend. But I refuse to let their bad attitude get me down. I am an enlightened human being. One day, they will beg me for tips on achieving inner balance.

I pick up the pace and Jed reaches in front of the driver to lay on the horn. Julian immediately steps out of the craft truck with a coffee in hand and hops into the van. The guys point in my direction and Julian turns and sees me. He says something to the driver as the van starts to roll forward.

"Wait for me!" I yell, running the last few steps.

The van kicks a cloud of dirt into my face as it accelerates.

★ ★ ★

Sir Nigel is signing autographs at the center of an excited crowd when I arrive outside the grocery store. He graciously fields questions about his movies (can't possibly choose a favorite), his marital status (doting husband and father of three), and his knighthood (an undeserved but delightful honor). Even when people ask really stupid questions, he just rattles off a joke in his

English accent and everyone is charmed. Now that is class. If I'm ever that famous, I will use Sir Nigel as my role model.

Chaz elbows his way through the crowd, wearing an ivory silk cravat intended to impress our resident knight. "Lex," he bellows into a megaphone. "Get the plebs away from Sir Nigel." Slinging an arm around Nigel, he whacks a few people with the megaphone until they move back.

"Now, now," Sir Nigel protests. "I'm absolutely fine."

Lex drops pylons around Sir Nigel to create a "safe zone," which the good knight immediately ignores to mingle with his people.

Meanwhile Drake beckons urgently to me from inside the store. When I join him, he pats my cheeks with tissues and clucks with dismay. "What did you do?"

I explain that the guys left me to walk in the rain, and Drake flags down Lex to say he'll need half an hour to fix my makeup.

Drake doesn't even have time to open his kit before Chaz arrives, followed by Jed, Rudy, and Julian. It's like there's a telepathic connection between them and I've never been hooked up.

"Do you think you're important enough to keep Sir Nigel waiting while Drake powders your nose?" Chaz demands.

"*Reattaches* her nose," Drake corrects him. "And it's not her fault she had to walk to set in the rain."

"She was supposed to take the cast van," Chaz says.

"Our diva prefers private transportation," Jed says.

"Ideally a limo," Rudy says. "With crushed velvet seats."

"Divas only sit on designer names," says Julian, who is standing across from me. "Does Narciso Rodriguez do upholstery?"

Interesting that my "killer dress" is still on his mind. "I wouldn't know," I say. "Because I am not a diva." My voice sounds snooty, so it's no surprise that everyone laughs.

"Could have fooled me," Julian says. "Oh right," he adds under his breath, "you already did."

Before I can even think about impulse control my arm swings back and fires. My script hits Julian in the chest and falls to the floor, scattering pages everywhere.

Chaz advances on me so fast his legs are a blur. He raps on my snout with his pen. "Scarlett, if you even think about showing that temper in front of Sir Nigel, I will personally see to it that you never work in this town again. Understood?"

"Understood," I mutter. I turn away from the pen and it jabs into my temple.

★　★　★

Oddly enough, my day improves once we start shooting the stunt. I manage to get through the hand-to-hand combat with Sir Nigel without a hitch. We move on to the tackle and Sir Nigel hits the ground as gently as a feather. Then he pulls me to the ground and I pretend to tear into his hand with my tusks until he screams.

After Chaz cuts the camera, Sir Nigel gets to his feet and gallantly helps me to mine. "Nicely done," he says.

No one can tell because of the prosthetics but I am beaming.

Chaz ambles over. "I'd like to run the sequence again."

"Really?" Sir Nigel asks. "I thought the young lady sold every single hit."

The young lady tries to cast a secret glance toward her costars, but her long snout hits her own shoulder.

"The hits were good," Chaz says, only because denying it would mean disagreeing with Sir Nigel. "But I think I want the scene to be more campy."

"Campy?" I ask, not quite sure what he means.

"We need to ham it up a little, Effluvia," Chaz says. He looks over at the guys and they smirk. "Get it?"

Sir Nigel smiles. "He just wants us to have some fun with it. We can do that, can't we?"

"Sure," I say. With Sir Nigel on my team, I'm ready to try anything.

"Okay, so here's what I had in mind," Chaz continues. "Effluvia will eat throughout the fight."

"Eat!" I say, alarmed. I can barely nail the stunts when I'm not trying to chew at the same time.

"Not to worry," Sir Nigel says, patting my shoulder reassuringly. "Since we're in a grocery store, why don't we just improvise?"

Chaz hesitates, but out of respect for Sir Nigel agrees to give it a try, as long as we keep the key elements of the stunt.

He returns to his chair and I scuttle after him. "Chaz, I can't eat and tackle Sir Nigel. I might bite my tongue off."

Straightening his cravat, he says, "Scarlett, nothing would make me happier than to make Effluvia a mute."

★   ★   ★

Sir Nigel and I try to chat about our new approach, but Chaz interrupts to send us to our marks. Freddy is tugging at his sleeve but he shakes her off and says, "We going to run the scene in a single steadicam shot, so there won't be time for a spit bucket."

Normally, I'd be in a state of panic by now but I'm not. That's partly because I did some improvisation during my acting course last summer, and Professor Kirk thought I had a flair for it. But it's mainly because Sir Nigel is calmly towing me toward my mark as if I were his protégé. His confidence makes me believe I'm capable of revising the scene on the fly.

INTERIOR GROCERY STORE, DAY

Effluvia creeps down the dairy aisle, eyes, ears, and nose on alert for the killer. Suddenly, she stops. There's a special on potato chips.

                          EFFLUVIA
                 That's a good price.

*She selects a bag and tears it open while walking over
to the cooler. After perusing the dip selections, she
pulls the lid off one and starts eating.*

The Panther is right behind her, rolling his eyes.

                          PANTHER
                       [whispering]
                 Effluvia, the crunching is going to give
                 away our position.

                          EFFLUVIA
                 [shoving a handful of chips into her mouth]
                 The killer is as good as dead, chips or no
                 chips.

*Rounding the corner, she comes face-to-face with
Sebastian, international double agent. He presses his
gun to Effluvia's snout.*

*Effluvia stares down the barrel of Sebastian's gun
for a moment before raising her right hand.*

                          EFFLUVIA
                 Dip?

*Sebastian glances down for a split second and Efflu-
via instantly knocks the gun out of his hand. He
tries to retrieve it, but she drops the food and stops
him with a quick combination punch to his jawline.*

Sebastian reels backward and she charges, knocking him to the floor.

Effluvia grabs a jar of peanut butter from another display and unscrews the top. She steps on Sebastian's neck as he struggles to rise and waves the jar under his nose.

> EFFLUVIA
> I have the peanut butter, Sebastian, but
> you seem to be the one in the jam.

Sebastian grabs Effluvia's foot and yanks. As she tumbles, he springs to his feet and grabs a bunch of fresh herbs.

> EFFLUVIA
> Is that supposed to be camouflage?
> Because I can still see you.

> SEBASTIAN
> It's rosemary. I'm roasting a pig tonight.

> EFFLUVIA
> Fat chance of that.

Effluvia clambers to her feet and picks up the peanut butter. She dips one cloven hoof into it and shoves it into her mouth. Then she tackles Sebastian again.

"No bite," I whisper to Sir Nigel through clamped teeth. The peanut butter has dislodged my tusks.

Ever the pro, Nigel immediately pretends to lose consciousness.

Julian, however, hasn't finished improvising.

PANTHER
Just take a bite out of the guy, Effluvia.

I work the tusks apart with my tongue in time to fire back:

Nah. I'm trying to watch my figure.

Chaz calls cut and the crew cracks up. Sir Nigel, still lying beside me on the floor, is laughing harder than anyone. He gives me a high five.

Drake approaches with a tissue and I spit the tusks into it. "Way to go, Leigh," he says. "You were hot."

Chaz lifts his shades so I can see his baleful squint. "I said you could improvise, not rewrite the entire script."

"You wanted camp," I argue.

"Camp, not crap."

"Chaz," Sir Nigel interrupts. "If you'd care to hear the opinion of someone who's been in this business a long time . . ."

"Of course, Sir Nigel, sir," Chaz says, practically groveling. "I'd be honored."

"My advice is to leave well enough alone. It was rather cleverly done, if I do say so myself."

He looks to the crew and they applaud. The cast doesn't make much effort.

"The credit goes to the young lady," Sir Nigel continues. "I do believe she's a comedienne in the making."

Who cares about bloodlines? In my book, knights rule.

★   ★   ★

I feel fifty pounds lighter when I step off Drake's truck, and it isn't because I've shed Effluvia's costume for the day.

Sir Nigel thinks I'm clever. And funny. Clever and funny

and talented! The new and improved Leigh can't let things like that go to her head, but she can enjoy them for a few moments when she's alone. Encouragement has been in very short supply lately.

I plug in my headphones, hit PLAY on my iPod, and sing along with Destiny's Child. *"I'm gonna work harder, I'm a survivor, I'm gonna make it . . ."*

The song dies in my throat when my trailer comes into view. It's listing at a forty-five-degree angle, like a ship that's run aground. Both of the tires on one side are flat. I knew it was a wreck, but I didn't think things were this bad.

I walk up the two steps and try to push the door open, but the sofa has slid over to block it. Since my purse and script pages are still inside, I decide to try using force.

I reverse my steps and charge at the door, Effluvia style.

Unfortunately, the old toaster is stronger than she looks.

"Ouch," someone says, as I pick myself up off the ground. It's Julian and as usual, he's smirking. "That must've hurt."

Suddenly, I realize what happened to my trailer. "You slashed my tires."

"What?" He looks stunned, probably because I figured out his game so quickly.

"It wasn't enough just to slash them," I say, getting madder by the second. "You had to stick around and see my reaction. You really are a jerk."

"And you really are a diva if you think I'd go to the trouble of vandalizing this heap just to bug you."

"Well, if you didn't do it then why are you here?"

Before he can answer, we see a driver coming toward us rolling two spare tires. "Sorry about the flats, Miss Reid. We must have run over some broken glass when we got you parked this morning. We'll have you back to normal in no time."

"She wasn't normal in the first place," Julian points out.

"Why don't you just shut up and go?" I say.

He's already walking away and he wiggles his fingers in a backward wave.

The driver looks up from the tires. "You got it bad for him, don't ya?"

eight

I didn't give Professor Kirk nearly enough credit last summer. It's only now that I'm beginning to realize how much I learned from him during my acting course. If it weren't for his lessons on improvisation, for example, I wouldn't have impressed Sir Nigel the other day.

Now I'm using another of his techniques and this time I'm off set. Professor Kirk says that actors can only give their best performance when they're unconscious of the audience, so he taught us how to block out external distractions. My favorite technique involves imagining myself walking into a soundproof room and shutting the door. When I use it, I can tune out anything I don't want to hear.

Well, almost anything. Sometimes, like now, the soundproofing leaks a little. I am sitting on the sectional sofa in the Cohen living room trying to watch a DVD documentary on warthogs. I asked Sir Nigel for some advice on developing my character and he suggested that studying real warthogs in action would help me fine-tune Effluvia's movements.

The house was empty when I sat down, but naturally Sasha and Gray arrived soon afterward and joined me to deliver a scathing commentary. Fortunately, Gray's hormones eventually overrode their need to shtick and now there's so much suction at their end of the sofa, the house might implode. Disgusted as I am, I won't give them the satisfaction of leaving.

Gray started his stint on Sasha's show this week and he has driven her home every night. Usually they start out in Sasha's bedroom, but Gray is always on hand to schmooze when Jake's BMW pulls into the driveway.

Sasha climbs on top of Gray, obviously determined to get my attention. Every so often there's a gap in the suction as she turns to make sure I'm taking it all in.

I turn up the volume and start taking deep breaths to regain my focus.

"Do you hear heavy breathing?" Sasha asks. "Someone's getting all worked up over warthog mating rituals."

"Or maybe she just wishes she were you, sweetie," Gray says.

My soundproof room collapses around me. "Always," I say. "But if Jake has another job to offer, maybe I'll find a user boyfriend of my own."

"That's not what happened," Sasha scoffs. "Daddy just recognizes talent when he sees it."

"He didn't recognize it four months ago. That's when Gray asked me to put in a good word for him, but I didn't feel right about it. And guess what? Gray didn't get the part."

"You're making that up," she says, but she slides off Gray's lap. "Tell her, Gray."

Gray slides his arm around Sasha. "She's just trying to wind you up, babe."

"Notice he's not denying it," I say. "But maybe you could discuss it later when I'm not trying learn something."

Gray murmurs something to Sasha that includes the words "jealous" and "liar" and pretty soon, the suction machine is up and running again.

"Get your tongue back in your own mouth right now or I'll see that it's permanently removed," Jake says.

We all jump but Gray is airborne long after I've relaxed. "Sorry, Mr. Cohen," he mutters.

"Daddy, don't be so mean," Sasha says. "I'm almost seventeen and I can kiss my boyfriend if I want to."

Jake shakes his head in disgust. "Show some discretion. Leigh is trying to study for her role and you're letting that boy slobber all over you."

"It's all right, Jake," I say. "This is the first night they've bothered me. Usually he's slobbering in Sasha's bedroom."

Gray is running to the front door before Jake can even form the words "Get out." Sasha starts after him but Jake stops her. "Upstairs," he commands.

"But we're seeing a movie tonight."

"You won't have time after reviewing your lines."

"But Daddy . . ." Sasha wails.

Annika walks through the front door with Brando under one arm. "What's going on?" she asks.

"Your daughter is trying to ruin my life," Sasha says, stomping toward the stairs.

"Sasha, come back," Annika says. "Let's talk about this."

"Let's not," Jake says, leading Annika to the sofa. "This is the three-week anniversary of our engagement and I don't want anything to ruin it." He pulls a Henry Winton box from a shopping bag and presents it to her.

Sasha forgotten instantly, Annika beams. "You are the most romantic man in the entire world."

If you ask me, it's not romantic, it's creepy. Jake is always going overboard as if he's afraid of losing Mom. According to the talk shows, normal men forget birthdays and anniversaries. Jake must be one of those guys who's in love with the idea of being in love.

One day, his delusion will pass and he'll be shocked to discover how much work Annika really is. Then he'll dump her. When that day arrives, I'll be right there helping Mom pack her bags. I've realized that there are worse things than living in a small house in the valley. Specifically, living with Sasha Cohen.

Annika unwraps a delicate silver bracelet and promptly launches herself into Jake's arms. I stand to leave. Watching Sasha make out with Gray was bad enough. I am not sticking around to witness Mom thanking Mr. Romance.

"Leigh, wait," Jake says, disengaging my mother, "I have a gift for you too." He reaches into the shopping bag again and passes me a DVD.

Big deal, more dailies. Jake brings home the unedited footage from my show most nights and I never watch it. It's not that I wouldn't like to. Seeing how lame I am would probably help me improve. But there's no DVD player in my bedroom and Sasha would have a field day critiquing my performance. I have enough insecurities already.

"There's more," Jake assures me, smiling. He takes a box out of the shopping bag. "It's a DVD player for your room—so that you can watch your dailies in private."

Obviously, I was a little hasty before. Jake is not a freak but an exceptionally thoughtful man.

Sasha must take after her mother.

⋆ ⋆ ⋆

At least I am in the privacy of my own bedroom when I come to the part of the script that is going to make tomorrow a difficult day: *Panther kisses Effluvia.*

I didn't see that coming. Why would I? In our two previous episodes, Panther has gone out of his way to let his former girl-friend know that she revolts him—that while he may respect her talent for fighting bad guys, he can't think of her in that way any-more. But in this new episode, Effluvia visits Panther's apartment, where the former lovebirds finally confront their past relationship and their current feelings for each other.

Who knew Chaz had such a romantic streak? It's an interesting storyline, and a great opportunity for me to develop my character further. Effluvia isn't just a fierce fighting machine with a big appetite. Earlier this week I discovered her wit, and tomorrow I will explore her capacity to forgive someone who has hurt her so much.

Fortunately, I don't have to explore my own capacity to forgive. I am not about to forgive Julian Gerrard for the way he has treated me. Effluvia, on the other hand, is free to make up her own mind about the Panther. I will do what is right for the character. Leigh Reid is a pro who doesn't let personal feelings get in the way of her performance. I could kiss a cockroach if I had to. In fact, I'd prefer it. I'd rather kiss a chimpanzee or even a snake than Julian.

Okay, not a snake.

But any sort of primate would be fine. Or a wildebeest. Possibly a mongoose.

A knock at my bedroom door prevents me from working my way through the entire animal kingdom. Jake has arrived to hook up the DVD player.

When he's done, he hands me the remote. "I've already watched the dailies and I was really impressed by your scene with Sir Nigel."

"Thanks," I say, careful not to show too much excitement. I'm not sure whether he's speaking as the show's executive producer or my mother's overeager boyfriend. I guess as long as I work for Jake, I'll always have to walk that line. "What did you think of the improv? That was Sir Nigel's idea."

"Really?" He looks surprised. Chaz probably took credit for it since it worked so well. "I thought it took the show in a whole new direction and I've asked Chaz to do more. Did you enjoy it?"

"It was fun. And challenging."

"How about the next episode?" he asks, grinning. "That looks like fun too."

"It's a great storyline, but I think it's a little soon for Effluvia to be kissing the Panther."

"Why? They were a couple in their former life."

"But he's a dirt bag in *this* life. He tried to kill her, remember?"

"Only when he was infected by the venom of a mutant beast," Jake says.

"Yeah, well he still treats her like crap. She'd be crazy to trust him."

Jake laughs. "Deep down he still loves Effluvia. He just doesn't know how to show it—especially with his friends around. That's what guys are like."

"You're not," I say.

"I'm not eighteen. Guys that age are idiots. I don't have to care what anyone thinks anymore. I can tell the whole world how I feel about your mother. When you experience the absolute bliss of loving someone—"

"Jake?" I interrupt. "I say this as your future stepdaughter, not your employee, but you're grossing me out."

He laughs again. "Sorry. I get carried away."

It's hard to dislike this man, and if it weren't for his evil spawn, I might enjoy having him as a stepfather.

As if sensing my thoughts, Sasha appears in the doorway. "Daddy, I need you."

"I'll be there in a minute," Jake says. "Leigh and I are having a chat."

She pouts. "I need you *now*. The door of Olivier's crate is squeaking. It's hurting his ears."

"Well, we can't have that," he says, winking at me. "It's obviously a c*anine*-one-one." He disappears down the hall, chuckling at his own joke.

Sasha lingers in the doorway. "You do realize you're going to have to pay for ratting me out?"

"I did it for your own good," I say, with mock sincerity. "I was worried that Gray was taking advantage of you. You deserve better than that."

"Stay out of my business, Farthog. Or else."

I see I didn't miss much by being an only child.

★   ★   ★

Rudy, Jed, and Julian are already complaining because we had to assemble early—and in costume—for a cast photo shoot. The show's current promotional glossies were taken before I joined the cast, and now that I'm receiving fan mail of my own the publicist insisted we update them.

"Can't you just add Katrina to our photo digitally?" Jed asks the publicist. "You could make her smaller than the rest of us since she didn't have to audition."

The publicist giggles at his wit. She's in her early twenties and she loves the guys—so much that she's responding to all their fan mail for them, whereas I have to answer my own. Not that I mind. Sir Nigel probably answers his own fan mail. Besides, so far I've only received four letters, and I don't have to answer the one from the convict.

"Leigh, can you move a little closer to Julian?" the photographer says. "I can't get you in the shot."

"Try switching to a wide-angle lens," Julian suggests.

"He's already using it to get your ego in the shot," I say.

"Play nice," the photographer says. "The sooner you show me some teeth, the sooner we're done here."

I move two steps closer to Julian, making sure there's still air between us. Everyone smiles and the photographer clicks off the "team" portrait.

The publicist says, "Let's do a few action shots. Julian, why don't you flip Effluvia backward?"

"There's no mat," I say.

"You have padding," Julian points out. "Lots of it."

He steps forward quickly and flips me over his leg. Hard. Thanks to Jake, I realize that this is a revenge hit. Julian is proving something to his pals. I almost don't mind because maybe now he'll be able to move on. I even make a show of rubbing my arm as I get up, so he'll think he really made an impression.

"You call that a flip?" Rudy asks. "Let me show you how it's done." He darts at me and tosses me down.

I hit the floor much harder this time, but spring to my feet to prove I can take it.

"My turn," Jed says, stepping forward.

"No," I say.

"No," the publicist echoes.

But Jed is determined to have his turn and grabs my arm. Because I'm resisting, he ends up flipping me forward and my front padding drives into my diaphragm as I land. I lie there for a few seconds, catching my breath and blinking away tears.

So, this is what it's like to be bullied. There's zero tolerance for this sort of thing at the Nerd Academy, although I can't imagine it ever happening there anyway. Still, I know that the worst thing you can do with bullies is to let them know they're getting to you.

"Are you okay?" Julian asks, as I heave myself to my feet.

"Sure," I say, smiling at the camera. "Ready for my close up."

"Not just yet," Freddy says, stepping out of the shadows off set. "First, I want to demonstrate a proper throw on Jed."

Jed's amber eyes widen. "How about later in the gym?"

"No, when I see something that needs to be corrected, I like to get right on it." Almost before she finishes speaking, she grabs Jed's arm and flips him. He hits the ground hard and stays there. Fred looks down at him. "Want to run that again?"

He shakes his head.

"Then act like a professional so no one gets hurt."

★　★　★

Jed and Rudy stand beside Julian, apparently in moral support, as they have finished shooting for the day. Julian must be dreading the big kiss as much as I am.

We're on the set of Panther's loft apartment and it's the coolest set the designers have built so far. It's been raised off the studio floor to allow for a huge terrace outside of the modern living room. The green screen that currently serves as a backdrop will later be replaced by a computer-generated skyline. Inside the loft, there are fake brick walls, thick timber beams, and a marble-fronted gas fireplace that actually works.

I take my mark beside the refrigerator so that the cameraman can adjust his lighting. Julian takes his mark at the kitchen table. When the cameraman asks him to turn my way, he does, but without making eye contact. Maybe he should ask his henchmen to do it for him.

"Rolling in five minutes," Lex announces, leaping onto the set. "Chaz wants you to run the dialogue up to the kiss. Then he's going to cut and cover the kiss in a separate shot."

"You better hope she flosses," Rudy tells Julian. "Warthog breath can be deadly."

"I already asked for danger pay," Julian says, earning a round of high fives from the henchmen.

Drake leads me to my cast chair for a touch-up. "I'm going to ask Chaz to send Jed and Rudy home," he says. "You've got enough of a challenge ahead of you."

I'm actually not that fazed. Sure, it's a drag that my costar finds me repellent, but it's his job to act like he doesn't. Besides, Annika has always said that a little tension between actors can lead to good chemistry on screen.

But then, she's never had to kiss someone she kicked in the crotch.

★   ★   ★

INTERIOR PANTHER'S KITCHEN, NIGHT

After a long day of fighting evil together, Panther has invited Effluvia back to his apartment for dinner. While he mixes a cocktail, Effluvia rifles through his fridge and cuts herself a slab of cheese.

EFFLUVIA
Remember the first time I came for dinner? You served spaghetti and meatballs. And strawberries for dessert.

PANTHER
I remember. You barely ate.

EFFLUVIA
[eating a slice of leftover pizza]
You made me nervous.

PANTHER
I see I no longer have the same effect.

EFFLUVIA
Times change.

PANTHER
You were the first girl I really loved.

*Effluvia puts the pizza down and her eyes fill with
tears.*

EFFLUVIA
You used to say I was the *only* girl you'd
ever really love.

PANTHER
That could still be true. But like you
said, times change.

EFFLUVIA
[breaking down]
None of this is my fault. Do you think I
wanted to be hideous? My life is ruined!

PANTHER
Effluvia, this isn't permanent. The
smartest guys in this country are trying
to figure out how to turn us back into
normal human beings.

                      EFFLUVIA
        It will never happen. We're of more use to
        the government like this. I'm a monster
        and I'll probably stay this way forever.

Panther opens the fridge and pulls out a pint of
strawberries.

                      PANTHER
                    [soothingly]
        Look what I got. For old time's sake.

He feeds her one and pats the bristles between her ears.

        I'm sorry I've been so distant. It's just
        hard to accept how much has changed.

Effluvia selects the biggest strawberry to feed to
Panther.

Seeing a chance to improvise, I pull a can of whipped cream
out of the fridge and squirt a dollop onto a strawberry before
feeding it to Julian.

Chaz waits a beat and calls a cut.

Julian spits the strawberry into his hand. "What did you do
that for?"

"The script says I'm supposed to feed you a berry. I fed you a
berry."

He holds out the script. "Where does it mention whipped
cream? I'm lactose intolerant. You can't just improvise like that.
You could send someone into anaphylactic shock."

"Lactose intolerance just gives you the runs, drama queen," I
say. He's not going to walk all over me forever.

Chaz comes over. "That was good. We're moving on."

"Don't you want one more take?" I ask. "Maybe something a
little more subtle?"

I was crying pretty hard in that one—more than Effluvia should be crying over such a jerk. I'm extra emotional today because of the bullying earlier.

"If I wanted a different performance, I wouldn't be moving on," Chaz says. "So quit fishing for compliments."

"I'm not I'm just—"

"Stalling? There's no getting around the kiss, Pork Chop, so pucker up."

★ ★ ★

"And . . . action!"

Julian stares at me, unmoving.

I lean forward to meet him halfway.

He turns away. "Chaz, I can't do it! Her snout is *glistening!*"

"It's fake!" I say. "Drake, tell them!"

★ ★ ★

"And . . . action!"

Julian leans forward.

I lean forward to meet him halfway.

We both tilt our heads in the same direction.

We both tilt our heads in the opposite direction.

Julian sinks to come at me from below and says, "Does it even have lips?"

★ ★ ★

"And . . . action!"

Julian leans forward and tilts one way.

I lean forward and tilt the other way.

"Ow!" he yelps. "Her snout pushed my visor into my eye socket."

★ ★ ★

"And . . . action."

Julian flips up his visor and leans forward.

I lean forward, raising my snout to give him easier access to my mouth.

One tusk drives straight up his nostril.

★ ★ ★

"Okay, people," Chaz says, pacing in front of the cameras. "We can't let one stupid kiss put us into triple time, so here's what we're going to do. As soon as Drake stops Julian's nosebleed, we'll go again—but without the tusks. If we keep the camera shot wide, no one will know they're missing."

Drake escorts Julian back to the set. There's a plug of tissue in his nostril.

Julian takes his mark and whispers to me, "Can you try to *act* like you've kissed someone before?"

Ignoring this, I call to Chaz, "Could we overlap some of the action from the last scene to help us get into the right place emotionally—say, from where Effluvia feeds the berry and whipped cream to the Panther?"

Surprisingly, Chaz agrees. "Anything to get this scene."

"Wait a second," Julian protests. "I can't eat dairy."

"Suck it up, Sexy Eyes," Chaz says. "And then tell Effluvia you've missed her."

The camera assistant sticks a slate in our faces and I smirk at Julian behind it.

"Witch," he says.

"Crybaby," I counter.

"And . . . action!" Chaz calls.

Effluvia sprays a dollop of whipped cream onto a strawberry and pops it into Panther's mouth.

PANTHER
I've missed you, Effluvia.

Julian and I coordinate our movements perfectly this time. He puts one hand on my waist, I put one on his shoulder. He tilts, I tilt. Our lips connect. Still, I have trouble staying in the moment. Julian's kiss feels normal—even nice—but I can't help thinking about how horrible he is and I almost pull away.

He has some nerve suggesting that I'm a novice just because I was tusk challenged. I've done plenty of kissing and to prove it, I wrap my arm around his neck and pull him toward me. Closing my eyes, I concentrate on my character: *I am Effluvia, and I'm kissing my old boyfriend, the guy I will love forever.*

Effluvia starts to enjoy the process. In fact, she's got a bit of a flutter in the pit of her stomach. The Panther wraps both arms around her tightly. His kiss is gentle but there's an intensity to it that hints at more. It's like he's conflicted and fighting his passion for her. But she can sense it and that's enough to cling to, for now.

"I said, *CUT IT!*"

I open my eyes to see Chaz and Lex standing right beside us. Julian and I jump apart. He looks as dazed as I feel.

"What's going on?" I ask, finding my voice first.

"We're wrapping, that's what's going on," Chaz says. "Jacket!"

Lex holds out a jacket and Chaz slides his arms into the sleeves before walking away.

"Actors," he mutters. "Always lost in their own friggin' world."

nine

"Listen to this," Karis says, lowering her copy of *Entertainment Weekly* and looking at us with suppressed excitement.

"Another article about me?" Sasha asks, nudging Ursela.

"No, *this* article is interesting," Karis says, winking at me.

We've gathered once again to support Annika in her quest for the perfect wedding dress. To ease the pain, she offered to treat us to lunch at the Urth Café in Beverly Hills, which is one of my favorites. Sasha loves it too because it's a great place to see and be seen.

Folding back the page, Karis reads the headline aloud. "'Effluvia Never Smelled So Good.'"

Sasha slumps back in her chair. "Oh, who cares?"

"I do," Annika says. "Please go on, Karis."

Karis continues theatrically:

A breath of fresh air has blown through the set of Freak Force, *the new prime-time action-adventure series.*

Effluvia, the most endearing warthog ever to hit the small screen, is just what this testosterone-driven show needed to set it apart in a highly competitive time slot. The studio has decided to withhold the name of the actor playing Effluvia. The show's creator and director— a newcomer known only as Chaz—says keeping the warthog's identity a secret creates an air of mystery. We say you don't need that kind of mystery when you have a good show, but we'll cut Chaz some slack as long as he keeps Effluvia around. We do give him full credit for casting this dynamo, who's as quick with a quip as a kick. Her wit and heart are a delight, especially in view of the positively hideous costume.

If you haven't watched Freak Force, *make sure you tune in next week to see Effluvia hold her own against the revered Sir Nigel Wanley. Long live the warthog!*

Annika applauds. "Bravo, darling! And you, Karis, did a wonderful reading. How would you like to join Team Annika?"

"Are there membership fees?" Karis asks, dubiously.

Annika laughs. "I'm talking about the wedding party. I'd like you to do a reading for us at the ceremony."

"Really?" Karis says. "I'd be honored."

It's not much of an honor but I'm happy Karis is officially coming on board. I could use a regular ally.

Sensing the balance of power equalizing, Sasha stands and pulls Ursela to her feet. "Come on. We need more caffeine."

As they join the line at the counter, the door opens and Roger comes into the café. "We meet again, my beauties!" he says, laying a wet one on Annika's cheek and another on mine. "Viola, let me borrow your mother for a moment." He takes Mom's hand. "Join me outside for a smoke, Annie."

"Remember, you don't smoke!" I call, as she follows him out. She flutters her lacquered nails at me to let me know that smoking and flirting are two different things. The former damages lungs, the latter only reputations.

"Did he just call you Viola?" Karis asks.

"He did," I say. "It's a long story." I watch as Roger and Annika giggle together on the patio and wonder again if anything is going on between them. We only saw Roger twice the whole time I was here in the summer and now he's everywhere.

Karis snaps her fingers in front of my face. "Did you hear me?

I said you should leave copies of the article all over the *Freak Force* set to make the guys jealous. Especially that loser Julian."

"He's not as bad as the others," I say.

Karis squints at me for a moment before asking, "So, what happened during the kissing scene?"

Note to self: Choose dumber friends.

I try to change the subject. "Hey, how was your date with Jon last week?" Jon works with Karis at Abercrombie and Fitch and they recently started dating. We've already discussed every detail of course but she might fall for it.

She grins at me. "You're just trying to throw me off the trail."

I check to make sure Sasha and Ursela are still out of earshot before filling her in on the details of the kissing scene. "He's still a jerk," I conclude. "But a jerk with talented lips."

"Ah, I get it," Karis says. "He was an idiot before because he *likes* you. It's classic guy behavior. If he were ten years younger, he'd be flipping you on the school lawn instead of on set."

"I don't think so. He called me a witch."

"Words don't mean anything. If Chaz had to pry him off you with a crowbar, he likes you."

I'm not sure I was the one who needed to be rescued but I don't say that. "He just got caught up in his character. I know I did." That's the only explanation I've come up with for my getting carried away on set. Otherwise, I'd know better than to stand around kissing some guy who goes out of his way to be mean to me.

"She totally wants him," Sasha says.

I turn to see how much she and Ursela have overheard but they aren't looking at me. Their eyes are on Annika, who is tossing her head as if being repeatedly shocked with low-volt electricity. I turn so they won't know I'm eavesdropping but slide my chair a little closer.

"You're crazy," Ursela says. "He's too old."

"If he wasn't too old for her ten years ago, he isn't now," Sasha says. "Plus, his marriage is on the rocks. He's always on the phone screaming at his wife."

"But Dad's a way better catch," Ursela says.

"He may be a lot smoother but Roger has more money and influence," Sasha says. "Plus, he's a lot closer to kicking it. She'd be loaded."

"We should say something to Dad."

"He won't hear a bad word about his Nika," Sasha says. "All we can do is help him figure it out on his own."

★   ★   ★

I hold Annika back as the others enter the exclusive bridal shop. "So, what did Roger have to say?"

"Oh, this and that. Nothing important." She tugs on my arm, anxious to get her hands on some taffeta. "I have the feeling we're all going to find dresses today."

"What kind of 'this and that'?" I press.

Annika stops pulling and focuses on me. "Why are you so curious about my friendship with Roger lately?"

"I always was," I say. "And now others are too." I point through the open door to Sasha and Ursela, who are already pulling dresses from the racks. "I overheard them talking about it."

"It's no secret, darling. Jake knows Roger and I were involved once."

"Sasha isn't using the past tense. You should watch your back, Mom."

"Annika!" Sasha calls from across the store. "Isn't this gorgeous?" She holds up a long white dress covered in lace.

"I'll be right there," Annika calls back to her. "Now, Vivien, would Sasha be choosing wedding dresses for me if she were conspiring to break up my relationship with her father?" She steps into the shop. "I appreciate your concern, darling, but you're being paranoid."

Karis joins me as Annika bustles off. "What did she say?"

"That I'm paranoid and that the Sisters Sashela are totally innocent."

"Sashela! Like Brangelina?"

"Only nastier."

Annika examines the dress Sasha pulled off the rack and says, "It's lovely but I look better in something more structured."

"It's not for you," Sasha says. "It's for me."

Annika plasters on a brittle smile. "Sasha, guests generally avoid wearing white at a wedding."

"I'm not a guest," Sasha says. "I'm in the wedding party."

"Yeah," Ursela says. "And Daddy would want us to wear whatever we like."

A saleswoman infiltrates our group before fists fly. "Fallon!" she exclaims, seizing Sasha's arm. "I love your show. Is this your—" She turns to Annika and switches gears. "Oh my gosh, you're Fiona—from *Danny Boy!*"

As always, Mom is happy to be recognized. "I'm Annika Anderson. Fiona is my character in *Danny Boy.*"

The saleswoman calls to an assistant, "ECA!" To Mom and Sasha, she whispers, "That's our code for Elite Customer Advisory." She has a brief chat with the assistant about ECA protocol and turns back to Mom. "Fiona, you must be so proud of your daughter."

"Oh, I am," Annika says.

"Fallon is such a lovely girl."

Switching gears on a dime, Mom wraps an arm around each Cohen girl. "As is her sister, Ursela. I'm very lucky to have such a wonderful family."

Karis fakes a wretch behind me.

The saleswoman locates a digital camera and passes it to me. "Do you mind?"

I take the camera and she gets into the frame with Annika and Sasha. I snap off several shots as Mom and Sasha try to outpose each other.

Meanwhile, the assistant has returned with a silver tray holding chocolate truffles and champagne. I step forward to help myself to a glass but she raises a warning hand. "This is for Elite Customers only," she says. Setting the tray on the coffee table, she motions Karis and me away. "Please don't pester the Elites for autographs, girls. In our shop, we make a point of treating famous people just like anyone else."

Sasha examines the truffles and frowns. "No white chocolate?"

The saleswoman snaps her fingers at the assistant. "Pop out and get Fallon some white chocolate."

"Raspberries would be nice too," Sasha says. "They put me in the mood for shopping—as long as they're organic."

Gathering several dresses, Sashela heads toward the changing rooms, while Annika and the saleswoman adjourn to the racks.

Once everyone is distracted, I pour champagne into two flutes and hand one to Karis. "I could get used to this."

"Everyone loosens up around the holidays," Karis says. "Are you celebrating Christmas, Hanukkah, or both?"

I explain that I'm heading home to Seattle for a few days to meet with my Nerd Academy teachers and spend Christmas with Dad and Gran. Mom is making me come back on the twenty-sixth for a holiday celebration with the Cohens.

"How about work?" she asks. "Is there a *Freak Force* party where you could catch Julian under the mistletoe?"

"I have no intention of kissing Julian again—unless it's scripted."

She gives me an evil grin. "And then?"

"And then I intend to enjoy it," I say, and take a nonchalant sip of champagne.

"With or without tongues?"

I spit champagne back into the glass. "Karis! Effluvia doesn't kiss and tell."

"Then Effluvia is a very dull pig."

We both laugh and then Karis continues more seriously. "Are you going to give Julian a chance? Maybe it's time to move on from Rory."

"Maybe it is but I was hoping I could find someone who's actually nice."

"Well, he's nice to look at. That's a start."

The saleswoman sneaks up behind me and snatches the champagne flute from my hand. "I told you that this is reserved for Elites," she says. "You girls should leave."

"But we're here to shop," I say.

She gives me a patronizing smile. "I think you're here to gawk at the Elites."

"We're Elites too," I say, trying to keep a straight face. "We may not be as famous as Fallon, but we've got some Hollywood connections. Karis here is the daughter of academy award–winner Diana Russell. And I'm the daughter of your pal Fiona."

She glances from me to Annika. "You look nothing alike."

"What about the beauty mark?" I protest, as she starts to herd us toward the door. "Mom! Come over here and show off your mole."

Annika is staggering toward a changing room under a towering pile of white tulle and doesn't hear me, so I carry on alone. I don't even want to stay, but someone has to stand up for the Hollywood little guys. They're the backbone of the industry. I mean, where would Rory Gilmore be without Paris? Bart without Lisa?

"I had a part in *Danny Boy*, you know," I say. "Don't you remember Danny's sister Sinead? I had a couple of big lines."

"Pivotal lines," Karis adds, playing along.

"Danny's sister would have an Irish accent," the saleswoman scoffs.

I deliver Sinead's closing dialogue in my best Irish brogue: *"I'll miss you, Danny."*

By this time, we're at the door and the saleswoman opens it. "You're not fooling anyone with that accent. Out."

I studied with a professional dialogue coach for that role! Obviously, she has no ear for languages. I feed her another line: *"It won't be the same without you."*

Karis says, "Maybe if you cry like you did in the movie."

"I can't turn on the waterworks just like that. I have to feel it."

Pinching my arm until I yelp, Karis says, "It's an old trick my mother taught me."

My eyes fill with tears and I continue the performance: *"I'll visit you but I'll never stay."*

"No, don't visit," the saleswoman says, shoving me out the door onto Rodeo Drive. "And if you bother my Elites again, I'll call the police."

Karis follows me out and the saleswoman closes the door and locks it behind us. I press my face to the glass and shout my final line: *"I'm Irish through and through!"*

"Undercover again?" someone asks.

Karis and I turn to see Julian standing behind us. He's wearing faded jeans and a leather jacket that looks like it's been run over by a motorcycle a few times. As usual, he's smirking.

"Just giving the fans what they want," I say.

The saleswoman is standing just inside the door, glaring.

"I guess some people are harder to impress than Sir Nigel," Julian says.

"Give me a break, I'm working without a snout."

He actually laughs and then looks as if he regrets it. Glancing up at the name of the bridal shop, he says, "Not shopping for Effluvia, I hope?"

I wonder if he's thinking about our recent scene together. "My mother, actually. They're holding her hostage inside."

"Maybe you could rescue her," Karis says, stepping forward. "I hear you're good with stunts."

"He's better than I am," I say, unsure whether to be grateful or annoyed that she's trying to be nice to him. "But I guess that wouldn't be hard."

Out of courtesy to Karis, he doesn't agree with me. Instead, he introduces himself and shakes her hand. "My father has worked with your father," he says, after making the connection. "I hear he's an excellent director."

Karis smiles, clearly quite charmed. Wait until she sees what he's really like.

The door of the shop opens and Annika appears in the doorway wearing a white satin gown and a matching floor-length cloak.

With the fur-trimmed hood pulled over her blond curls, she looks like an extra from *Lord of the Rings*. "Vivien Leigh Reid, what are you doing out here?"

"I got kicked out," I say. "My pedigree isn't good enough."

"Don't be ridiculous," she says. "Get back in here right now. I need you." Noticing Julian, her eyebrows shoot up. "You're that boy from her show."

"Yes, ma'am," he says. "I'm Julian Gerrard."

Annika crosses her fur-trimmed arms. "You haven't been very nice to my daughter."

"Mom," I interrupt. "Don't."

Annika ignores me. "I heard what you said about nepotism and I want you to know that it's wasn't Leigh's idea. I pressured Jake into giving her a part. It doesn't mean she's not a good actress."

"*Mom!*" She's fighting my battles for me. It's excruciating and touching at the same time.

Julian says, "I know."

"If you know, then stop this silly hazing and be professional," she says. "Vivien is very talented. She's just new to stunts. Obviously, she didn't mean to kick you in the—"

"*Mom!*" Now it's just excruciating.

Julian's face reddens and he flinches perceptibly.

Annika relents. "At least you put your heart into the kissing yesterday."

I turn to Karis. "Did you tell her?"

"Of course not!" she exclaims.

"Pillow talk, darling," Annika says. "Chaz mentioned it to Jake."

This is awful. Now Julian will think we were all talking about him. And we were.

"I'm sorry," I say, turning back to see Julian disappearing into the distance.

★   ★   ★

Karis wisely waits outside as I follow Annika back into the store. "If you want to kill me, why not just push me under a Hummer and get it over with?" I ask.

"I didn't realize how much you liked him," she says. "Why didn't you say so earlier?"

"I do *not* like him. If I did, obviously I'd be throwing myself under the Hummer."

"If he likes you, he won't be so easily put off."

"How would you know?"

She rolls her blue eyes. "I may not know much but I know how the male mind works. A hint of interest is better than too much. Think about Brando: When he's had a glimpse of a bone, he can't think of anything else.

"Julian is going to tell the other guys that my mother came into the street to fight my battles—while wearing a hooded cloak."

She whirls in front of the mirror delightedly. "It's very *Dr. Zhivago,* don't you think?"

"Who's he? Your plastic surgeon?"

"Vivien, your ignorance about classic film shocks me. What are they teaching at that academy? And for the record, I do not have a plastic surgeon."

"For the record, you'll look like an idiot wearing a rabbit-trimmed hood at a beach wedding."

"Ermine, darling. Rabbit is cheap. And I haven't settled on the beach."

Sashela emerges from the changing rooms. The Ursela half is wearing a black sequined number so low cut it reveals her pierced navel. The Sasha half is in a white satin dress nearly identical to the one under Mom's cloak.

"This is the one, Annika," Sasha says.

Ignoring this, Mom says, "I've already picked out something for all of you."

Karis comes back into the store and the saleswoman promptly

apologizes to us. The new and improved Leigh Reid doesn't give her a hard time; the store is already filled to the brim with divas.

Turning to Annika, I say, "I want to pick my own dress."

"Trust me," she says, pointing to the gowns hanging from the changing-room doors, "I know what suits people."

On Ursela's door, there's a glittery copper dress and on Sasha's a sequined blue one. Hanging from the next is a pink dress so plain I could wear it practically anywhere.

"Don't judge a dress on the hanger," Annika warns.

I flop into a chair. "I hate it."

Ursela is the first to capitulate. After trying it on and admiring herself, she says, "Okay, I'll wear it. For Daddy."

"Why couldn't you choose something like that for me?" I whisper. "You want me to be the ugly stepsister."

Mom sighs. "Just try on the dress. If you hate it, we'll find you something else."

I head into the changing room to get it over with. Up close, I notice the pink fabric is shot through with fine gold threads. And as I pull it on, I find it is more fitted than it appeared on the hanger. It drapes low in the back, nips in at the waist, and kicks out in a little fishtail at the bottom.

I step out of the changing room and Karis says, "Very red carpet. You look fabulous."

Even Ursela nods grudging approval.

Turning to the mirror, I'm surprised by what I see. The dress fits perfectly and under the lights, the gold threads give off a subtle sparkle.

"I knew it," Annika says, well satisfied. She turns to Karis. "Now that you're in the wedding party, I'd love to buy a dress for you, Karis."

Karis's smile disappears. "Thanks, but I don't really wear dresses."

"You'll wear this one," Annika says. She pulls a flirty, aqua dress with a three-quarter length skirt off the rack and hands it to Karis. "Consider it a thank-you for agreeing to do the reading."

"Do it for the team," I tell Karis, and she scowls at me.

Annika leads Karis to a changing room and I spin again to admire my reflection. There's a wolf whistle behind me.

Gray is leaning against the sales counter, blatantly leering. "Nice dress."

Sasha steps out of her changing room, wearing not the blue dress, but her street clothes. Running her eyes over me, she says, "Don't worry, Leigh, most bridesmaids lose a few pounds before the wedding."

The sales assistant finally re-enters the store carrying a shopping bag. "I'm so sorry, Fallon," she says. "It took ages to track down organic raspberries."

"I'm not hungry anymore," Sasha says. "But you can bag these and charge them to Fiona." She sets Ursela's copper dress and the white one she liked on the counter.

"My mother doesn't want you to wear white," I say.

"Daddy said we can wear whatever we want," Sasha replies, leading Gray and Ursela toward the front door.

"Where are you going?"

"Venice Beach," Ursela answers. "Not that it's any of your business."

"We're supposed to get a trial run on our makeup this afternoon. Annika booked appointments at her spa."

"We don't need a trial run," Sasha says. "You can't improve on perfection."

Ursela picks up the open bottle of champagne on the way out and Sasha grabs my half-full flute.

"Later, loser," Sasha says.

I smile as she takes a big swig of my backwash.

ten

The space between the Dumpsters where my trailer usually sits is empty.

I'm still standing there staring at it when Lex appears and greets me with a cheery "Good morning."

My stomach sinks instantly. Like his role model, Lex never wastes energy on pleasantries, at least not with me. Come to think of it, the only time Chaz ever really warmed up to me was the day he learned I was being fired.

I have a very bad feeling about this.

"Where's my trailer?"

Lex shakes his carefully unruly bleached mop and says, "Don't worry about it."

"But it's *missing*." My voice spikes up a few notches.

"Relax," he says. "It's not a pet."

Easy for him to say. I've grown attached to that heap. The *Charlie's Angels* poster Abby gave me and my signed photo of Sir Nigel are still in it.

Lex turns and heads back toward the studio, snapping his fingers at me to follow.

"Was it stolen?" I ask, close on his platform heels.

He snorts. "The drivers probably sold it for scrap."

Scrap! As in, refuse? Trash? No longer needed?

Somewhere there's a list of Top Ten signs an actor is about to be fired and having your trailer sold for junk is on it. Sure, I've been working hard and I've had a glowing review in a respected industry magazine, but glowing reviews didn't save my butt on *Diamond Heights*. If Chaz wants to fire me, he'll find a way.

I clutch at Lex. "What's happening? Where are we going?"

He stares at my hand on his sleeve. "Versace. Back away slowly."

I release his arm and he explains that Chaz wants me to join him for breakfast in his trailer.

That's got to be another Top Ten sign. The director wouldn't want you sobbing in public and making your costars nervous. Better to feed you a last meal in private and hope that you'll die quietly.

Chaz's trailer stands out from the others, not only because it's forty feet long, but also because it's the only trailer with a huge wooden deck, teak patio furniture, and planter boxes full of flowers. Lex climbs the stairs ahead of me and holds the door open. I follow slowly, as if walking to the gallows. I remember reading about Anne Boleyn, one of the wives of Henry VIII, who was unjustly beheaded when the king decided to replace her with someone who had more sex appeal. Anne had a rep too.

We find the executioner sprawled on his orange leather sofa marking up a script with a silver Tiffany pen. Judging from his extensive edits, Chaz is trying to strike just the right note with Effluvia's demise.

I croak out a nervous greeting and Chaz flicks his pen at the kitchen counter. "Get something to eat, Scarlett. I'll just be a minute." He scratches at the script and adds, "Lex, be a doll and whip up a couple of sterile skinnies."

"He's invented his own coffee lingo," Lex explains, setting up the coffeemaker with decaf espresso and skim milk. "He's such a scream."

"A scream," I agree. Of horror. But like Anne Boleyn, I am determined to be brave in the face of impending doom. After all, this isn't my first firing. I will hold my head high until it is rolling on the immaculate hardwood floor of this trailer.

Taking a croissant and some strawberries, I sit down at the

table and Chaz gets up to join me. "Do you know why you're here?" he asks.

"No." I'll be dammed if I'm going to be the first to say the word "fired" out loud.

Chaz snaps his fingers. "Article."

Lex rifles through a stack of magazines and produces a copy of *Variety*. Opening it, Chaz taps one page with a manicured finger. "You've heard of Cameron Carter?" I nod but he explains anyway. "He's the most influential columnist in all of Hollywood. And do you know what he has to say about Effluvia this week?" I shake my head and he hands the magazine back to Lex. "Read."

" 'Effluvia is inspired,' " Lex pronounces. " 'A unique and riveting character.' "

"Did you hear that?" Chaz asks and I nod. "He's referring to my writing, of course, but the point is, he loves Effluvia."

I'm still struggling to read the obituary between the lines. "That's good, right?"

Chaz bugs his eyes at me. "Are you slow, Scarlett? It's better than good. It's huge. Lex?"

"Massive," Lex says.

"Cameron Carter is always the first to recognize a show that taps into the zeitgeist," Chaz says. "Lex?"

"Zeitgeist: The general intellectual, moral, and cultural climate of an era."

"Any show Cameron endorses becomes a hit," Chaz concludes.

My throat unclenches, allowing me to take a sip of my latte. "Did you see the review in *Entertainment Weekly*?" I ask.

He nods. "Nice piece."

" 'Long live the warthog,' it said." I may be humble about my work these days, but a termination scare activates anyone's urge to self-promote.

I take a bite of my croissant, scattering crumbs on the table. Chaz snaps fingers at Lex, who instantly wipes the table.

"Five minutes till your next appointment," Lex tells Chaz.

Chaz stands. "Thanks for joining me, Scarlett, but I'll have to excuse myself."

Lex snatches my plate out of my hand and empties it into the trash. "That's your cue to exit."

"Oh. Okay, well, thanks for breakfast."

"My pleasure," Chaz says, kissing the air on either side of my cheeks. "If you need anything, your director is always here for you."

With that, he steps into another room and closes the door in my face. Lex motions for me to leave but I hesitate, knowing I may never have a private audience with Chaz again. I need to make the most of this opportunity.

I reach out and knock. "Actually, Chaz, there is something I'd like to ask you."

Behind the door there's a loud sigh. "Lex?"

Lex pulls me to the trailer door. I don't put up much of a fight, even though I could fully take him. As he opens the door, however, I activate my healthy BMI, shove him out the door, and lock it behind him. "Lex got called away, Chaz. I'll only take a second of your time."

Chaz steps back into the living room wearing a white silk kimono with the word RELAX embroidered across the chest in ornate lettering. "What now?"

"It's about Effluvia," I say, raising my voice over Lex's knocking. "I'd never presume to know where you're going with the storyline, but if things are heating up with the Panther, Effluvia would want to slim down a little. Every girl wants to look her best in a romantic situation."

"Effluvia isn't a normal girl," he reminds me. "She's a warthog."

"She's got the *heart* of a normal girl and she's upset that her former boyfriend finds her repulsive. Don't you think she'd do whatever she could to be more attractive to him? You know what it's like to be in love, Chaz."

Chaz ties the belt on his silk robe into a perfect bow before answering. "Don't bother appealing to my heart, Scarlett. I don't have one."

"Reviewers wouldn't be reacting so well to the show if that were true," I say.

I can barely communicate with my lips glued to his butt but I'm not ashamed. This isn't about being a diva; it's about doing the best thing for my character. Shaving a few pounds off Effluvia won't just make her more attractive to the Panther, it will also improve her ability to fight crime.

"It won't hurt the character, Chaz," I continue. "She still has warts and a tail. But she'll move a little better, which means I'll be able to nail the stunts faster." I'm almost shouting now because Lex is hammering on the door with something heavy. "The money you'll save in crew time can be used for more special effects. You know our viewers love special effects."

"For god's sake, keep it down," Chaz yells toward the door. He flicks a finger at me. "Open it."

Lex threatens me with a gardening trowel but Chaz shuts him down. "Tell wardrobe to design a new backside for Effluvia. Make it twenty-five percent smaller than the old one."

"And the stomach?" I press. "The costume has to be balanced. For the stunts, you know."

"Scarlett, the best shiatsu masseur in the city is about to arrive. He charges three hundred bucks an hour, and if I miss one second of his time because you're still here yapping, it's coming out of your salary."

It's a price I'm willing to pay. "Twenty-five percent off the gut and I'm gone."

Chaz rolls his eyes at Lex. "Do it. Have the dresser deliver them to her trailer."

"I don't have a trailer," I point out. "Mine disappeared."

"That's not the only thing that will disappear if you don't back off."

★ ★ ★

Pointing down the row of cast trailers, Lex says, "Last one on the left."

It's so much older and shorter than the rest that I don't need the little EFFLUVIA sign on the door to tell me it's mine. Still, it's a palace compared to my former crap can and there's no Dumpster anywhere within smelling range.

Inside the trailer, I find a copy of the latest *Freak Force* script on the counter, along with copies of *Variety* and *Entertainment Weekly*. The tiny kitchen is stocked with snack foods. And best of all, someone has hung the *Charlie's Angels* poster over my new sofa. Beside it is Sir Nigel's photo that reads, *Look forward to working with you again. Your friend, Nigel xo.* I happened to notice that all he did was scratch his name on everyone else's.

There's a knock at my door and I open it to find the driver captain. "Just making sure you've got everything you need," he says.

"Yes, it's perfect, thank you."

"It's on the small side but I didn't have the budget for a bigger one—not after building Chaz's new deck."

"This one is big enough for me. Mostly I'm just here to do homework anyway."

He looks relieved. "I wish every actor were as easy to please as you are."

Obviously, I am making good progress with my professional makeover. The spoiled brat who got the boot from *Diamond Heights* hasn't resurfaced on this show. I may only be a few months older but I am years more mature. Hopefully, with constant vigilance, my ego will never get the better of me again.

One day, I could start up a school to teach other actors, artists, and performers the fine art of being gracious.

Scene 7: Leigh Gives Back

EXTERIOR STYLISH NEW BUILDING, DAY

CLOSE UP ON a magnum of champagne as it breaks against the building's marble entrance. Dozens of cameras flash, and the crowd erupts in a cheer.

WIDEN OUT to reveal Leigh standing beside a platinum plaque that reads: THE VIVIEN LEIGH REID FOUNDATION.

                         REPORTER
        I understand this is your fifth facility, Ms. Reid.

                          LEIGH
        That's right, Harry. One in New York and
        four in Los Angeles.

Harry smiles as this renowned legend of film and TV refers to him by name.

                          HARRY
        Please tell us more about your foundation.

                          LEIGH
        With all the red carpet coverage you do, I
        hardly need to say it, Harry, but actors
        are prone to getting a little full of
        themselves. Men and women alike fall prey
        to the Diva Syndrome, and they become in-
        creasingly unreasonable and insensitive.
        I'm ashamed to say I was once one of those
        divas. But I had a harsh wake-up call
        and turned myself around. Eventually, I
        started to speak up about the problem
        and created my revolutionary program,
        RAD—or React Against Divas. Quite sim-
        ply, RAD's goal is to clean up the acting
        community, one diva at a time.

The crowd cheers.

HARRY
Could you tell us how RAD accomplishes
this?

LEIGH
Mainly through an intensive in-patient
program. But people keep coming back
for more even after graduating. One of
our most popular outpatient courses
is Tips for the Autograph Session,
designed by my good friend Sir Nigel
Wanley.

HARRY
RAD's a huge success, Ms. Reid. What's your
secret?

LEIGH
My good reputation, Harry. My professional attitude and solid work ethic pro-
mote my program.

HARRY
Your mother, Annika Anderson, is also famous for being grounded.

LEIGH
It wasn't always that way, Harry. Annika
was actually one of our first patients
and thanks to intensive therapy, she's
now a RAD spokeswoman.

HARRY
Is there any truth to the rumor that
Sasha Cohen has checked herself in?

                        LEIGH
        I'm afraid it wasn't a voluntary admis-
        sion. Her father and sister held an in-
        tervention. I only hope we're not too late.

                        HARRY
        I wish you luck, Ms. Reid. Thank you for
        your time. And don't be surprised to re-
        ceive a nomination for a Nobel Prize one
        day. You're a real humanitarian.

                        LEIGH
        It's not about the recognition, Harry. I
        just want to give back.

                    ★   ★   ★

Freddy has taped the reviews from *Variety* and *Entertainment Weekly* to the wall of the gym. I'd be pleased if that's where her interest ended. Instead, my higher profile has made her more critical of my stunt technique because it reflects on her training. As a result, she's amped up my strength training to include one hundred and fifty crunches, sixty squats, forty lunges, and worst of all, three men's push-ups.

She applauds as I complete the last push-up and tosses my warm up jacket at me. "Let's call it a day, Champ. The reviews have put Chaz in such a good mood that he's treating everyone to sushi at wrap."

"You go ahead," I tell her. "I'm going to cool down with some yoga."

After she leaves, I take a position in front of the mirror and move through my sequence of poses. Thanks to my new and diminished paunch and butt sacks, now attached to my sweats, I am able to do a proper Downward Dog at last.

"What are you doing here?"

I straighten up to find Julian looking at me in the mirror. "I work here, remember?"

"But you aren't in any scenes today," he says.

It's hard to say whether his keeping track of my schedule is good or bad. But he could avoid me easily enough now if he wanted to. "I had some voice-over work and trained with Freddy afterward."

"Mind if I join you?" he asks.

"It's your gym too," I say. I notice that he's wearing regular street clothes instead of work-out gear. It seems that he wasn't intending to break a sweat until he saw me.

Hopping onto the bench press, Julian moves the key to one hundred and ninety pounds and whips off a quick set of ten. He must be benching his own body weight.

When he's done, I say, "Impressive. But I did three push-ups today."

"Oh yeah? Watch this." With his feet still on the bench, he does ten push-ups off the ground—clapping his hands between each one.

Okay, he's showing off and this time it doesn't involve any injury to me. I'll consider that a peace offering and extend one of my own. "So, listen. About the other day . . . My mother was—"

"Right."

"Pardon?"

"Your mother was right. I haven't been very professional. I apologize."

"Really. Well, I accept your apology and re-apologize for . . . you know."

"Kicking me? Or telling everybody about the making out?"

My face explodes right off my neck, leaving only a stump. "Whatever."

He grins. "Does that mean you don't have a crush on me?"

If I hadn't already lost my head, that would fluster me even more. "Of course not!"

"So, you *do* have a crush on me."

I have to regain the upper hand here. "There's no crush, unless you're counting the one you have on yourself."

Julian laughs and does another set on the bench. I repeat my yoga postures, although I'm not exactly finding my inner calm.

"Are you a method actor?" he asks, pointing to my stomach and butt attachments. "It looks like you're blurring the line between life and your character."

I roll my eyes. "Yeah, because I want to be a warthog twenty-four-seven."

I wait until he's finished his last set before continuing, "I only wear these to train. The more comfortable I get in them, the less they'll affect my performance. Besides," I add, giving him a pointed look, "crash pads come in handy around here. You never know when your costars might decide to toss you around."

"That got out of hand," he says, sheepishly. "You were a good sport about it."

"You called me a crybaby."

"Actually, I called you witch. You called *me* a crybaby."

He might be right about that. The details have become a little fuzzy.

"I'm willing to call a truce if you are," he says, extending his hand.

"Okay, truce," I say, offering my hand in return. He has a good handshake, but I make a point of being the first to let go. Getting to my feet, I pick up the five-pound free weights to do some curls. Just to do something.

"Don't take this the wrong way," he says, "but your butt looks different."

"It's twenty-five percent smaller. Chaz agreed to let Effluvia slim down."

"So, she's been hitting the gym, just like her alter ego?"

"It's the only way I'm going to master those stunts."

He moves behind me to demonstrate positioning and lines his arm up with mine. "Don't let the momentum take the weight down. Make sure your muscles always do the work."

I try to focus on my arm instead of his but it isn't easy. In fact, I have no idea how many repetitions I've done. He moves away and a cool breeze blows over my arm, lifting the hairs on it.

"You've been doing a lot better lately," he says. "Even Cameron Carter said your moves are solid."

"That just means I have to work harder," I say.

He moves toward me again. "Don't hyperextend your spine." He puts one hand over my stomach attachment and another on my butt attachment. I correct my posture immediately, but he doesn't hurry to move his hands. "Where are your tusks?"

"My tusks?"

"I thought you liked to train in costume."

I roll my eyes. "My tusks don't affect my performance."

Julian raises his eyebrows. "Well, they affect *mine*. And if *you* were professional, you'd want to do something about that."

⋆　⋆　⋆

"More to the left," Julian says.

I tilt my head to the left and he flinches as one of my tusks gouges his upper lip. "Sorry," I say, and pull away.

His arms tighten around my waist. "That's only take one. Go again."

This time I accidentally stab his lower lip and he yelps. "Cut," he says. "And I don't mean that literally."

"Maybe we should give up," I say, as he dabs at his mouth with his sleeve.

"Professionals rehearse until they get it right," he says. "No pain, no gain."

We persist until our lips finally connect properly in spite of the tusks. Then we keep going until it feels almost natural.

After a long spell of successful rehearsing, Julian's hands slide south to squeeze my butt attachment.

"Hey," I say, disengaging myself. "Effluvia and the Panther haven't even had a real date."

"They were a couple before the explosion," he says. "A little groping is in character."

"They weren't a couple for long."

"Long enough to take an African safari together," he points out. "They would have been sleeping together."

"You don't know that," I say.

"Sure, I do," he says, grinning. "It's in my back story."

I haven't worked through all the details about their past yet, but I do know that I don't want a hot guy groping my fake butt—still seventy-five percent larger than my real one—in front of millions of viewers. "Even if they were, Effluvia wouldn't be in a rush to get serious again," I say. "She's hardly going to trust someone who dumped her as soon as she got a few warts."

"That's not how it went down," he says. "There's more to the story than that."

He's obviously done more homework than I have, and I don't want to be influenced by his ideas before I've worked the story through myself. "All I'm saying is that the Panther has to prove himself. Until then, he keeps his paws off the tail."

Still grinning, he puts his hands on what passes for my waist. "Eric is a good guy, you know."

"Who?"

"Eric. That was my character's name when he was still human."

I shake my head. "His name was Sam."

"My character. My back story."

"I thought you wanted to rehearse," I say.

"Action," he says.

He leans down to kiss me again and this time it feels totally natural.

eleven

Julian presses me into the limo's soft leather interior.

"That was the best date ever," he says.

"You're telling me," I whisper, now practically horizontal. His weight is crushing me into something sharp and his hands are traveling, but I'm not about to complain. Not when things are going so well.

"Looking good," Chaz's voice crackles over the walkie-talkie. "Stay in the clinch, but I want to see the Panther caress Effluvia's warts. It's symbolic of his starting to accept her for who she really is."

Keeping his lips on mine, Julian raises a hand to stroke one of my facial protrusions.

"Great," Chaz says. "Let's cut it there."

Julian gives me a last kiss before pulling me upright to face the camera in the front seat. Although this scene will appear to take place on the city streets, it's actually being filmed in the studio. While the camera rolled, the crew rocked the limo with wooden levers to simulate the motion of driving and panned red and white lights through the windows to create the illusion of passing other cars and brightly lit buildings.

"Nice job, you two," Chaz says, still over the walkie. "Very convincing. Any blood on the tusks, Scarlett?"

I spit out the tusks and take the walkie from the cameraman who's filming us from the front seat. "Not a drop."

"If I didn't know better," Chaz says, "I'd say you two have been practicing."

Julian is wearing his visor so I can't guess what he's thinking. After our "rehearsal" the other night, we parted as casually as if it had been any other run-through. I hoped he'd suggest a coffee or something but he didn't even walk me to my trailer. Of course, mine is pretty far from his, being in the studio equivalent of skid row.

Not that it matters. If this is just professional for him, it is just professional for me. Contrary to what he might think, I am not the type of actress to blur the line between art and reality.

Okay, I used to be that type of actress but I've evolved since then.

Someone yanks open the limo door and clambers over me in a blur of dark hair and white vinyl.

"What are you doing here?" I ask, as Sasha settles between Julian and me.

"Didn't Chaz tell you? His guest star had a car accident. My show broke early for the holiday so I offered to fill in."

Fabulous. Now I can't even escape her at work.

She takes the walkie-talkie out of my hand and says, "Chaz, I was watching the last take on the monitors and Julian looked terrified that she'd sever an artery with those things." She gestures with distaste at the tusks in my hand. "Plus, she gave him bristle burn."

Julian doesn't move when Sasha reaches out to stroke his cheek. I imagine his paralysis has something to do with the fact that she's wearing a low-cut white vest above an acre of bare midriff followed by a white miniskirt.

To remind her I'm still here, I ask, "Didn't Roger find this a bit odd?"

"*Daddy* was all for it," she says. "He knows you guys could benefit from some star power around here, even if it's only for one episode."

Julian has been silent through this discussion, his eyes falling occasionally to Sasha's bustline and darting away again. If he could focus on the conversation, this would be the perfect opportunity for one of his cutting comments about nepotism.

"Then why don't you go get into costume?" I ask.

She giggles. "Silly. This is what Dr. Ram wears."

Dr. Ram, the villain of the week, is a computer scientist with a genius level IQ and a hidden agenda.

"Interesting," I say. "In my script, she's wearing a lab coat."

"You don't hide star power under a lab coat," Sasha says.

Apparently, you showcase it in a skintight outfit, shiny white boots, and a high, sleek ponytail. As a clichéd nod to the intellectual, she's wearing dark-framed glasses.

Dr. Ram is teaming up with the Freak Force to help them decode a microchip embedded in the neck of a dead government official. While the guys fall prey to Dr. Ram's charms, Effluvia uncovers her connections to a Russian spy agency.

"Have you even learned your lines?" I ask, knowing she was out late with Gray.

"Plenty of time for that. I was hoping Julian would rehearse with me."

Julian nods as if his head is hooked onto his neck with a spring.

"Don't worry, I'm a quick study," she assures him.

I stare at Julian but he appears to have forgotten I'm alive. "He loves rehearsing," I say. "Don't you, Julian?"

He looks over at me, bewildered, and bobbles his head again.

★　★　★

The full cast is on the computer lab set waiting for Chaz when the publicist arrives to announce that the show has been rated number two in its time slot.

There are jubilant high fives all around, with the guys making a point of including Sasha, rather than me. The boom man finally gives me a pity high five.

The publicist waits for the hubbub to die before telling us that the fan mail has been pouring in; she's had to order reprints of the new glossies.

"Which one of us is most popular?" Rudy asks. "I bet the horns are breaking hearts."

"You're all popular," the publicist says, diplomatically.

"Come on, you can tell us," Jed says. "We can take it."

Sasha decides to weigh in. "I'll bet Julian has the biggest fan base. Panthers are the sexiest animal on the planet."

Jed and Rudy jump on Julian and playfully pummel him until they collapse in a heap on the floor. Sasha backs away in her stiletto boots, squealing.

The publicist, who prefers having the guys all to herself, changes her mind about sharing the ranking. "Okay, I'll tell you who's causing the stir."

The guys immediately break apart and leap to their feet to hear the verdict.

"It's Effluvia," she says. "There were one hundred and sixty-two requests for her photo last week alone."

Jed's face falls. "One hundred and sixty? For Effluvia?"

"One hundred and sixty-*two*," I say. "Do I have to answer them all?"

"All you have to do is sign the photos," the publicist says. "I've hired a student to deal with the letters."

"I demand a recount," Rudy says. "There's no way that warthog is more popular than we are."

Sasha walks over to Rudy and consoles him with a close-up of her costume. "Don't worry," she says. "Leigh was popular on *Diamond Heights* for a while too but it didn't last. Do you know why?"

"Because she got fired?" Chaz asks, galloping onto the set and kissing Sasha's cheek.

"That's right, she got fired." She gives his frayed tie a fond tug. "I *never* get tired of saying that."

★ ★ ★

INTERIOR DESERTED GOVERNMENT OFFICES, MIDNIGHT

Dr. Ram hacks into a computer as the Freak Force looks on.

GAZELLE
Thanks for helping us out, Dr. Ram.

Dr. Ram pushes her chair back and smiles flirta-tiously at the Panther, staring up into his eyes.

DR. RAM
It's my pleasure. I'd do *anything* for my country.

"Cut!" Chaz's disembodied voice floats over from the monitors. "Sasha, doll, you're supposed to be flirting with Gazelle, not Panther."

"Really?" she asks.

"Yeah, it's right in the script, Sasha," I say. "I thought you and Julian rehearsed."

"We did." She giggles. "Well, sort of."

Julian laughs too, which makes me want to throw something sharp at them.

Sasha calls to Chaz, "Sorry, sweetie. I could have sworn it said Panther. I guess there's a natural chemistry that makes me gravi-tate toward Julian."

"Please adjust your chemistry and gravitate toward Rudy," Chaz says. "And stay on your mark, kiddo. You stepped in front of Leigh and blocked her."

I sense that Chaz knows it wasn't an accident and I wonder if he'll have the strength to stand up to the boss's daughter.

"I couldn't find my light," Sasha says. "Leigh's butt is casting a huge shadow."

Jed and Rudy snicker but Julian doesn't join in. He doesn't get any credit for restraint, though, because Sasha is clinging to his arm like a big game hunter showing off her kill and he isn't complaining.

★ ★ ★

INTERIOR DESERTED GOVERNMENT OFFICES, MIDNIGHT

Effluvia points to the computer screen.

> DR. RAM
> As you can see, there are encoded files in
> the documents.

That's my line! I pointed at the computer screen and opened my mouth, but Sasha spit the words out before I could. Is she that unprepared or is this a deliberate hijacking?

Leaving her mark, Sasha strolls to the window, which forces the cameraman to follow her, effectively cutting me out of the shot. Chaz should call a cut but when he doesn't, Sasha delivers my next line as well.

> DR. RAM
> I think someone in this office is working
> for the SIB.

Panther, Gazelle, and Cheetah all migrate toward Sasha, who has perched on the window ledge. They continue the dialogue as if everything is normal.

Not only is it a deliberate hijacking, the hostages are enjoying the ride.

PANTHER
The Russian spy agency?

Now off-camera, I say my next line:

EFFLUVIA
Exactly. I'll have Head office—

DR. RAM
Run a background check on the entire
staff? That's an excellent idea, Effluvia.

"Cut," Chaz calls. "Let's run that scene again," he says. "And how about sticking to your marks and your lines, people?"

I'd like to point out that I did, but it would probably open the door for comments that I'm a whiny diva. I'll look more professional if I suck it up.

"Sorry, Chaz," Sasha says. "It just *felt right* for Dr. Ram to be the one to raise the possible connection to the Russians and suggest the background check. It shows she's trying to be part of the team. Everyone will feel even more betrayed when the truth comes out later."

Chaz doesn't usually welcome comments on his script, but because it's Sasha, he listens. "Well . . ."

Jed drags his eyes away from Sasha's chest for a moment. "The scene was working well. She's got great instincts."

"I can't afford to lose *all* of Effluvia's lines," Chaz says. "Cameron Carter loves her."

"Think of our demographic," Rudy says. "Would guys my age prefer to watch Sasha or *that?*" He jerks a thumb toward me.

Chaz glances from Sasha to me and back. "Good point. We'll leave it."

Okay, so Sasha won that round. That's what I get for playing it safe. Next round, I'll have to play to win. Jake said he wanted more improvisation so I'll give it to him today. Sasha's acting skills have improved since *Diamond Heights,* but I doubt ad-libbing will come easily to her. She doesn't know this show or these characters as well as I do, and she's barely rehearsed. If I stick to the key points Chaz needs to cover in the scene, he might let me take a few liberties.

> DR. RAM
> Your ex may have lost her looks but she hasn't lost her brains. Are you attracted to smart women, Mr. Panther?

> PANTHER
> Oh yeah. And I understand you're a genius, Dr. Ram.

> EFFLUVIA
> Are we here to do a job or flirt?

Julian gives me a startled look, trying to figure out whether my improvised comment is supposed to be part of the scene. He decides to run with it.

> PANTHER
> I don't see why we can't do both at the same time.

> EFFLUVIA
> Who's the one who refused to let relationships get in the way of our mission?

Sasha is watching us with her mouth hanging open. She has no idea what's going on, but Rudy and Jed quickly catch on.

                    CHEETAH
     [glancing from Panther to Effluvia]
     Don't tell me you two are hooking up
     again.

                    GAZELLE
     [sliding an arm around Dr. Ram]
     That would be a huge mistake.

                    PANTHER
     We're not.

                    EFFLUVIA
     You're right about that. Not if you were
     the last man on earth.

Sasha finally jumps into the fray.

                    DR. RAM
     See, that's your problem, Effluvia. He's
     not a man—he's so much more than that
     now. And if you keep focusing on your
     past relationship, it will affect your
     ability to protect your country.

                    EFFLUVIA
     If I need your advice, I'll ask for it.

                    DR. RAM
     You need it. And if you don't take it,
     you'll live to regret it.

                    EFFLUVIA
     That sounds like a threat.

"Cut," Chaz calls. There's a silence as he collects his thoughts. "Scarlett?"

"Yes?" I ask, steeling myself for a blow.

"The next time you intend to improvise an entire scene, let your director know."

"Sorry," I say. "It just *felt* right."

Chaz emerges from the shadows. His tie is askew, as if he's been trying to strangle himself with it. "You're lucky it worked," he says. "But if you two don't rein it in, I'm calling a family meeting."

By family, he means Jake, and the warning helps Sasha and me discover that we can stick to the script after all.

★ ★ ★

Jab, jab, hook.

I throw punch after punch at the bag. Dad always warned me not to underestimate my opponent and today I finally see what he meant. I made the mistake of assuming that Sasha was incapable of thinking on her stilettos, but there's more to her than silicone and a mean streak a mile wide. She almost ran away with my role.

Jab, jab, uppercut, cross.

Not that it was an incredible acting feat. Playing a villain comes naturally to her, especially one like Dr. Ram. Sasha was born knowing how to use her good looks to get what she wants and with her defective conscience, she'd make a fine double agent. It seems like the Dr. Rams of the world get to take what they want, while the warthogs stand on the sidelines waiting for their luck to turn.

Jab, jab, hook.

On the other side of the flimsy gym walls, the music is pumping. The cast and crew are enjoying an impromptu party to kickstart our holiday hiatus. I decided to work out instead. I'm not going to go in there and pretend I'll miss those people during my week off. They are not my friends.

I picture Sasha's face on the bag.

Jab, jab, uppercut, cross.

Now I picture Julian's face. I thought he was smart enough to see past the vinyl surface to the fiend within. If he isn't, they deserve each other.

Jab, jab, hook.

Sweat is pouring into my eyes now, but I keep the punches coming.

"You're not working your feet," someone says.

Julian steps behind the punching bag and holds it steady while I swing.

"Without the proper footwork, you'll never knock me out," he says.

"Not everything," I puff, "is about you."

"Did I do something wrong?"

I may not have the footwork, but I can sidestep a question I don't like. "What do you mean?"

"I got the sense that Effluvia had issues with Panther this afternoon."

I land another punch on the bag. "Effluvia and Dr. Ram didn't take to each other, that's all. It was scripted."

"Not all of it. Effluvia went off on a bit of a rant."

I stop punching to glare at him. "Of course she did. The panther tossed her aside for the genius in the tight top."

"It was scripted."

"Not all of it," I say. "One moment he's making out with Effluvia and the next he's all over Dr. Silicone. You said Panther was a good guy."

"He is a good guy. But he's still a guy and that outfit was—"

"Never mind."

I abandon the punching bag and climb onto the stationary bike. Surely pedaling is basic enough that he won't feel the need to offer advice. I'm not in the mood for private tutoring tonight.

Julian follows and leans on the handlebars to face me. "You're not taking this personally, are you?"

"Nope." I prop my elbows on the handlebars, wheezing a little as my stomach attachment presses into my diaphragm.

"You're missing a good party."

"If it's so good, why are you here?"

"Just trying to reunite the Force. One freak is missing in action."

I snort. "Jed and Rudy are pining for me?"

He grins. "Actually, they're pining because Sasha is chatting up Chaz instead of them."

"Typical."

"I take it there's a little step-sibling rivalry?"

If he thinks I'm going to confide in him now, he's wrong. "It's been a while since we acted together and I don't think we clicked today. That's all."

He laughs. "Well, she did steal your light and your lines."

Now he says so. Where was he when she was doing the stealing? That's right, he was cheering her on. If I say anything negative about her tonight, he'll probably say I'm being catty. I know that trap. Better to take the professional high road. "Improv is all about risk. I respect her skills."

"Yeah? Then what was all this punching about?"

"Just getting in a last workout before the break."

He sits down at the leg press and does a set before speaking again. "No one gets along with stepbrothers or sisters—at least not right away."

"I didn't say we don't get along. And how would you know, anyway?"

"I became an expert at age four, when my stepbrother locked me in a neighbor's garden shed overnight. The police found me eventually—but not before I developed some unusual phobias."

I don't want to laugh but it happens anyway. "Did your parents send him to reform school?"

"Nah. I think they figured they deserved some grief after breaking up two marriages to be together."

"Messy." At least Jake and Annika have been divorced for a while.

"Very. One reason they didn't want me going into show biz is that it's hard on relationships."

"How do you feel about your stepbrother now?"

He rolls his eyes. "My stepsisters from Dad's first marriage are crazy too."

"How do you deal with it?"

"Two basic rules . . . One: Reduce overall exposure to the offending parties. And two: Surround yourself with allies when exposure is unavoidable."

"Sounds like war tactics."

"When you strategize, it doesn't come to war." He gets off the leg press and leans on my handlebars again. "If you need an ally when your Mom marries Jake, I make an excellent wedding date."

"We tried that once," I remind him. "It didn't end so well."

Julian leans closer until his face is inches from mine. "Second-time lucky."

The door opens and Julian moves away but not before Sasha sees him. Genuine surprise flickers across her face but she recovers instantly. "Your Mommy sent me to get you, Effluvia. She's here to drive you home."

"To drive *us* home," I say, hopping off the bike.

She looks me up and down. "So you wear your costume all the time. How cute. But it must stink if you sweat like that in it."

I automatically move away from Julian. "It's washable," I say.

She grins and comes over to take Julian's arm. "I told Annika that I'm catching a ride with Chaz, later. So, you'd better get going."

"If you want to stay, I can take you home, Leigh," Julian says.

If he'd just worded that sentence to indicate that *he* wanted me to stay, I'd do it. But my war tactics don't include battling my future stepsister for some guy who isn't sure what he wants. "I've already made plans for tonight."

"Too bad," he says.

I think I hear disappointment in his voice, but someone is already talking over him. "Come on," Sasha says. "I want to see how a panther moves on the dance floor."

I wish Julian a good hiatus but he doesn't hear me. The big game hunter has already chased him out the door.

twelve

Recipe for Disaster

Ingredients:
1 well-seasoned Male*
1 overly ripe Female*
(*desensitized to the feelings of those around them)
*2 Daughters of Male, extra bitter, with all traces of humanity re-
   moved*
1 Boyfriend of bitter daughter, stuffed with false sincerity
1 Daughter of Female, thorns intact

*Combine ingredients with a generous dash of pressure and allow
to simmer for several hours, or until combustion occurs.*

Enjoyment optional.

Annika is tense. There's already a waxy ring of Glazed
Poppy lipstick around her champagne flute, although our festive
gathering with the Cohens has barely begun. Plus her eyes have
become shallow blue pools in which panicky thoughts seem to
surface like goldfish.

"Isn't it lovely that we're all together for our first holiday dinner?" she says, rearranging her cutlery.

"Lovely," Jake agrees.

It's our first dinner together, period. With our varied schedules, we've managed to avoid ever using the dining room. That explains why I took Sasha's seat by mistake and had to be scalded out of it with caustic remarks. Then I moved to the other side of the table and Ursela refused to sit in *her* usual seat because it's next to mine. So now, Gray and I are side-by-side facing Sashela, while Annika and Jake try to keep the conversation going from either end.

"Isn't the kugel lovely?" Annika asks. As if she'd actually eat a mouthful of carbs.

"Lovely," Jake agrees. "Try the latkes."

It's a true Hollywood festive gathering, with manufactured good looks lighting up the room. Gray's laser-whitened teeth and golden highlights gleam under the chandelier. Sasha's breast implants are on prominent display in a white corset. Ursela's nose job is brighter than Rudolph's. Jake's normally silver hair, on the other hand, is darker and richer. And Annika . . . well, it would be easier to point out what *hasn't* been done. I'm the only one here who'd qualify as natural.

"Did you wear your smelly costume on the plane, Farthog?" Sasha asks.

Jake runs interference. "Sasha, tell us what you bought at the sales today."

He has no interest in bargain hunting, but he does want to keep the dinner civil. It's more effort than Annika is making, but then she's lost in her own world where reconstituted families are lovely and perfect and polite.

I appreciate Jake's efforts but I'm actually fine. My anti-Sashela force field is functioning at peak capacity due to prolonged exposure to Dad and Grandma Reid in Seattle. Not that my stay was all peace and goodwill. Because of what happened on *Diamond Heights,* Dad had his ego detector going full blast the whole time and delivered several unnecessary sermons about values. I thought he'd outgrown his lecturing problem, but the threat of L.A. corruption has caused a relapse.

Gran and Stan came on Christmas Eve, as usual, and we drank Dad's eggnog (heated to eliminate the risk of salmonella), ate Grandma's shortbread, and opened our gifts. Also as usual, Dad's gifts were disappointingly practical: a lamp for my desk, a thesaurus, some collectible coins, and a gift certificate for a course called "Women on Wheels" that will teach me what goes on under a car's hood. Gran's were no better: perfume that smells like fabric softener, a hot water bottle with a fuzzy pink cover, and a flannelette nightie she wanted me to bring to L.A.

"It's warm year-round in L.A., Gran," I said.

"A little too warm, if you ask me," she said. "I saw you kissing that boy."

"On television," I said. "That was acting."

"It didn't look like acting."

It didn't feel like it either but apparently it was—on Julian's side. "It's amazing what you can fake, Gran."

She pointed to my last gift and said, "If he ever takes you out on a real date, you can wear this."

Inside was a long kilt in the Reid tartan and a sweater with the family crest on it. Dad said later that Gran is worried I'll change my name after Annika remarries because "Cohen" carries so much weight in Hollywood. I could tell from his expression that he's worried too so I reassured him I won't. One day I might drop the "Vivien" just to bug Annika, but otherwise my name will never change, even if I get married.

Whether Mom gives up *her* last name now that she's finally worked it onto the A list remains to be seen. She's already making other compromises. For example, Mom loves choosing nice gifts for people but today she gives Sasha, Ursela, and me receipts for charitable donations made in our names. "It seemed silly to spend money on you girls when you already have so much," she says.

The words come out of her mouth but the sentiment is Jake's. Annika's idea of *charity* is offloading free makeup samples at the local women's shelter. I'm all for holiday donation, but would it kill her to slide her real daughter a little something on the side? Sashela looks equally underwhelmed.

The only good thing about the Cohen festive event so far is that Mom poured me a glass of champagne. It's an odd pairing with kugel and potato latkes, but I'm making the best of it. For the reconstituted family.

"So, Leigh," Ursela says. "Did you see your friends from the Turd Academy?"

Jake swiftly tosses out a conversational chicken for his feral offspring to maul. "Girls, someone you know is getting some work done."

There's a shrill chorus of: "Who? Who, Daddy? Is she on one of your shows? Who's her surgeon?"

I use the distraction to slip Brando some brisket. Annika dropped a slab on my plate, thinking I'd set vegetarianism aside for the holiday. Not. I compromise my principles only when it's convenient for me.

Gray, who is sitting beside me, says, "Easy does it, Cowgirl. That's a lot of meat for a little dog."

I scowl at him. "It's none of your business."

"Brando's well-being is my business," he says. "I chose him for you."

Gray did not choose this dog. I'm the one who saw the puppies in the pet store window. All Gray did was scoop him out of the display and plunk him in my arms. To be honest, I was so infatuated by Gray that if he'd handed me a lizard, I'd have taken that too.

"And I named him," Gray adds.

That much is true. Marlon Brando is his idol, not mine. "I wanted to name him Poochino," I say. "After Al."

He laughs. "That was such a great night. Remember?"

I stare at him, suspiciously. Gray has been varying degrees of rude to me since I moved in here. Why this fond trip down memory lane now? "You were so busy laying the groundwork to use me, I doubt you can remember anything else about it."

He hooks one tanned arm over his chair. "You were wearing black pants, a pink T-shirt, and a white hoodie—and sunglasses although it was dark. You ordered pizza without cheese, and Karis was pissed because we'd dumped Skippy on her."

Okay, that's impressive. "I guess actors need to be observant," I say. "Even when they plan to get by on connections."

Sasha parachutes into our conversation. "What's going on?"

Gray turns his smile on her and demonstrates his acting skill. "I was just congratulating Leigh on her review in *Variety*."

"Here, here," Jake says, raising his glass. "A toast to Effluvia!"

Sasha and Ursela refuse to raise their glasses, even though Annika encouragingly tops up their champagne. My glass she ignores.

"To Effluvia," Gray echoes, giving me a wink.

He's flirting with me! Obviously he thinks I'm making enough of a name for myself to be useful to him again. It's sickening but I giggle anyway to provoke Sasha. I could provoke her even more by telling Gray about how she flirted with Julian, but I won't because Annika is spinning her engagement ring dazedly and Jake's forehead has beaded in sweat. The dinner is already ugly enough.

"And here's to our girls working together again," Jake says, raising his glass again. "Tell us about your day on *Freak Force*, Sasha."

"It was great working with Chaz," she says. "What a relief to have a director who focuses on the action instead of his crumbling marriage."

Jake's fork freezes in mid-air. "What do you mean?"

"Don't make a big deal about it, Dad. The show is fine. I'm just worried about Roger. At least he has friends like Annika to help him through it."

Annika stops playing with her engagement ring and says, "I didn't know Roger was having marriage trouble."

Sasha widens her eyes innocently. "I assumed he confided in you about everything. He seems so much happier the days you come by our set."

"My Nika has that effect on people," Jake says, giving Mom a strained smile.

"Enough divorce talk," Annika says. "Let's talk about weddings."

I'm amazed we've gone this long *without* talking about weddings.

"If we hurry," she continues, "we can make it to Henry Winton's before it closes. I want to buy Team Annika some bling."

I've got to give credit to Sasha: Thanks to one well-timed bomb, the Cohen family holiday isn't a complete write-off after all.

✦　✦　✦

I'm surprised to see someone with red dreadlocks standing beside the security guard at Henry Winton's when our cab pulls up.

"I could tell he didn't trust me," Karis says. "So I stood here to freak him out."

"My mother calls you now?" I ask.

She nods. "I think she felt outnumbered with you in Seattle."

Herding us into the store, Annika announces, "I want you to choose something to wear to the wedding as a thank-you for participating in our special day."

An older man in a pinstriped suit hurries over and greets Annika with a hug. "It's so lovely to see you," he says, in an upper-class English accent.

It's Henry Winton, the store's owner, and if he's being that nice to Annika, more of her jewelry is real than I thought.

He waves us toward the display cases, saying, "Just let the clerks know what catches your eye. And do look at the Bombshell collection: I designed it with beautiful young starlets like you in mind."

Sneering, Sasha pulls her sister away. "I saw something more my style on our way in."

"Probably from the Fast and Loose collection," I whisper to Karis.

Annika flits from counter to counter like the butterfly she is, while Karis and I examine the silver bracelets Henry sets on a velvet cushion. Karis chooses one, but I ask to see a simple chain with a pink stone on it, which would look great with my dress.

"What do you think?" Sasha calls, waltzing toward us wearing an elaborate diamond and sapphire choker.

Henry says, "You have exquisite taste, Miss Cohen. That's the most expensive piece in the store."

"It's stunning," Annika says. "Now, put it back before something happens to it."

"But this is what I want," Sasha says.

Annika's tolerant smile fades. "You can't be serious. That must be worth—"

"You don't want to know," Henry says, laughing.

"Please put it back, Sasha," Mom says.

"No. You said we could choose."

Henry discreetly excuses himself, leaving Annika to fight the battle alone. "You're being silly, Sasha, and you're embarrassing me."

That's precisely the point and Mom is just fueling the fire.

Sasha saunters back to the counter to ask for matching earrings and Annika follows her, entreating, "You know I can't afford those."

"Daddy can," Sasha says, trying on the earrings. "And he pays the bills, right?"

"He'd have to sell the house to pay that one."

Sasha's cold blue eyes meet Annika's in the mirror. "Or he could have a smaller wedding."

Annika takes a deep breath and releases it very slowly, probably counting to ten. "I realize we're all under pressure, with this being our first holiday together . . ."

"And hopefully our last," Sasha mutters under her breath.

Annika continues as if she missed this, "So, I'm going to give you a few moments to think about this while I choose some cuff links for your father. When I come back, I expect that jewelry to be under lock and key."

Sasha pushes her sleek hair behind her ears and tilts her head to admire the earrings. "And if it's not?"

"Then," Annika says, her voice spiking, "I'll remove it personally."

Sasha turns to face her. "Just try it, Annika."

Ursela moves to her side. "Don't you dare touch my sister!"

I move to Annika's side. It's the showdown I've been waiting for, but unfortunately, I can't let it happen. "Mom," I say, giving her a little push toward the cuff link display. "Henry is waiting."

She gives Sasha one last glare before reluctantly walking away.

"You'd better keep your mother in line," Sasha tells me. "If she lays one finger on me, I'm charging her with assault."

A man's voice prevents my answering. "Good evening, ladies. Does anyone need my assistance?"

We turn to see a tall, dark man in his mid-twenties standing behind us, smiling. He has olive skin, eyes the color of bittersweet chocolate, and lashes long enough to rival Sasha's. His expensive-looking suit is paired with a cream shirt, and as he reaches out to shake her hand, I see the glint of gold in his French cuff.

If Prince Charming ever came to life, this is exactly what he'd look like. And he'd have an English accent like this too.

Sasha apparently agrees because she stutters as she says, "Yes, please."

He takes her by the hand and leads her to a quiet corner. The rest of us follow so closely that I step on Ursela's foot almost by accident.

"I'm Edward Winton, Henry's nephew," Prince Charming says, offering a courtly little bow as he releases Sasha's hand. She leaves it hanging, as if hoping he'll take it again. Karis and I exchange amused glances. Unless this guy is Prince William incognito, he's taking himself too seriously.

Sasha introduces Ursela and the three chat for a bit. I listen in, noting that Edward sounds more Australian than English. In fact, the more he speaks, the less convincing his accent becomes. The dialogue coaches I had on *Diamond Heights* and *Danny Boy* would be cringing right now.

"What brings you to L.A.?" Sasha asks, too overcome by pheromones to notice the lame accent.

"I've moved from London to work for the family business," he says.

I notice that his eyes are actually darting all over the store instead of focusing on Sasha. She'd better not dump Gray just yet.

"Really?" Sasha says. "So, all of this . . ." she fondles the jewels around her neck, ". . . will be yours someday?"

Prince Charming laughs. "Well, we'll see about that. In the meantime, I'm learning the ropes from Uncle Henry. One thing he's taught me is to be honest with clients, and that's why I need to say that this necklace is all wrong for you, Sasha."

Sasha pouts. "Why?"

"Because sapphires compete with your stunning blue eyes. Emeralds, on the other hand, would complement them."

"I've always liked emeralds," Sasha says.

"Top-quality emeralds are more valuable than diamonds. And Sasha." He rests a hand on her shoulder here. "You deserve the best. You are a very beautiful woman."

She steadies herself on a display case. "Thank you. Do you have any emeralds I can try?"

"Of course. Let me return the sapphires and I'll choose something for you."

While Sasha starts to take off the necklace, I study Edward. Instead of helping her with the clasp, he's glancing around the shop again. And his hands, now at his sides, are clenching and unclenching. It brings to mind what Professor Kirk used to say when he sent us off to observe people in cafés or at the mall: *Lips may lie but body language tells the truth.* He wanted us to learn how to use nonverbal cues to communicate our characters' true feelings.

Edward's body language suggests that he isn't the calm, helpful employee he says he is. With every second Sasha fumbles with the necklace, his breath seems to get shallower and faster. A flush is creeping around the crisp collar of his shirt.

I have no idea why he's so nervous but something is off here. I take a look over my shoulder at the cuff link counter and see that Annika and Henry are head-to-head, whispering. She may be choosing a gift for her future husband, but that doesn't mean she can't flirt with the salesman.

Sasha finally offers the necklace to Edward and I intercept her hand. "I'll take it back to the clerk who gave it to you so that she doesn't worry."

Sasha tries to shake me off but I pry the necklace out of her fingers.

Edward steps toward me and his smile looks less princely and more wolflike at close range. "I'll take the necklace back. It's no problem, really."

"I've got it," I say.

"And I want it," he replies, all trace of an English accent vanishing. His hand closes around my wrist and squeezes.

"Darling," my mother carols, joining us suddenly. "It seems that everywhere we go these days you're meeting young men. Who's your handsome friend?"

Sasha's eyes flick from Annika to Edward's hand on my wrist. Confused, she says, "Edward is *my* friend."

Annika smiles flirtatiously at Edward and extends her hand. "It's a pleasure to meet you, Edward. If you weren't a decade too young for me, you'd be in *big* trouble."

Edward pauses for a moment, his dark eyes unfathomable. The flush has climbed to his jaw line. Finally he releases my wrist and extends his hand to Annika. She takes it and with one swift move, spins and flips him over her shoulder. I barely get a glimpse of Edward's black Oxfords flying over his head before he's on his back and Annika is herding us to the front of the store.

Meanwhile, the security guard charges past us and hurls himself on top of Edward's prone form. Police officers are suddenly everywhere.

"How did you know?" I ask my mother.

She calmly takes a tube of Glazed Poppy out of her coat pocket and freshens her lipstick. "Would you believe it was mother's intuition?"

"No," Karis and I chime in unison.

She laughs. "Well, you're right. Henry recognized the guy's face from a story about some previous robberies. He called the police and they warned him not to startle the thief before they arrived. But I refused to wait, of course. How could I, when my daughter was in peril?"

"How about the rest of us?" Sasha grumbles.

A police officer leads Edward, now handcuffed, outside to a patrol car and another officer approaches us to collect witness statements. "I heard about what you did," he tells Annika. "Are you a martial arts expert?"

"Actually, I'm an actor," Annika says. "Perhaps you've seen me in—"

"Mom."

"Well, darling, my filmography is relevant."

"Not to his police report."

"It was my ability to act under pressure that got Edward to drop his guard," she says.

Acting like a flirt is a breeze for Annika in any situation, apparently even a robbery-in-progress.

A yowl causes all eyes to turn toward Sasha who is crouching in a corner with tears streaming down her face. "The guy was all over me," she says. "He was an animal!"

The officer excuses himself and leads Sasha outside for some fresh air. Ursela follows with her cell phone to her ear. "Daddy, you won't believe what happened!"

When the officer returns, he explains that Sasha's panic attack is abating and asks how we're holding up.

"We're fine," Annika says, having questioned Karis and me at length. "Thank god I was here! When I saw that man grab my daughter . . . Well, my life flashed before my eyes. And I'm telling you this: I did not suffer through nine months of being fat and twenty hours of labor to lose her now."

Annika brags a bit longer about using "all the tools in an actor's arsenal" before mentioning to the officer that I'd already figured out that Edward was up to no good.

"You're a brave girl," the officer says, after I describe what happened.

I wave away his praise. "My dad would say a stupid girl. He's going to kill me."

"And me," Annika says. "But he'll be proud too."

The officer explains that everyone reacts differently to this type of situation. Some, like Sasha, lose it right away, whereas others experience Post-Traumatic Stress Disorder—or PTSD—long after the event. He offers a card with the name of a crisis counselor on it.

I won't need counseling. I understand that this could have become a dangerous situation, but it's over now and no one was hurt, so there's nothing to be upset about. If Sasha put as much effort into yoga as she does into picking on me, she'd be a lot calmer right now.

Still, I accept the card from the officer. Annika has taken to her bed for far less.

★   ★   ★

Henry escorts Annika, Karis, and me to the door. "I can't thank you enough. When you're ready to come back and choose your jewelry, it's on the house."

"Thank you, Henry," Annika says, kissing his cheeks. "That's very generous."

"If Miss Cohen would like to keep the sapphire earrings overnight, it's fine with me," he adds. "But I will need them back eventually."

Annika is horrified. "I'm so sorry. I didn't realize she still had them."

As we step out of the shop, dozens of cameras flash, blinding me momentarily. When the dots clear, I see two dozen reporters, cameramen, and photographers crowding the sidewalk.

"Sasha!" someone calls. "Over here!" A reporter jabs a microphone at Sasha, who has recovered enough to fix her hair and makeup. "Tell us exactly how you did it."

"It was nothing," Sasha says. "One flip and he was down. I didn't even break a nail."

Everyone laughs. Except Annika, Henry, and Karis and me.

Sasha smiles at another camera and tosses her head so the sapphire earrings twinkle. "That thug was *between a rock and a hard place* when he met up with me."

At the reporters' urging, Sasha explains how she realized Edward was a conman. "There was something shifty about the way he was coming on to me. I mean, I'm used to compliments, but guys are usually more interested in me than the jewelry."

"Tell us how you felt," someone calls.

"Well, I was nervous but there was a voice inside my head saying, 'You can *act* your way out of this.'"

"Unbelievable," a reporter calls and there's another round of flashes.

"It's unbelievable, alright," Henry's voice rings out. The reporters turn as one and thrust microphones toward him. "I am the owner of this shop and I must tell you that it wasn't Miss Cohen who saved the day, but Annika Anderson and her daughter, Vivien Leigh Reid."

Henry pushes us forward and describes the event in detail. When he finishes, reporters swarm us.

"Annika, where did you learn that move?"

Annika fluffs her hair and assumes her red carpet pose. "I've always done my own stunts. Take a look at *She Devil*, or *Where, Wolf?* You'll see similar moves, only this time my heels were even higher!"

"How do you stay in such amazing shape?"

"I work at it, believe me. You never know when you might be called upon to defend your family."

"What have you learned from this experience?"

"Well, I know it will make me a better actress. Now I don't just have to imagine what terror feels like—I've experienced it."

Annika fields a few more questions before reluctantly yielding the spotlight to me.

"How did you figure out the guy was up to something?"

With the lights shining in my eyes, my mind immediately goes blank. Karis quickly comes to my rescue. "She's had on-the-job training. No one can sniff out trouble faster than Effluvia, the superhero wart—*Ow!*"

Karis stops speaking as Annika's nails dig into her but the reporters are on it.

"So, you're the mystery girl from Freak Force! *Is that Vivien with an 'e' or an 'a'?"*

Finally, someone asks the question I've been waiting for: *"Can you tell us why Miss Cohen would lie about what happened today?"*

A scream prevents our answering. We turn to see Ursela standing over Sasha, who is sprawled on a bench. Or, more accurately, neatly arranged in case anyone wants to snap more photos.

The reporters surge over to them.

"She fainted," Ursela says. "One minute, she was standing here and the next she was down."

Not a bad performance, although Ursela's exaggerated gestures are a sure sign that she trained in live theater.

Sasha's eyes flutter open. "Wh-what happened? Ursela? Is that you?"

"Don't try to speak, honey," Ursela says. "You've had a terrible shock."

A reporter leans over the bench. "Sasha, do you remember telling us all about how you saved the day inside Henry's?"

"Wh-what day?" Sasha asks. "Who's Henry?"

Ursela makes grand, sweeping gestures with her arms. "Please back away. The officer warned us about this. My sister is obviously suffering from PTSD."

I roll my eyes at Karis. "Make that PT*B*SD."

thirteen

Jake slides the newspaper across the kitchen table and beams at us. "You made page four of the *LA Times*."

Under the headline MOTHER-DAUGHTER TEAM SAVES THE DAY, there's a shot of Annika and me outside of Henry Winton's.

Annika reads the caption aloud. "'Renowned actor Annika Anderson and her talented daughter, Vivien Leigh Reid, use actor's intuition and movie stunts to foil jewel thief.' Did you hear that, Jake? I'm *'renowned.'*"

"Of course you are," he says, smiling delightedly. "I hope you don't plan to give up acting for crime fighting."

"I'll stick to make believe," Annika assures him. "How about you, Vivien?"

"I guess so," I say, staring at a smaller photo of Effluvia in full warthog regalia. Something tells me Chaz is going to be in one of his moods today.

"Your grandmother called," Jake tells me.

That's the second time this morning and it's only eight o'clock. Gran and Dad are totally overreacting about what happened at Henry Winton's. It's not like it was a life or death experience or anything. I'm absolutely fine. I finally had to ask them to get off the phone so that I could learn my lines.

Jake continues, "She's booking a flight down here and I offered her a place to stay."

"You what?" Annika and I both say at once.

He holds up both hands defensively. "I couldn't let her pay for a hotel. She's Leigh's grandmother."

"But I've just gone through a very difficult experience," Annika says, her voice suddenly fragile. "I can't play hostess right now."

"I'm sure she won't be any trouble," he says. "She sounds very pleasant."

"Well, she's not," Annika says. She looks at me and corrects herself. "I mean, she's *not strong*. The flight will be too much for her."

"Nice save, Mom." I actually understand why Annika wouldn't want Gran trolling the halls of the beach house, especially with the wedding-planning kicking into high gear. And I don't want to have to referee between them all the time. Hopefully Gran will lighten up on Mom now that she's demonstrated proper maternal instincts. "Don't worry, I'll call Gran and convince her I'm fine."

"If you're not, you should take a Valium with your orange juice," Sasha says, entering the kitchen.

Jake gets up from the table to hug her. "Sasha, honey, you sound upset. Still shook up?"

"Well, I was the one who nearly died, Daddy. If I hadn't taken off the necklace when Edward asked me to, I might have been shot!"

"Shot!" I scoff. "He wasn't even armed."

"He had a gun," she insists. "I could tell."

"Then, no wonder you're upset," I say. "But you don't have to deal with this alone, Sasha. The police gave me the name of a crisis counselor."

"That's a great idea," Jake says. "I'll go with you, honey."

I speak over Sasha's protests. "Maybe you could take her tomorrow, Jake. She isn't filming."

"It's my three-month anniversary with Gray," Sasha says. "I have plans."

"Nothing is more important than your health," Jake says. "You're lucky Leigh is so concerned about you."

I smile at him. "Well, since Sasha feels the guy had a gun, then I guess I saved her life. It sort of bonds us."

Sasha gives me a withering look. "You did not save my life."

"She might have," Annika says. "And she probably saved you from a robbery investigation, too. If *your friend* Edward had walked out with the necklace, the police might have considered you an accomplice."

Looks like Mom has finally aborted her mission to win over the Cohen Coven. Had she listened to me earlier, she could have saved herself months of fruitless sucking up.

"That's stupid," Sasha says. "Obviously I knew Edward was up to something. I was just waiting for the right time to manage the situation—with words, not violence."

"That might have worked, honey," Jake says, as Annika and I roll our eyes. "But even so, you do owe Leigh a thank-you."

"Okay, fine," she says, turning to the coffee pot. "Whatever."

Jake pats her back and I realize that was my thank-you. "Sasha, please," I say. "You're embarrassing me with all the fuss."

Wagging a warning finger at me, Annika walks to the door. "Let's go, girls. I have a rehearsal this morning, so I'll need to drive you to work now."

"I want Dad to take me today," Sasha says, pouting. "I'd feel safer. Please, Daddy?"

"Sure, I'll take them," Jake agrees.

"But you've got a meeting, sweetie," Annika says. "And it's out of your way."

"She wants to check in on Roger, Daddy," Sasha says. "Now that she knows his marriage is on the rocks."

Annika's eyes narrow to the blue slits that spark fear in my heart. They have zero effect on Sasha, who nonchalantly fills a travel mug.

Jake is already gathering his things. "You go ahead, Annika. I've got this. I should check in on Roger myself, anyway."

As we trail after him to the car, Sasha says, "Dad, don't worry about Roger and Annika. Even if he were single again, Annika would never leave you for him. He's already made her famous, so she doesn't need him anymore."

I reach out and pinch the back of Sasha's arm until she squeals. Jake turns in time to see her heave her cup at me, and I make a show of wincing as a trickle of hot coffee runs down my leg.

Taking Sasha by the shoulder, Jake propels her to the driveway. "I'll book that appointment for you today."

★　★　★

When I see Julian coming toward me, my heart does a high kick in my chest. No matter how much I've tried to drive him out of my mind over the hiatus, I've missed him. The wide smile under his visor gives me hope that he missed me too. Maybe I read too much into his fascination with Sasha. After all, she was practically naked.

He falls into step with me. "I hear you've become a real life superhero."

I wave my hand dismissively. "Annika's the one who took the guy down."

We cross the lobby of the office building the studio has rented today as a *Freak Force* location. The cameras are set up out front for our first scene.

Julian stops before we reach the door and squeezes my arm. "How are you doing?"

"I'm fine," I say. "It was no big deal."

"It sounded like a big deal." He gives me a quizzical look and then smiles. "Or was this just another method-acting exercise for you?"

"Of course not. Otherwise, I'd have been wearing my butt attachment."

Julian laughs. "With the publicity the show gets from this, you might be able to talk Chaz down another twenty-five percent."

"I like the way your mind works," I say.

He reaches out to open the door and then wraps it around my shoulders instead. "I was worried about you."

He was worried about me! Worried! About me! That means he likes me, for sure. Plus he is practically hugging me where anyone could see us.

I lean against him for a fraction of a second to let him know that I'm glad he worried about me. And then I repeat that I'm fine. In fact, I am now much better than fine, thanks to him. If it weren't for my sore wrist where Edward grabbed me, I'd probably forget last night even happened.

As he opens the door, we notice the commotion outside. "There's the publicity I was talking about," Julian says.

A crowd of about fifty people cheers as we walk out. A few girls practically dissolve into tears as Julian passes, but even more people yell my name. Someone is waving a poster that reads EFFLUVIA KICKS ASS! I give the crowd a tentative wave and the cheer grows louder.

"Stop winding them up, Scarlett," Chaz says. "We can't work with this noise."

The scene we'll be shooting is a conversation between Effluvia and the Panther. Chaz has decided to do a "walk and talk," which means Julian and I will deliver our dialogue as we walk toward the building; a steadicam operator will capture the action while walking backward ahead of us.

We do a quick rehearsal for the cameraman and afterward, the crowd applauds. Chaz snaps his fingers at Lex, who puts a megaphone into his hand. "SHUT UP!" Chaz yells.

"Chaz," I say, "you can't talk to our fans like that."

"We never had a crowd problem until you spilled the beans about Effluvia."

Julian steps in, a white knight in a black bodysuit. "It's great publicity, Chaz."

"All I care about is finishing today's shoot on time and staying within budget," Chaz says. "That's what'll get us renewed. By the way, Scarlett, has Jake dropped any hints about that at home?"

I shake my head. If Jake thinks I'll be sticking around longer, he hasn't let on. I'm not sure how I feel about that idea anyway. It would be nice if *Freak Force* was renewed, but the prospect of on-going incarceration with the Cohens isn't appealing. Mom would have to let me fly home often to recharge my anti-Sashela force field.

Behind us, the crowd is getting louder. Chaz raises the mega-phone, but this time I boldly take it from his hands and walk back to the crowd.

"Welcome to the *Freak Force* set, everyone," I begin and the crowd hushes immediately. If I weren't so grounded, that kind of power might go to my head. But now I have Sir Nigel's example to live up to. "Thank you so much for your support today. While we're shooting, we'll need to ask for silence."

There's a murmur of assent and then someone asks me to sign an autograph. Julian joins me and together we chat to the fans while signing everything from parking receipts to an empty Star-bucks cup. One guy even gets me to sign his boxers. Normally, I'd refuse that sort of request, but I have my knight with me. Julian and I are already turning into one of those royal Hollywood cou-ples. Maybe we'll live and act together until we're old and gray, like Tom Hanks and Rita Wilson.

A girl who appears to be about fourteen gushes, "I loved you so much in *Diamond Heights* that I cried when you died. The show hasn't been the same since. And they should *never* have given Fallon a spinoff. She's horrible."

A high five wouldn't be gracious, so I settle for beaming at her. "That's so nice of you to say."

She beams back. "You're so *normal*."

"I'm just like you, only my part-time job comes with a really ugly uniform."

"No argument there," Julian says.

"Shut up," I say.

The girl looks from one of us to the other. "Are you two dating?"

"Effluvia and the Panther are going through a tough time," I say, although I know she meant in real life. "He has a wandering eye."

He lifts his visor to direct emerald eyes at me. "Remind me which one wanders?"

"You *are* dating," the girl says.

Julian shrugs. "Wait till you see Dr. Ram."

He had to bring up Sasha. Until now, I was feeling pretty good about him.

The girl holds me back as Julian moves on. "I think what you did yesterday at the jewelry store was so cool."

"It was no big deal," I say.

"But the guy had a gun," she says. "I just heard it on the news."

"A gun?" I ask. "A real gun?"

The girl nods. "Yeah. They said he shot someone during another robbery."

Chaz saves me from having to respond to this.

"Warthog front and center," he barks into the megaphone. "Some of us have a schedule to keep."

I head over to Effluvia's mark, trying to push what the girl said out of my mind. It doesn't matter what *might have* happened. It didn't happen. Everything is fine.

Julian pulls me to another mark. "That one's mine," he says. "Are you okay?"

"Sure, I'm fine." I've said that over and over since last night, but this is the first time it hasn't been true.

★   ★   ★

EXTERIOR OFFICE BUILDING, DAY

Effluvia and Panther have been dispatched to snoop around the offices of Dr. Ram's colleague, a possible Russian spy. Effluvia is still angry with Panther about his flirting with Dr. Ram.

                    EFFLUVIA
        I think Dr. Ram is trying to lure us into
        a trap.

                    PANTHER
        A trap? Why would you say that? She's
        helping our team.

                    EFFLUVIA
        I'm telling you, she's dangerous. And if
        you don't watch your step, you could end
        up dead.

Just like I could have ended up dead last night. Instead of being here filming, I could be lying in some cheesy L.A. funeral
home. I can picture it all now:

*Gran and Annika are fighting over the service because
Annika wants to give her wedding caterer and florist
a trial run and Gran finds that tacky. Karis is throwing evil looks at Sasha, who's wearing white, as usual.
Ursela is spiking the punch. The press is interview-
ing everyone, musing over how my star has set far too
soon. Dad, stoic as always, is making sure no one trips
over the camera cables. Gran and Annika are fighting
again because Gran wants me buried in the family
tartan and Annika prefers the Narciso Rodriguez
dress. Jake is trying to keep Roger away from Annika.
Chaz is trying to get private time with Jake. Meanwhile, poor Julian sits weeping in the front row, wondering if he has lost his one chance at true love.
There's Sasha, undoing a few more buttons as she approaches Julian from behind, ready to make her play,
even as Gray—*

A blast from the megaphone startles me. "You dropped a line, Scarlett. Hiatus is over. How about joining the rest of us at work?"

Obviously, Chaz wouldn't miss a beat if I died. He'd put some crew member with my build into the pig suit and keep right on shooting.

"Sorry," I mumble, embarrassed to screw up in front of so many fans.

"That was pathetic," he says. "Where's the emotion? The guy you thought you'd be with forever likes someone prettier, even though she might be an enemy spy. Some anger wouldn't go amiss."

Geez, he could lighten up. There's no need to humiliate me. It's not like I've ever zoned out on a performance before. Still, it's unprofessional and it can't happen again. People came out of their way to see me perform and I won't let them down.

I take a deep breath and try to clear my mind.


```
              PANTHER
Does this have something to do with the
other night?


              EFFLUVIA
You're damn right it does. Why did you
even ask me out if you didn't mean it?
You've got to start thinking before you
act. Otherwise, people get hurt.
```

Last night I wasn't the only one who could have been hurt. The article in the *Los Angeles Times* could have been a mother-daughter obituary. I may feel like I want to kill Annika sometimes but not for real. Especially not when my name and credits would be buried under a pile of crappy B-list titles, like *Love on the Dark Side*.

"Cut!" Chaz bellows. "That was the sixth take, Scarlett. What the hell is wrong with you today? You don't get paid to *read* lines, you get paid to *act*." Turning, he plays to the crowd. "Would anyone here like to see some real acting before we run through the entire day's film stock?"

The crowd cheers, proving how quickly popularity turns to bite you in the butt.

★　★　★

Julian pulls me aside as the camera is being reloaded. "You sure you're okay?"

"Yeah, I'm fine. Just distracted. I'll nail it this time."

"You'd better," he says. "Or Chaz will find someone else who fits the costume."

Great, he's reading my mind now. "Is that supposed to be encouraging?"

"I'm just saying that Chaz has no mercy. He could turn Effluvia back into a human and cast Sasha in the role. She's pretty good."

"Are you upsetting me on purpose?" I ask, my voice now a squawk. "To motivate me for the scene or something?"

He shakes his head. "Nope. Just trying to help."

"Pointing out that you prefer Sasha's work isn't helping."

"I didn't say I prefer it. It doesn't matter to me either way as long as the show gets picked up." He waits a beat before adding, "Not that any guy in his right mind would complain about working opposite Sasha."

I shake off his arm. "Get away from me."

★　★　★

The thing about guys is, they're pigs. Not fancy savannah warthogs, but regular, roll-in-the-manure swine. They come at you with guns, both literally and figuratively. One day you're all la-la-la, life is great and then *BANG!* You're on the ground shot full of holes. There is absolutely nothing you can do except take every possible chance to kick the crap out of them—literally and figuratively—before they get to you first.

And, when all else fails, you pretend that they've got nothing on you. You plug up the holes and you *act*.

> EFFLUVIA
> You're damn right it does. Why did you
> even ask me out if you didn't mean it?
> You've got to start thinking before you
> act. Otherwise, people get hurt.

> PANTHER
> [staring at the ground]
> I'm sorry if I gave you false hope, baby.

> EFFLUVIA
> Don't you dare call me that, you patron-
> izing jerk.

> PANTHER
> I thought I could pick up where we left
> off but I can't. Looking at you now is too
> painful. It reminds me of everything I
> lost.

> EFFLUVIA
> [voice splintering with hurt and rage]
> All that you've lost is a pretty face
> on the pillow beside yours. Inside, I'm
> the same person you fell in love with.
> Probably a better person. Isn't that
> enough?

*Effluvia stares at Panther but instead of answering,
he looks away silently in shame.*

EFFLUVIA
[barely audible; as if it's painful to speak
the words]
You disgust me.

Her eyes fill with tears for all that is lost and she
turns and walks away from Panther into the building.

Chaz calls cut and the crowd cheers. I'm aware of both of these things, but it's as if the sounds are coming from far away. My heart is thundering and my breath comes in shallow, rapid bursts.

"Welcome back, Scarlett," Chaz says, still using the megaphone. "That was powerful stuff. Let's move on, people."

I'm not in the next scene so I continue walking away.

"Leigh, wait," Julian says from behind me.

I pick up the pace until I am almost running. I will not give him the satisfaction of watching the plugs pop and the guts spill out.

★   ★   ★

Julian opens the office door and says, "I've been looking everywhere for you."

I should have gone to my trailer, but this was the first place I came to with a door. It turned out to be a perfect refuge, complete with a soft leather couch.

"I don't want to talk to anyone," I say. "Especially you."

He closes the door and sits on the couch beside me. "I'm sorry I pulled that motivational crap on you earlier. I didn't mean what I said about Sasha, I was just trying to get you in touch with your anger for the scene."

I know he's telling the truth. And at the moment, it doesn't really matter anyway. "The guy had a gun," I say. "I could have died yesterday."

He reaches out and pulls me close. "But you didn't. And thanks to you, he's behind bars right now."

I try to find a comfortable position for my snout against his shoulder but eventually give up. "The police officer told me I might experience Post-Traumatic Stress Disorder but I didn't believe him. I guess I should have taken the day off."

"I don't know about that. It was a good performance. I really believed I disgusted you."

"Good. Because you did at the time."

Julian pulls me to my feet and over to the computer. "The manager gave me the password to log on so I could show you something." He sits at the desk and types www.warthogsrule.com. Effluvia's picture pops up on the home page. "It's an entire Web site dedicated to you. I found it when I googled your name over the holiday. Or rather, Effluvia's name."

He googled me! It's the first time a guy's done that—at least, that I know of.

Leaning over Julian's shoulder, I click on the Bio & Vital Stats page. Someone has gone to the trouble of inventing an entire history for Effluvia. According to this, she was born Ashley Ellison, grew up in Connecticut, and met Julian in first year Biochemistry at Yale.

Wrong. That is so not Effluvia's back story. But scanning the site helps me relax. Some people—however misguided—love this character, and I owe it to them to pull myself together. A thief with a gun may have thrown me off track for a few hours, but I won't let him take much more of my time. From now on, I'm going to try to keep my eyes forward.

Julian clicks on the Romantic Status tab. "Apparently, Effluvia is single but obsessed with the Panther."

"Not anymore," I say. "She isn't going to waste another minute on some guy who can't see past inflated cleavage. Effluvia is moving on."

"Call me a hopeless romantic," Julian says, "but I think those two will get together yet." He catches my hand and pulls me around alongside the chair. "The Panther is going to mend his ways. He is not as shallow as you think."

"Then maybe he'll get another chance," I say.

He pulls me onto his lap. "Third-time lucky."

★ ★ ★

Julian springs out of the chair so suddenly that I hit the floor.

The office door opens to reveal Lex. He looks from me to Julian and his jaw drops. "Whoa."

Julian's black hood is twisted and one of the ears is bent flat. His visor is still on the chair, crushed.

Julian helps me to my feet and whispers, "Your snout."

I discover that it's shifted to the right. I can't see properly out of one eye.

"You were due on set half an hour ago, Julian," Lex says. "Everyone's looking for you."

"Oh, sorry. We were rehearsing a stunt and we lost track of time." He taps the end of his nose.

Touching the end of mine, I find the nostrils dangling by a rubbery thread and try to push the piece back on. "You know the scene," I add. "The one where we kill Dr. Ram in a room about this size? It's a very complicated stunt."

"Right . . ." Lex says. "The one where you roll over her with a desk chair? I'll let Chaz know you're learning the moves. And, in the meantime, you should know that your ass is dragging on the ground."

I glance behind me to see that my butt attachment has detached from one side of the costume.

I call after him as he leaves, "It's a very complicated stunt!"

★ ★ ★

"Sorry I'm late, darling," Annika says, as she answers her cell phone.

In the background, Jake yells something unintelligible.

"He sounds pissed," I say.

"You know I don't like vulgar language," she says. "And that goes for you too, Vivien."

"What is going on?" I ask.

Annika says, "I told you, I was just watching the dailies."

"What?"

She hangs up on me.

Looks like I'm not the only one battling Post-Traumatic Stress Disorder today.

★ ★ ★

I'm sitting on the stairs of my trailer when Julian comes by.

"Need a ride?"

I think about calling Annika back and decide against it. She's already teetering on the edge; no need to push her over. "Thanks, but my mom's on her way. Why are you still here?"

He sits on the step beside me. "Just wanted to make sure you're okay."

I nod. "I spoke to the police officer who said the guy didn't have a gun after all. That's not even his MO. They call him the Gentleman Thief because his weapons of choice are good looks and charm. Apparently, they've been after him for three years and now they're going to put him away for a long time."

"That's great," Julian says. "You should be proud."

"Well, I'm relieved anyway. Sorry for freaking out on you earlier."

"No problem—although Chaz wasn't too happy about the delay in shooting."

"Drake wasn't thrilled either: Effluvia needed a full rhinoplasty."

Julian laughs. "I guess we'll have to keep it under wraps from now on."

I'm not sure what "it" is or what kind of wraps he has in mind. This is a weird situation—at least for me. Julian and I haven't even been out on a date, yet we've spent more time making out in a few weeks than Rory and I managed in a year.

Fortunately, Julian saves me the trouble of asking him to define "it." "I checked the production schedule and we both wrap early on Thursday. How about dinner at Kate Mantilini's?"

"Perfect," I say. Kate Mantilini's is a favorite of mine, not because it's a hot spot for actors, but because it's the first place I had dinner in Hollywood.

Peering to the right and left to make sure the coast is clear, Julian leans toward me. "Do you mind if I try it again without the snout?"

Before he gets the chance, Annika screeches up in the BMW. It's surprising how much weight a skinny woman can apply to a horn.

fourteen

Scene 8: Vivien Leigh Reid and the
Perfect Guy

EXTERIOR SANTA MONICA BEACH HOUSE, EARLY
EVENING

*Julian parks his vintage Mustang convertible in
front of the house.*

JULIAN
So? How does it feel to own your own home?

LEIGH
Our own home. And it feels great. It was
nice of Jake to let us buy it when he and
Annika moved to Malibu. I just hope the
feng shui guy can cleanse Sasha's bad energy.

JULIAN
How did she take it when you told her
she was out?

LEIGH
Very well. You won't believe how much
she's changed because of RAD. Today she

actually admitted that her divatude was always unfounded and that she's not that good an actress. In fact, she's decided to become a documentary filmmaker instead.

JULIAN

That seems like a stretch.

LEIGH

No more than her acting was. But she's going to keep it light. The subject of her first doc is white.

JULIAN

White!

LEIGH

Jake told her to go with her passion.... She's heading to the arctic to get some footage of polar bears.

JULIAN

They're pretty vicious, aren't they?

LEIGH

Yeah. I said we'd be happy to finance the film.

JULIAN

That's my girl. Generous to a fault.

LEIGH

Well, we can afford it. Our *Freak Force* dolls are raking it in.

                    JULIAN
They're not dolls, they're action figures!
Your *War of the Warthogs* video game is
doing great too.

                     LEIGH
Our game. You're the one who designed it.
I just star in it.

                    JULIAN
We make a great team.
 [pulling out a small Henry Winton box]
So great that I want us to be partners
for life.

Julian opens the box to reveal a huge diamond soli-
taire.

                    JULIAN
Vivien Leigh Reid, would you do me the
honor of becoming my wife?

                     LEIGH
              [tears streaming]
    Yes!

Julian slides the ring on her finger and it sparkles
in the setting sun.

                    JULIAN
Leigh? The sooner you get out of my car,
the sooner I can pick you up again.

"Huh?"
I'm staring at my bare ring finger.

"Is something wrong with your hand?" Julian gives me a curious look and I wonder how long I've been lost in my daydream.

"My wrist is still a little sore from the holdup." I make a show of rubbing it, hoping he doesn't point out that it's my right one that's bruised.

"I hope you can still work a fork," he teases.

I smile and climb out of the car. "No worries there."

"When I come back at six-thirty, I'll open the car door for you and everything."

"You'd better," I say. "It's a real date."

★　★　★

I have exactly ninety-seven minutes to make myself irresistible. I'll start with a face mask to shrink my pores and move on to a deep-conditioning treatment to add shine to my hair. After a body scrub in the shower, I'll smooth on some self-tanning lotion, and while waiting for that to dry, give myself a manicure and a pedicure. That should leave about forty-five minutes to blow dry my hair, and apply makeup, glitter lotion, and perfume. At precisely six-twenty-five, I'll put on the new dress I bought on the Third Street Promenade a few nights ago, plus sandals that by my calculation will make me exactly the same height as Julian, not a smidge more.

It may seem like a lot of effort, but Julian has spent so many hours romancing a warthog lately that he deserves a nice view.

In the upstairs hall, I find Brando standing outside Annika's room with his tail between his legs. There's a thumping coming from inside.

The bedroom door is partially open and I can see clothes, purses, and toiletries strewn everywhere. I push the door open a little more to see shoes flying out of the walk-in closet. Some of them land in the open suitcases on the bed. Others hit the wall. And, as I watch, an espadrille takes out a bedside lamp with a crash.

I shut Brando in the bathroom for his own safety before approaching with caution. Annika fires a last mule over her shoulder and sweeps an armful of scarves off a shelf. When she turns, I see she's been crying.

"Thank god you're home," she says. "Hurry up and pack your things."

"Pack? For what?"

"We're moving out. I will not stay another night with that horrible man."

I glance at the clock on her bedside table. If I skip the mask and the conditioning treatment, I can spend exactly twelve minutes talking sense into Annika. I'll have to cut to the chase. "All couples have fights, Mom. You can work this out."

"We can't work anything out because he won't listen to me," she says, starting to cry again. "It's over."

"It can't be over," I say. Not when the cutest guy on the planet is coming to pick me up in just over an hour. "You said Jake was 'the one.' You said it was destined."

"Destined for failure. He is a stubborn, unreasonable man."

To underscore her point, she takes a framed photo of them and hurls it at the wall. It bounces off and lands at my feet. The glass is cracked but they smile on.

I'm sure this is just drama. Annika hasn't had a major meltdown in a while, and with all the pressure around here, she was set to blow. If she were truly upset, she wouldn't be taking the time to fold her lingerie. Especially when there's so much of it. How many peignoirs does one woman need?

"Jake might be stubborn but he's not unreasonable, Mom. I bet an apology would go a long way toward making him listen." Since Annika thinks the world revolves around her, it's safe to say she owes him one for something.

She dabs at her eyes before asking, "Whose side are you on?"

I check the clock, realize that I am at risk of losing my body scrub and maybe even the fake tan, and decide to fast forward. "Yours. I'm trying to help you find a solution because being with Jake makes you happy."

And generally stable. As much as I want to escape Sashela, I can see that living with Jake has been good for Annika.

"What would make me happy right now is seeing you pack," she says, taking her second drawer full of lingerie and overturning it into a suitcase.

Annika is very particular about her things. If she's crushing the lingerie, this is more serious than I thought. Giving up on my manicure and pedicure, I clear a stack of designer jackets off a chair and sit. "Are you still upset about the robbery, Mom? Because it would be completely understandable. I think about it a lot too."

"This is not post-traumatic hoo-ha, if that's what you mean," she says, kneeling to retrieve the shoe she kicked under the bed.

"Then does it have something to do with the fight you had on Monday?"

"We've been fighting all week," she says, her voice muffled by the duvet. "I've talked until I'm blue in the face."

"But what happened on Monday?"

She gets to her feet. "*Nothing* happened. That's what I keep telling him."

"Okay, what does Jake think happened?"

"He read something into nothing. I was watching Sasha's dailies in her trailer while I was waiting for her and Jake dropped by unexpectedly."

"I don't get it."

"Well . . ." she overturns another drawer and adds, "Roger was there too."

"Ah. Just the two of you."

She nods. "He'd come for some reason and decided to watch the dailies too. When Jake flipped on the lights, he became totally irrational."

"Back up. You had the lights off?"

She rolls her eyes. "You can only appreciate the cinematography in the dark."

Right, everyone knows that. Except Jake, evidently, who's

been known to watch dailies in the family room in broad daylight. But then, he's a producer, not a director.

"So, you were appreciating the cinematography in the dark and Jake flipped out?"

Annika picks up on my tone. "I've heard enough accusations from him. I don't need them from you."

"I'm not accusing you of anything." At least not out loud. "I'm just wondering if Jake saw something that he could have misinterpreted. Like maybe Roger had confided in you about his crumbling marriage and you were giving him a platonic but comforting hug?"

Annika shakes her head. "I was watching the dailies. That's all."

"Maybe you were watching the dailies while holding Roger's hand in a platonic but comforting way?"

Annika fires a handful of bras into the suitcase. "I will not be interrogated by my own daughter," she says.

"I'm just trying to get to the bottom of this so that we can fix it." Ideally, while there's still time for a shower before my date.

"It's not fixable." She stares around the room dazedly. "Where's Jane?"

"Jane?" I ask, wondering if she's taken something to calm her nerves. "Who's Jane?"

She gathers her collection of limited edition Jane Austen novels from a shelf and heaves them into the suitcase on top of everything else. "Go pack your things."

"Mom, you can't run away. What kind of example are you setting for me?"

She pulls me up off the chair and pushes me toward the door. "A good one. I can't expose my daughter to a toxic relationship."

"Working through this is the way to go. Besides, you're doing more damage to me by moving around all the time. I want to stay here with Jake." In the end, a stable Annika is better for both of us. "Please, Mom."

"I know you're worried about your job, but I'm hoping Jake won't drag you into this."

I wasn't actually thinking about my job, but now that she mentions it, Chaz might very well take advantage of the change in my status. Regardless of my current popularity, he's never liked me and he never will.

Annika shakes her head sadly. "I'm sorry to do this to you, darling, but it's for the best, believe me. That man would just break our hearts."

★   ★   ★

When Annika pulls up in front the Beverly Hills hotel, the BMW is literally spilling over. There's a pink negligee trailing from the trunk. I pointed it out earlier and she actually said she didn't care.

This has turned out to be much worse than I thought. She wrecked such havoc over my own packing that I misplaced my cell and haven't been able to call Julian yet. He's going to show up at the beach house any moment expecting me to be ready. I'll have to call him the minute we're inside.

There's a cluster of paparazzi by the front door of the hotel.

"How could they have heard already?" Annika asks. "We just left."

She flips down the visor and checks her face. There's a gasp of horror and a flustered application of Glazed Poppy lipstick. Then she reaches into the glove compartment for her emergency shades and head scarf. Once the disguise is in place, she tucks Brando under her arm and steps out of the car.

"How did the press find out?" Annika asks the bellhop. "It just happened."

He gives her a puzzled look. "Bono's been booked for weeks."

Annika recovers from her disappointment while the bellhop unloads the suitcases, and by the time we pass the paparazzi, she's able to muster a strut.

"Hey," a reporter says, "I recognize her!" Annika pauses mid-step and the reporter continues. "It's that kid who stopped the holdup at Henry Winton's!"

All at once, there are cameras in my face. Through the flashes,

I see Annika's dejected expression and raise my hand. "Enough photos for now," I say. "Can't you see my mother—Annika Anderson, star of *Danny Boy*—is upset right now?"

The lenses immediately swing in Annika's direction and she shields her face with her arm. "This isn't a good time," she says, but her back straightens slightly and her legs move almost of their own accord into the red carpet pose.

"It looks like you're checking in, Annika," someone calls. "Don't you live with Jake Cohen?"

Mom hesitates just long enough to pique their interest. "This is a difficult time. I need some privacy."

Lowering her arm, she poses for several more photos before leading me inside.

"Honestly, Vivien. How could you blow my cover like that? Now everyone will be wondering if we've broken up."

★　★　★

There's a knock on the door of our suite and a woman enters pushing a trolley that holds shrimp, crab cakes, caviar, lobster, grilled asparagus, wild mushroom salad, a cheese platter, an exotic bread basket, two bottles of chilled champagne, chocolate-dipped strawberries, and an ice cream sundae.

Annika gets off the bed and examines the cart. "Where's the Peking Duck? I ordered it and I'd like it delivered, please."

The woman nods and Annika signs the bill, adding a fifty-dollar tip.

"That was generous, considering she forgot the duck," I say, after the woman leaves.

"What can I say? Jake is a very generous man."

"You can't put all this on his card!"

"Darling, he won't even notice the meal once he's seen the price of this suite."

"You didn't charge this room to his card too!"

"Of course. It's his fault there's no roof over my daughter's head."

She takes a bottle of champagne and a glass over to the sofa and switches on the television.

"Aren't you going to eat some lobster?" I ask. "I thought that was your idea of comfort food."

"No, darling, *this* is my idea of comfort food." She raises the champagne bottle. "That," she points to the food, "is my idea of expensive."

She flips through the channels and squeals with delight. "Vivien, it's *Casablanca!* My all-time favorite! Hurry!"

"I've got to make some phone calls, Mom." I've already tried Julian's cell, but he didn't pick up and his voicemail is full.

"Darling, I need your support tonight. Catch up on your calls tomorrow."

"I don't like old movies."

"You liked *Gone with the Wind,*" she points out. "And as I keep saying, if you're serious about acting, you need to learn from the classics. This is one of the greatest films ever made."

If you ask me, great doesn't come in black-and-white packaging. But since she's looking happier than she has all day, I sit down beside her and wait to be edified.

★   ★   ★

Annika blows her nose as the end credits role. "Now *that* is what love is all about." She passes me the tissues. "Did you like it?"

Wiping my own streaming eyes, I nod. I'm not sure I understood all the politics, but I certainly understood the love story between Rick and Ilsa. They meet and fall in love in Paris during the Second World War, and when they learn that the Germans are advancing on Paris, Rick proposes. The next day, he waits at the train station for her but she never shows.

Flash forward several years, and Rick, still heartbroken, is running a nightclub in Casablanca, Morocco. One day, an antifascist hero asks Rick to hook him up with travel visas so that he can flee to America with his wife. That wife turns out to be Ilsa. She explains to Rick that when they met in Paris, she'd believed her husband to be dead, but discovered the day they were to escape together that he was still alive. And because she wanted Rick to flee to safety, she let him think she'd jilted him.

Seeing Rick again makes Ilsa realize the power of their love and she vows to stay in Morocco with him. Rick ultimately chooses to sacrifice his own happiness—and risk his life—to send Ilsa to America with her husband because it is the right thing to do, both for her and the fight against fascism.

Annika grabs another handful of tissue. "I watched this movie a dozen times after your father left me."

I stare at her. "Dad didn't leave you, you left him."

She drains the last of the champagne. "Oh, that's what they told you. It was a conspiracy."

"What are you talking about? Grandma says you pulled up in a cab and dumped me on the way to the airport."

"On the way to the suburbs," she corrects. "I got a rundown apartment, found a job as a cable TV host, and saw you on the weekends." She gets up to collect the other bottle of champagne. "So, yes, technically I left but I didn't go far. And I was just making a statement."

This is news to me, but there have been other aspects of the story that Gran and Dad twisted a little, so I keep her talking. "A statement about what?"

"About how marriage is a two-way street. I'd given up my career in New York for your father's job in Seattle, but it was only supposed to last two years. Then you came along and *he* decided we should stay permanently because it was a good place to raise children. I was miserable and he wasn't listening. So I made a statement."

"Which he didn't hear?"

Annika's eyes tear up again at the memory. "I kept thinking he'd come for me. We'd had fights before and he'd always come. But this time was different. I think he was just . . . tired of me. So, after a few months, I decided to try my luck in L.A."

Dad probably missed his cue because he had his hands full

with a child and couldn't handle a drama queen too. "Why didn't you just talk to him?"

"Have *you* ever tried talking to your father?" she asks. "It's like the words hit the side of a mountain and bounce off." I have had that experience, actually. "I seem to attract that kind of man. Roger wasn't much better when we were together."

"What does your shrink have to say about all this?"

"He says I repeat the same patterns with relationships," she admits. "But when Jake and I got together, he thought it was a real breakthrough." She takes a swig directly from the champagne bottle. "Wrong. Jake is just another guy who won't listen. They're all the same, darling."

"No, they're not," I say. "Julian listens."

She lowers the bottle and stares at me. "Are you seeing that boy?"

"Maybe not after tonight. We had a date and I stood him up." At least that's what he must think because I've called nine times and he still won't pick up. I'm sure he'd understand about the family crisis if he'd just . . . listen.

"You stood him up for me?" she asks, surprised. "That's sweet. But it's for the best, darling. He would have broken your heart anyway. That's what men do."

"Not always. There are happy endings."

"Only in romantic comedies. Julian has already treated you badly and it could happen again."

I retreat to the bathroom to call Julian before her cynicism drags me under too. When I can't get him on his cell, I try his home number and his mother promises to tell him that I had a "family emergency." Then I call Karis and complain to her.

By the time I emerge, Annika has dug the cracked photo out of the suitcase and is rocking it in her arms and sobbing. We've passed cynicism and proceeded directly to maudlin.

"I really thought he loved me," she bawls.

"He does love you," I say.

"If he loved me, he'd trust me."

"He's just feeling threatened about Roger."

She throws herself back onto the couch and stares at the ceiling. "It would never have worked anyway. Because of those vipers."

Is she having delusions? "What vipers?"

"You know." She waves her hand, knocking the tissues off the table. "Sashela."

I try not to laugh. "It's nothing a good exorcist can't fix."

"What do I know about being a stepmother?" she continues, as if to herself. "I'm barely functional as a mother."

At one time, I'd have agreed with her but not anymore. "They're the problem, not you."

She doesn't seem to hear me. "I might as well die in this room."

I take the champagne out of her hands and pull her upright. "Enough. It's time for a fire drill."

"I'm not going anywhere," she says. "I'm a mess."

That, at least, I can change.

I pick up the phone and push the button for the hotel spa.

★   ★   ★

The waiter deposits two glasses of champagne at our table in the Polo Lounge. Annika relented only because of the fire drill.

"Here's to happy reunions," I say, raising my glass to hers.

Annika shakes her head. "To new beginnings." She lifts her sunglasses to gaze around the room with puffy eyes. "There's Bono." She points to the piano bar. "I suppose I should say hi or he'll think I'm snubbing him."

"Don't, Mom," I say. She met Bono a few years ago at a fundraiser and he won't remember her. "I'm sure he wants to be left alone. You said he was boring anyway."

"Boring! I'm sure I never said that. Why, the man supports any good cause."

"Exactly. You called him a 'tedious boy scout.' And also an 'Irish windbag.'"

"Vivien, that's terrible. I said nothing of the sort. I have the utmost respect for Mr. Bono and his music. I love that *Speed of Sound* and I'm going over to tell him so."

"I wouldn't if I were you: *Speed of Sound* is by Coldplay."

Annika smirks over her glass. "If you get bogged down in details, you'll miss all the fun in life."

After a while, I excuse myself to try Julian once more and when I return, Mom is standing with Bono at the bar. She's wearing his signature Bulgari wrap-around shades and I can hear her tittering all the way to our table. "I do so miss the Emerald Isle!" she says. "The beautiful green hills and all those darling sheep!"

Oh god. She's using an Irish accent and Bono is wearing the pinched smile of a cornered man. I cannot go over there. I've done more than any normal daughter would to keep her mother from going over the edge tonight and I refuse to peel her off Bono.

Annika sees me and calls, "There you are, darling! Don't be shy. Come and meet my good friend Bono." To show how close they are, she wraps an arm around his waist. Bono proves he really does know the meaning of charity by allowing Mom to plant a kiss on his cheek.

I am not the only one watching this spectacle: Jake has come through the door.

"How did you know we were here?" I ask, walking toward him.

He doesn't take his eyes off my mother and Bono. "Annika left a note. I guess she wanted me to see this."

"It's not what it looks like," I say. "Really. She's just upset, Jake." In case he hasn't noticed, I add, "And very drunk."

Annika's face lights up when she sees him and she abandons Bono in a flash. "Jake, you came for me! Vivien, he came for me!"

"I thought I'd overreacted," Jake begins. "But obviously I was wrong."

Annika's face falls. "Bono is just a friend."

"Not even that," I say, but they both ignore me.

"It just proves my point that you're unable to commit," Jake says. "I don't want to be part of a harem."

He turns to leave and Annika follows. I hear her call from the lobby. "Jake? Jake!"

And then the siren wails: "VIVIEN!"

fifteen

"Honey, don't take this the wrong way," Drake says, studying my reflection in his mirror, "but you look like roadkill."

I'm not sure there's a right way to take that but it's true. My eyes are bloodshot, there are dark circles underneath, and I'm so pale that my mole appears to be planning a hostile takeover. In short, I look like someone who's been burned by love. Julian may believe I burned him, but given how many times I've called, and left messages with his parents and even his rude stepbrother, I've been burned too. I guess Mom's right that there are no happy endings.

"Just cover it all up," I tell Drake. "I'll catch some sleep while you work."

With all the pacing, crying, and hand wringing, there wasn't much sleep to be had in our luxury suite last night. It was fine for Annika because she had nothing to do today except call room service to order iced cucumber slices for her puffy eyes. I, on the other hand, am facing my toughest stunt ever this afternoon and I'd like to be awake for it. Fortunately, all I have to do this morning is stand around in some party scenes and look uncomfortable. No real acting involved.

The door to the makeup trailer opens and Julian steps inside, looking well rested after his evening of avoiding my calls. Seeing me, he hits reverse. "I'm early," he tells Drake. "Sorry."

Yeah, sorry he ran into me. I catch his eye in the mirror, wondering what to say. Although I rehearsed a speech in my head, Drake wasn't supposed to be in the audience. "Look," I begin, "I'm really sorry the uh, *package,* wasn't there when you went to pick it up."

"Whatever," he says, fumbling with the doorknob.

"There were some unexpected and unavoidable complications," I blurt, before he can escape. "The courier company feels terrible about it and called you at least twenty times. I understand they spoke to your family too."

Drake continues to apply his products, seemingly oblivious.

"Maybe if the courier had called earlier, I wouldn't be so pissed off," Julian says, pushing open the door. "Obviously, they don't want my business badly enough."

"That's not true!" I say, trying to turn as Drake restrains me. "The courier really does want your business and very much regrets the screw up."

"It's too late," Julian says. "I've decided to find a new courier. There are plenty of others around."

He lets the trailer door slam shut behind him.

"Well," Drake says. "Someone's got his tail in a knot this morning. I'm sure you had a perfectly good reason for standing him up."

★　★　★

The cast chairs are arranged in a horseshoe, just off the set. I pick mine up and move it away from the others. I can't deal with any of them right now. My nerves are as frayed as Chaz's ties.

Sasha is back today to finish shooting her scenes. This time she's wearing a strapless ball gown with a poufy taffeta skirt. It's red rather than white, as Dr. Ram needs to look more dangerous than the average bride. Sasha is willing to make more concessions for her art than I expected.

She waits until I've settled into my chair before saying, "I was hoping you'd gone back to Loserville, Farthog."

"Well, life is full of disappointments. I was hoping you'd gone back to hell."

"Farthog!" Rudy repeats, as the guys arrive in a pack. "Good one, Sasha."

She turns to bask in the stifling gusts of testosterone, allowing me to focus on my script. It's a good thing I learned my lines yesterday before my life went off the rails.

Lex takes the script out of my hands. "We're working from a new version. Chaz did a rewrite yesterday. I delivered two copies to your house and left them with—"

"Sasha," I interrupt.

She offers me a beatific smile. "Yes?"

"Did you bother telling Lex I wasn't home?"

"I'm not your personal assistant," she says. "And if you want to stay out all night, that's your business."

"She stayed out all night?" Jed asks. "Alright!"

Rudy eyes me with new appreciation. "There's more to this pig than meets the eye."

"If you must know," I say, "I spent the night at the Beverly Hills Hotel."

The guys whoop again. I'm trying to decide whether adding "with my mother" will help or hurt the situation when someone arrives with my new script.

"Get to work," Lex says, tossing it into my lap. "If Chaz thinks your love life is interfering with his schedule, we'll all pay."

"Yeah," Rudy says, with a knowing leer. "Save your hormones till we're burning film."

★   ★   ★

Jed turns to Rudy as we take our marks. "Did you ever think you'd have to kiss a pig, dude?"

Actually, I'll be the one doing that. Thanks to Chaz's last-minute inspiration, Effluvia has to lay a big one on Gazelle as a ploy to make Panther jealous.

Never have I had to dig so deep for my motivation. Why

would Effluvia even bother? I don't believe she'd expect Panther
to be threatened by a stupid gazelle. As for the actor who plays
him, Rudy's good looks and buff bod can't hide the moron inside,
but at least there's a paycheck involved.

Rudy catches me checking him out and nudges Julian. "She's
checking me out."

"Don't let it go to your head," Julian says. "Warthogs aren't
picky."

Chaz claps his hands to end the snickering. "This is serious
business, people. Effluvia is angry."

"And horny," Rudy adds.

Oh, the things I could say if I were less enlightened.

★   ★   ★

INTERIOR DR. RAM'S MANSION, NIGHT

*Dr. Ram moves through the crowded room. We widen out
to reveal the Freak Force observing her. Panther
believes she has invited them to a fund-raising ball
as a gesture of goodwill, but the rest of the Force is
suspicious.*

DR. RAM

So glad you could make it, Mr. Panther.
You look more handsome than ever.

PANTHER

And you, Dr. Ram, look divine.

*Panther wraps an arm around Dr. Ram and pulls her
aside.*

EFFLUVIA

He's a fool to trust her.

> CHEETAH
> For what it's worth, I think you're right.

> GAZELLE
> I don't know what he sees in her, except for
> the fact that she's hot. But you were even
> hotter when you were human, Effluvia.

> CHEETAH
> This guy had it bad for you in college,
> Effluvia. Used to bug the hell out of
> Panther.

> EFFLUVIA
> [getting an idea]
> Really.

*Effluvia glances at Panther just as Dr. Ram reaches
up to stroke his cheek. In retaliation, Effluvia does
the same to Gazelle.*

> GAZELLE
> Don't think you can use me to make
> Panther jealous. I'm not that kind of guy.

> EFFLUVIA
> Come on, you're exactly that kind of guy.

*Effluvia pulls Gazelle toward her and kisses him.
Panther sees this and does the same to Dr. Ram.*

I break the kiss for a moment and look over to see Sasha's hands
on Julian's butt. That is not in the script. Nor is he supposed to be lifting her right off the ground as if she were as light as dandelion fluff.

Well, the game isn't over. I happen to know my way around these tusks, and if the Gazelle has been pining for Effluvia all these years, he deserves a reward.

I grab Rudy's horns with both hands and pull his body closer to mine. It would be easier to fake some passion if Rudy weren't such a sloppy kisser. Plus, he tastes like bacon. Hasn't he heard of the courtesy brush? But that's why they call this acting. By the time I am done with Rudy, Julian is going to be very sorry about taking his business to another courier.

Using his horns, I steer Rudy around so that I can get a clear view of Julian. He does the same, only with Sasha, the horns are figurative. Then he dips her. I consider doing the same to Rudy, but decide it won't have the same effect. Instead, I lift my leg and wrap it partway around him. It's the best I can manage with the gut attachment but Rudy seems to like it because he pushes me against the wall of the set.

"Cut!" Chaz calls.

Both couples part, puffing harder than after a real stunt. I wipe my mouth on my sleeve and notice Julian does the same.

"Let's go again," Rudy exclaims. "Julian, why didn't you tell us the warthog was such a hot kisser?"

"If you think so," Julian says, draping an arm around Sasha's bare shoulders, "you need to get out more."

"Let's move on," Chaz calls. "One more take and the camera will explode."

★　★　★

Scene 9: Leigh Laughs Last

INTERIOR FANCY AUDITORIUM, NIGHT

Presenter Adam Brody pulls a card out of a golden envelope.

ADAM
And the People's Choice Award for "Best
On-Screen Kiss" goes to my friend, Vivien
Leigh Reid.

Adam kisses Leigh as he presents the award.

ADAM
Hey, you really are a good kisser.

LEIGH
Thanks, Adam. You're not bad either.

ADAM
This is your fifth win in this category.
What's your secret?

LEIGH
Practice. Years ago, an actor named
Julian Gerrard suggested that I'm not a
good kisser and I decided to prove him
wrong. Now, dozens of love scenes later, I
guess I have.

ADAM
Julian Gerrard? Never heard of him.

LEIGH
No one has, Adam. He worked on the first
season of *Freak Force* but didn't make it
to the second. He got sidelined by ego
problems so serious that RAD declared
him untreatable. These days, he sells toilet bowl cleaner on late-night infomer-
cials.

★   ★   ★

I can't decide which will be harder: faking passion for a creep, or faking courage while shooting down a twenty-five-foot drop.

In our next scene, Effluvia comes to the Panther's rescue after Dr. Ram lures him into her private garden and spikes his drink with a paralyzing drug. When Dr. Ram makes a move to drown Panther, Effluvia leaps off a brick wall and pushes the wicked doctor into the pool instead.

Sasha is going to deprive me of the pleasure of shoving her into the pool because she demanded a photo double. As a result, we have to shoot the scene in two parts. First, we'll take the action to the point where I land on the pool deck. The cameras will cut and a Sasha look-alike wearing the same dress will take her place. Then the cameras will roll again and I'll push the look-alike into the pool.

Freddy offered to hire a double for me but I wanted to do the stunt myself. I figure if I can take on a wanted criminal, I can take on a twenty-five-foot wall. After all, I'm a lot stronger, fitter, and more agile than I was two months ago. Not that any of that will keep me from doing a face plant if something goes wrong.

A guide wire will be clipped to my safety harness at the center of my back and fed through a system of pulleys back down to the guys controlling the wires. During rehearsals, I found the worst part was leaning over the edge of the wall until the tension on the cable stopped me from plunging into freefall. Not that it got easy after that: While being lowered quickly to the ground, I have to keep my feet moving against the wall to make it appear as if I'm running. And near the bottom, I have to push off from the wall and rotate my legs under my torso so that I can land on my feet.

Today the mats will be gone and there will be nothing between me and the concrete but air. The risk of injury means that there's pressure to get it right the first time.

With so much at stake, it's time to search for my inner calm; fortunately, I know where I might find it.

Dr. Ram's walled garden has already been built in another studio and it's beautiful. The in-ground swimming pool (formerly a concrete pit in the middle of the studio) is lined with blue tiles and lit from beneath. Around it are trees and iron planters filled with exotic flowers.

I take a seat in a chaise lounge and focus on the sweet, heavy scent of the flowers. After a few moments, however, the peace is destroyed by voices on the other side of the garden wall.

"It's been great having you on set," Chaz says. "You're a much better fit with the guys than Leigh is."

"I know," Sasha says. "They all hate her."

This shouldn't bother me, considering the source, but somehow it still does.

"Where's your father these days?" Chaz asks. "He hasn't come to set all week."

"Trouble at home," Sasha explains. "But the blond parasite moved out last night, so he should be fine now."

"Moved out as in they split?" Chaz asks, surprised. "Jake must be upset."

"He is." She laughs and the sound echoes jarringly in the massive studio. "But he'll get over it."

"I don't get it. He was so excited about the wedding."

"Annika wasn't good for him," Sasha says, impatiently. "And living with the Farthog wasn't good for me."

"Wait a second," Chaz says. "What did you do, Sasha?"

There's a long pause, as if Sasha is listening for eavesdroppers. I hold my breath until she continues. "Nothing any daughter wouldn't do if she saw her father getting bled dry. I just helped him see that Annika isn't one of us. She's C list with the wrong zip code and she was dragging us down to her level."

"I have the feeling it took more than a father-daughter chat to bring Jake to reason."

"All I had to do was drop a few hints that Annika's seeing Roger on the side."

"Is she?"

"Who cares? She's a flirt and Dad's sensitive to that sort of thing because Mom cheated on him all the time."

At Chaz's urging, Sasha describes how she set Annika up by throwing her together with Roger and letting Jake know where to find them. He jumped to the conclusions Sasha hoped for and it's been downhill ever since.

"It was almost too easy," she concludes. "I thought I'd have to get a lot more creative than that."

"But what if your Dad finds out you were involved?"

"He'd never believe it," she says. "I was up half the night giving him an emotional transfusion and he's already seeing it's for the best."

"Remind me not to get on your bad side," Chaz says. He laughs but there's an undercurrent of seriousness in his voice.

"Don't worry, sweetie: For you, I'm all good sides."

★   ★   ★

EXTERIOR DR. RAM'S GARDEN, POOLSIDE, NIGHT

Dr. Ram is lying on a lounge chair in the light of a dozen candles sipping a glass of chardonnay.

DR. RAM
You're awfully quiet, Mr. Panther. Don't
you like my garden?

Dr. Ram laughs and as the shot widens out, we see Panther is unconscious and chained to a heavy iron chair.

PANTHER
[slowly opening his eyes]
Where am I?

> DR. RAM
>
> Don't you remember? You came home with
> me. But I'm afraid you haven't been much
> fun.

Panther tries to focus on Dr. Ram.

> PANTHER
>
> You drugged me.

> DR. RAM
>
> Indeed I did. And now I'm going to kill
> you.

*Dr. Ram crosses to Panther's chair and unlocks the
chains. He tries to lunge at her but flops onto the
deck instead. Dr. Ram laughs again and pulls her
skirt away.*

> DR. RAM
>
> The paralysis won't wear off for another
> hour. In the meantime, why not take a nice
> swim?

*Dr. Ram starts to roll Panther to the edge of the
pool.*

> EFFLUVIA
>
> Cats don't like water, Dr. Ram. Everyone
> knows that.

*Dr. Ram spins and then looks up to see Effluvia stand-
ing on the top of her garden wall. She recovers
quickly and continues to roll Panther toward the
pool.*

                    DR. RAM
        Since pigs can't fly, I'm not too worried
        about it.

                    EFFLUVIA
        You should be: I'm no ordinary pig.

*Effluvia runs down the side of the wall and lands in
front of Dr. Ram. She charges and knocks Dr. Ram into
the pool.*

Sasha's scream echoes throughout the studio, but the cameras continue to roll. As she thrashes around in the cold water, she fires a string of expletives at me that Chaz will have to overdub later. She wipes her eyes with her hands and smears mascara and makeup down her cheeks.

Staying in character, I help Julian into a lawn chair. Then I walk to the edge of the pool and watch as Sasha heaves herself onto the deck and collapses in a sodden heap of taffeta. Her strapless dress is drooping to X-rated.

Improvising, I say,

        It doesn't take a genius to keep a dress
        on, Dr. Ram.

Then I deliver a dramatic—and unscripted—kick to Sasha's head. I'm too professional to connect, but Sasha's screech confirms she has her doubts.

                ★   ★   ★

Chaz catches up with me before I make it out of the studio lot. "Where do you think you're going?"

"I'm wrapped," I say. "I've got things to do."

Chaz grabs my arm and forces me to stop. "Yeah, like meet the press. Lex told you the publicist set up interviews for the full cast tonight. *Teen People* came especially to meet you."

I've been so distracted by *The Annika Show* that I forgot about that. "I can't do it tonight, Chaz. I have family obligations."

"YP, not MP, Scarlett. Professional obligations come first. Effluvia is popular at the moment and you need to be here. Disappointing the press can mean the difference between a second season and cancellation."

"I'll do the interviews tomorrow. Tonight, there's a blond parasite that needs my help."

Chaz's mouth drops as he realizes I overheard his conversation earlier. "What are you going to do?"

"I'm not sure but I wouldn't tell you anyway."

"Let them sort it out alone," he advises. "Jake won't believe a word you say against Sasha and he'll end up turning on you."

I shrug. "I might have to take that chance."

He squeezes my arm harder. "Let me put this another way: Making Jake mad at you could cause trouble for me. He could fire you, or worse, cancel the show. Either way, it's bad news for *Freak Force*."

"I'm touched that you think I have that kind of influence," I say, shaking him off. "But this isn't about you, Chaz, it's about Jake and Annika."

He bellows after me, "If my show loses a single viewer because of you, I promise I won't rest until your name is mud in this town!"

sixteen

Roger opens the door of his trailer. "Well, this is a surprise," he says.

"Do you mind if I come in?" I push past him without waiting for a response. Otherwise, I might lose my nerve.

His trailer is twice the size of the one he had in Ireland and much nicer. It's furnished in the spare, modern style Annika loves, which makes me wonder if she helped him decorate. Someone has obviously been giving him style advice lately. The man was a wreck on *Danny Boy*, but now he's almost dashing. He barely qualifies as a troll anymore.

Still I can't picture Roger and Annika as a couple. They don't look right together. Jake and Annika, on the other hand, look like Barbie and Ken—perfect, if artificial. More important, Jake dotes on Annika. If he's sitting across from her at breakfast, he can barely focus on the newspaper. He keeps asking her opinion on issues, from recycling to global warming. Surprisingly, Annika seems to *have* opinions about issues. Pre-Jake, she was only interested in discussing acting, aging, and aging actors.

Roger may not debate global warming with Annika but I know he has a thing for her. It was particularly obvious when we were working together in Ireland where there was so much tension on set that they rarely got through a day without a fight. You just don't waste that much energy on someone you don't care about. He prodded her into the best performance ever, thereby relaunching her career at an age when most actresses find roles getting scarce. Annika is grateful to Roger for that—so grateful that I worry she might go back to him if he asked. Especially when life with Jake includes the evil Sashela.

"To what do I owe the pleasure, Verna Lou?" Roger asks.

Since he doesn't ask me to sit down, I get straight to the point. "Annika left Jake."

He nods. "I saw the photos from outside the hotel."

"It's your fault."

"Mine!"

"Yeah. I think she left Jake for you."

"That's the first I've heard of it," he says. But I notice his bulbous brown eyes become unfocused behind his glasses as he speculates.

"You've confused her," I say. "You keep giving her mixed signals and stirring up old feelings. Now she's too weak to fight for Jake."

"Last time I checked, I was still married, Violet. Your mother knows that."

"Yeah, but your marriage is on the rocks."

His brow furrows. "Is that so?"

"According to the Sasha Cohen newswire, it is."

He turns to walk into the kitchen without commenting either way. "How about an espresso?"

"I'd rather have some answers."

"Do I look like one of your girlfriends, Velvet? If you want to dish, dish with your mother."

I'd never confront Roger so aggressively on set but this is personal. Of course, if he wants to hold it against me professionally, there's nothing I can do.

For the moment, however, he seems amused by my boldness. Firing up his industrial-size cappuccino machine, he asks, "What kind of mixed signals have I been sending?"

"You've been paying more attention to her and paying more attention to yourself. Your clothes are nicer. Your hair is nicer. Even your glasses are cooler."

"I'm flattered you noticed," he says. "Maybe I'm trying to keep my wife interested. Ever consider that?"

I didn't actually. "But if Mom thinks you're doing it for her, it's the same thing."

Roger carries our coffee to the living room and motions me to take a seat. "Has she really left Jake or is it one of her 'statements'?"

Clearly Dad isn't the only one Mom has put to the test. "Like I say, she's confused. And she's been really stressed lately."

He sips his espresso and waits for me to continue.

"I mean, I know she loves Jake, but you seem to have this hold over her."

"We had quite a run together," he muses. "She's a beautiful, dynamic, talented woman. Sometimes I wonder why I ever let her go."

"But you did let her go. It took her years to find someone else and that's when you really had second thoughts." He doesn't argue, so I continue, "Don't you think she deserves a chance to be happy with Jake?"

"I haven't stood in the way," Roger says. "But if she leaves Jake of her own accord, why wouldn't I let her know how I feel?"

"Because the last time you checked, you were still married," I point out. "That means you're not sure what you want. But Jake is. Or at least he was, until Sasha screwed everything up. Mom could be happy with him."

"What do you want me to do about it? She's a grown woman and has to make her own decisions."

"I want you to let her go." Just like Rick did for Ilsa in *Casablanca*.

"In other words, you want me to do the right thing," Roger says.

"Exactly!" I congratulate myself for getting through to him so quickly. If my name really does become mud in this town, I should explore a career as a diplomat.

Roger laughs. "Do you think I became one of the biggest directors in town by doing the right thing, Viola?"

Then again, some people are slippery negotiators.

"I do what I have to do to get what I want," he continues.

"And what I want right now is to enjoy my coffee in peace."

Vivien Leigh Reid does not give up that easily. Nor do Verna, Violet, Velvet, or Viola. Appealing to Roger as a normal human being was the wrong approach, that's all. This is Hollywood, where no one is normal. Besides, as a director, Roger's number one love is film. Women may come and go but celluloid lives on.

If I can't get through to him, maybe *Casablanca* can.

CASA ANNIKA
A Vivid Imagination Production
Starring Vivien Leigh Reid

EXTERIOR RUNWAY, NIGHT

Leigh and Roger are wrapped in trench coats, their collars turned up against the swirling fog. In the distance, we make out a small plane being prepared for takeoff. Jake waits by the plane for Annika, who stands in the middle of the runway in tears, torn between leaving with Jake and staying with Roger.

LEIGH
Roger, we both know Annika belongs with
Jake. He needs her.

Roger looks on as Jake entreats Annika to come with him.

JAKE
Nika, you know we're meant to be together. *You complete me.*

Annika throws herself into Jake's arms.

> ANNIKA
> Wrong movie, Jake, but I adore you any-
> way. If only I weren't so confused.

Roger and Leigh watch them embrace.

> LEIGH
> Roger, if you stand in the way of their
> happiness, you'll regret it. Maybe not to-
> day, maybe not tomorrow, but soon and for
> the rest of your life.

> ROGER
> Verna, I'm no good at being noble, but it
> doesn't take much to see that those two
> were meant to be together.

> LEIGH
> [hopefully]
> Does that mean...?

> ROGER
> Yes. I'll do the right thing.

Annika looks back at Roger and he nods, signaling that he's setting her free to go with Jake. She throws a tearful kiss to him before turning and boarding the plane.

Leigh and Roger wave as the plane departs.

> ROGER
> So, you're a sucker for old movies too.

LEIGH

I am now.

Roger slings an arm around Leigh as they walk off into the fog.

"Veronica, I think this is the beginning of a beautiful friendship," Roger says, delivering Rick's final line from *Casablanca*.

"Isn't it the best movie ever?"

"One of the best, certainly. Maybe I should look into remaking it. I vowed never to mess with a classic, but there's a whole generation that hasn't even heard of Humphrey Bogart and Ingrid Bergman. If a kid your age enjoys the story, maybe it needs to be told again."

"I loved it," I say. "A great romance like that never goes out of style."

Now that I'm speaking his language, Roger is chatting to me as if I'm his equal, not the pest who was constantly underfoot on *Danny Boy*. If I started talking Hitchcock, we'd be hanging out all the time.

He drains the last of his espresso. "You are your mother's daughter."

Hearing that doesn't bother me as much as it used to. "She loves a great romance, but she hasn't had much luck in real life."

"Well," he says, getting to his feet, "let's see if we can't fix that."

As I follow him out the door, he adds, "You can audition when I cast my Ilsa."

Look out, Hollywood: Mud's making a comeback already.

★ ★ ★

I brake at the red light and a black Audi TT convertible pulls up beside me and guns the engine. There's a Heath Ledger look-alike at the wheel and he gives me a wink. In the space of eight miles, guys have waved, shouted hello, and even thrown air kisses.

Roger's Porsche is a total guy magnet.

Mr. Audi TT rolls down his passenger window and calls, "Nice car."

"Thanks," I say, returning his smile. With options like this available, it's no big deal that it didn't work out with Julian.

The Heath clone is still watching so I casually pick up a CD and slide it into the player. A wolf howl blasts from fourteen surround-sound speakers and Mr. TT laughs as I scramble to lower the volume.

Humiliated, I peel away from the light with a squeal of rubber.

"Could you leave some treads on those tires for me?" Roger asks.

"Could you get some better CDs?" I ask.

"My sound mixer gave that to me to scare the squirrels out of my roof," he says.

We're on our way to the Santa Monica beach house where Roger is going to have a man-to-man chat with Jake. To make sure he doesn't chicken out, I decided to escort him there myself—and he actually agreed to let me drive.

I didn't bother mentioning that I've barely driven stick since I got my license because I mostly have to drive Gran's automatic. My shifting was a little rough for the first few miles but I didn't fully stall and things smoothed out eventually.

After pulling into Jake's driveway, I turn off the ignition and start to get out.

"Stay here, Virginia," Roger says.

"Don't you think I should come and help?" I ask.

"I think 'man-to-man' pretty much rules that out."

"At least let me give you some pointers before you go. I just saw the movie last night."

"I think I can handle it."

"Okay, but don't forget to say that Annika is his destiny. And that she's never been happier than she is with him. And if you could tell him Sasha's a sneak and a hag, the world would be safer for everyone."

"Get into the passenger seat," he says. "I'll drive you to the hotel when I'm done."

"I don't mind driving back," I say. Playing chauffeur is the least I can do for him since he's making such a sacrifice for my mother.

He holds out his hand for the keys. "Kid, I've had smoother rides on a camel."

★　★　★

I examine Roger's face for signs of injury as he climbs into the Porsche and starts the engine. "Well?"

"Well what?"

"How did it go with Jake?" I ask, exasperated.

"What happens between men stays between men," he replies.

"But she's my mother."

"Not tonight," he says. "Tonight she's Ilsa."

I ask a million more questions but Roger is a vault that cannot be cracked. And after a while, he turns on the wolf howls to drown me out.

★　★　★

The hotel suite is in darkness when I enter. I grope around for the light and find the living room empty. "Hello? Mom?"

Annika replies with a loud, lingering sigh.

I follow the sound to her bedroom where I smell the smoke before I see the glow of the lit cigarette. As my eyes grow used to the gloom, I make out Annika's form on the divan by the window. She's swaddled in an ermine-trimmed cloak that she bought for her wedding day.

"Have you been lying here all day?" I ask, switching the lamp on.

She squints at me for a moment and then switches the lamp off again. "Only since noon, darling. Before that, I had calls to make."

I take the cigarette out of her hand. "You know this is a non-smoking suite. And you're going to stink up your cloak."

"It doesn't matter," she says. "It's not like I'm ever going to wear it again. Mrs. O'Reilly offered to make throw cushions out of it."

"Mrs. O'Reilly from Bray?" I ask.

"One and the same." Her voice takes on an Irish lilt.

Mrs. O'Reilly is the crusty, bedraggled old woman who rented a cottage to us when we shot *Danny Boy* in Ireland. Despite the fact that Mom and Mrs. O had absolutely nothing in common except an addiction to nicotine, they developed an odd friendship. More than once, Mrs. O consoled Annika over Roger's mistreatment with a night of smoking and Irish whiskey.

"Talking to Bono made me realize how much I miss the Emerald Isle so I called her to catch up," Annika says.

"You hated the Emerald Isle. And you have friends in L.A., Mom." At least, I think she does. Annika is a bit of a loner.

"I know but none of them plays the fiddle."

Mrs. O, on the other hand, has quite a talent for it, especially when the whiskey is flowing. It gave me a few sleepless nights.

"You had her play the fiddle over the phone?" I ask. "It costs a bomb to call long distance from a hotel."

"It was quite a concert," Annika says. "Once she gets started, she doesn't stop."

"Mom, you've got to stop spending Jake into the poorhouse. You'll regret it if you get back together."

She simply lights another cigarette from the one she's already smoking, making up for lost time.

"Let's go downstairs. We can still grab a bite if we hurry," I say, trying to pull her limp form off the divan.

"Order room service. I'm not going anywhere."

"Are you sure?" I ask. "I poked my head into the Polo Lounge on my way in and Martin Scorsese was there."

She pushes her hood back. "Scorsese?"

"He was at the bar and Leslie Nelligan joined him. I heard he's casting a movie and I guess she's interested."

"But she's not even A list," Mom says, switching on the lamp.

"I know. I guess she saw her chance to make a pitch and went for it."

A spark is returning to Annika's eyes. "I can't imagine he'd take her seriously. Not with her résumé."

"Probably not," I agree. "But they did seem to be having a nice chat. And like you always say, this business is about relationships."

Annika is off the divan and heading for the shower. "Put something nice on, darling. And see if I have something pressed."

★   ★   ★

I glance nervously at my watch. I was supposed to have Annika in the Polo Lounge half an hour ago. "Hurry up. Scorsese won't wait forever."

She steps out of her bedroom, pale but beautiful in her blue Valentino. I chose it because it makes her looks like a movie star from the golden era of film.

"How do I look?" she asks. "I have to be perfect, Vivien. All I have left now is my career."

"Perfect," I say. She puts her cigarettes into her clutch and I take them out again. "I heard Martin hates smokers."

In the elevator, she fusses nervously with her hair but once we step through the door, her shoulders go back and she strides into the room, every flag flying. "Where is he?" she asks.

"Right there," I say.

She follows my gaze and whispers, "I don't believe it."

Jake is standing beside the grand piano wearing a white tuxedo with a black bow tie, very similar to Humphrey Bogart's in the *Casablanca* club scenes. On the piano is a vase filled with yellow gladioli, Annika's favorite flower.

Jake says, "Of all the gin joints in all the towns in all the world, she walks into mine."

I smile. That's what Rick said about Ilsa when she walked into his club.

Recognizing her cue, Annika slaps her purse into my hands and takes her mark in the center of the room. People at the tables around us stop talking to watch as she strikes the red carpet pose. And in a dark corner of the room, Roger raises a glass to his lips.

Jake taps the piano player on the shoulder. "Play it, Sam."

The pianist looks up from the keyboard: It's Bono. He starts to play "As Time Goes By," Rick and Ilsa's song.

The crowd heaves a collective sigh as Jake takes Annika's hand and they dance.

I slip over to join Roger. "I see Mom and I aren't the only romantics."

He shrugs. "Bono and I are having dinner so I asked him to do me a little favor beforehand. God knows how many causes I'll have to support in return."

I take the inch of wine he pours for me and raise my glass to his. "Thanks, Roger. For everything."

Roger winks and clinks his glass against mine. "Here's looking at you, kid."

Annika and Jake are still dancing. It's one of those scenes that I will remember for the rest of my life, no matter how long I live— like one of my daydreams come true, only with Mom as the star instead of me.

Bono finishes the song and Annika and Jake step apart. Her eyes are wet with tears.

"I'm sorry I was such a fool," Jake says.

"You should have trusted me," she says. "I'd never betray you."

"I know that now," he says, dropping to one knee. "Marry me, Annika."

She looks down at him for a moment and everyone, including Bono, waits in silence for her answer. At last she says, "It's too late. I've canceled everything."

I stare at Roger, stunned. "Is she out of her mind?"

"I've asked the same question many times," he says.

"But she was so miserable without Jake. And we went to so much trouble."

Roger gulps down the rest of his wine and stands to leave. "What can I tell you, Vera? Not every story has a Hollywood ending."

seventeen

The photographer looks over the viewfinder at me. "Lift your snout and angle it slightly to the right," he calls. "And could someone get Goat Boy and Leopard Man out of the frame, please?"

The *Freak Force* publicist quickly pulls Jed and Rudy out of the shot.

"Tell him I'm a *gazelle,*" Rudy says. "Doesn't he watch the show?"

The publicist explains that *Teen People* has decided to do a profile of me alone.

"Just the Farthog?" Jed asks. "Why?"

Lowering her voice, the publicist—no longer the guys' biggest fan—uses the words "breakout star." The guys guffaw in response and Jed actually belches to express his true feelings.

The reporter from *Teen People* gives me an eye roll but I resist the urge to laugh. Today I'm the face of the show so I have to be professional. She can draw her own conclusions about life on this set. If the burp makes the story, it won't be my fault.

"But Leigh blew off the first interview," Jed complains. "She's a diva."

The reporter comes to my rescue. "Putting your family first is not being a diva," she says. "Leigh is also an upstanding citizen who foiled a robbery recently. We think she's such a good role model that we've decided to expand our story to two pages."

Jed mutters, "It's just a *girl* magazine, anyway" and the publicist hauls him away before he can do any more damage.

At this rate, my RAD program will never be short of clients.

★   ★   ★

The entire cast and crew has gathered on the roof of a warehouse for a briefing on this week's special guest: an army helicopter.

Soaring ratings have meant a soaring budget so the show's stunts are getting bigger and more dramatic. In this episode, for example, the Freak Force will run through a ball of fire before escaping the bad guys in a chopper. Freddy has hired expert stunt people for the explosion sequence, but we have to do the chopper scene ourselves.

Some days, I long for the relative ease of the daytime soap where my biggest challenge was last-minute script changes.

Freddy paces in front of us shouting orders about securing loose objects against the wind before the chopper arrives. Only the actors and camera people will be allowed to get anywhere near the helicopter's rotor blades.

"Keep your heads down," Freddy warns. "I don't need to tell you what could happen if you don't." She slices a hand across her throat.

Once we're on board, the chopper will lift off and hover so that the Freak Force can shoot at the bad guys from the rear door. We won't be harnessed but the pilot is supposed to hover only ten to twenty feet above the roof. That's no higher than the garden wall I ran down last week, a stunt that went a long way toward taming my fear of heights. I'm actually more nervous about running under the rotating blades. Unlike the guys, I'm maneuvering in a cumbersome costume.

When Freddy is done, Lex helps Chaz onto an apple box and hands him the megaphone. "Good news, people," Chaz says, "*Freak Force* has been given the green light for a full second season!"

Amid the commotion that follows, I consider what that news

means for me. Dad won't be happy about it, but I've found that he doesn't hold me back when there's something I really want to do. Mom will be thrilled, although she'll have to make some decisions about where we'll live. We can't stay at the Beverly Hills Hotel forever, especially if Jake canceled his credit card after the *Casablanca* fiasco. I tried reasoning with Annika until late last night, but for once, she didn't want to talk. She was still smoking on the divan when the cab picked me up for work this morning.

My feelings about the show's renewal fall somewhere between the two extremes. I'd rather live with Dad in Seattle, but I enjoy playing Effluvia and am glad to continue the role. A second season would also bring in enough money to put myself through college. If we got a third, I might even be able to afford my own place.

Not that I'm counting on anything. Chaz could fire me anytime and Jake won't protect me. With an action series, it's easy enough to drop a character: *Oops, Effluvia fell out of the chopper over a remote mountain range.*

Mom always warns me not to get complacent: "If you show up and your name is still on your trailer, you're probably good for the day." It's a scary way to live. No wonder she's unstable.

Chaz hops off the apple box and walks toward me, filling me with dread, as usual. I'll never trust the guy but he isn't a bad director. He may not have Roger's vision and talent, but as far as popular TV goes, he's got the goods. The new and improved Vivien Leigh Reid can admit this and rise above her personal feelings.

"Congratulations, Chaz," I say, extending my hand. "You must be proud."

"I am," he says, ignoring my hand. "I'm proud that my show is so good that it survived your attempts to destroy it."

Some people will check into RAD and never leave.

★   ★   ★

I visualized the stunt in advance, like I always do, but in my imagination, the helicopter resembled a Volkswagen Beetle with a tail and propeller. The real thing is a lot more menacing. When it approaches the warehouse, the whole crew takes an involuntary step backward. It's like an airborne cube van with blades over thirty feet long. And while I expected noise, this is an earsplitting roar.

I look around at the guys and see I'm not the only one who feels intimidated. There's no roughhousing today and they're all paying attention. If we get this right the first time, everyone will be happy: the cast, because we're only risking death once; the crew, because the noise and dirt are uncomfortable; the pilot, because it's difficult to land between buildings and the wind could change at any moment; and Chaz because faster means cheaper. If we miss the shot for some reason, we'll be back tomorrow night and Chaz will eat into the dollars he needs for next episode's big bang.

The pilot brings the chopper in for a landing and the force of the wind drives me back at least a yard. For once I feel as light as a feather, but a lot more awkward, because my stomach and butt attachments create wind resistance.

The assistant director signals the cameras to roll before I can find my balance. The guys press forward while I struggle against the wind. Where's my healthy BMI when I need it?

Suddenly, someone grabs my hand and pulls. "Hang on and keep your head down!" Julian shouts in my ear.

Once I'm moving, I try to shake off his hand. As much as I could use the help, Effluvia and the Panther are not supposed to be holding hands, and I don't want to lose the shot because of something so minor.

Julian refuses to let go so I shout, "It's not in the script!"

"Screw the script," he yells back.

The other guys are close to the chopper and Rudy sinks almost to his knees to keep his horns out of the blades.

Julian and I continue to hold hands as we creep under the blades and climb into the belly of the helicopter.

Back on the roof, Lex signals the "bad guy" extras to charge after us, prop guns blazing. The pilot lifts off. There's a horrible shifting feeling, like hitting an air pocket in a plane only magnified. I brace myself on the wall and try to find my balance. Chaz said it would only be a few moments before he cued us to return fire with our own prop guns, but it seems to take forever.

Finally his shouts come over the walkie-talkie inside the helicopter. "And action on the gunfire from the chopper!"

As we hover over the warehouse roof, Julian, Rudy, and I move to the rear opening of the chopper. Julian stumbles and I help him to his feet. We peer out of the door and start firing our electric prop guns at the guys on the roof below.

"I can't see Jed!" Chaz hollers. "Step forward, Jed. The chopper can't hold position much longer."

Continuing to fire, I glance around and see Jed lying on the floor of the chopper. His face is pasty white.

"Cheetah down," I shout at the others. "Just keep firing."

It's a good thing Jed isn't miked. Superheroes aren't supposed to get airsick.

★　★　★

Freddy deposits Jed with the set medic and comes back to congratulate the rest of us. "Let's get the video guy to play back the take," she says. "You guys are going to be blown away."

"We almost were," Julian says, after Freddy and Rudy head to the monitors.

I'm surprised he's speaking to me again, but thanks to prosthetics, I don't need to *look* surprised. I will simply respond like the professional I am. "Yeah."

"It was pretty cool though, wasn't it?" he asks.

"Yeah," I say. Strictly professional, no more, no less.

"Is that the best you can do—monosyllables?"

"Yeah." Okay, just a little less than professional.

"Oh, come on, I'm the one who's mad," he says.

Professionalism deteriorates to a scowl that he may not be able to see but can probably sense. "Is that right?"

"Who showed up at your door with flowers only to hear from Sasha that you'd already left with some guy? One hour after I dropped you off! That's gotta be the fastest, rudest dump on record."

Ah, the Wicked Witch of the Beach House strikes again. No wonder he wouldn't take my calls. "You brought flowers?"

"It was supposed to be a real date."

I tell him about Annika's fight with Jake and our hasty departure.

"I know," he admits, smiling. "Your mother called me yesterday."

"She didn't! She's got to stop interfering in my life!"

"I hadn't noticed the Irish accent before but it was really strong yesterday. She actually called Jake a wanker."

It could have been worse: She could have called *Julian* a wanker.

I figure it's up to me to make the first move, so I say, "Should we try another take?"

"Fourth-time lucky," he says.

★ ★ ★

"Places, girls, places!" Lex barks at us as he passes. He's wearing a navy suit with a fine green pinstripe, green cut-off tie, and a massive peony boutonniere. When we don't move, he claps his hands. "The wedding will begin in precisely five minutes."

Karis and I watch as he continues down to the beach, checking his clipboard and issuing instructions into his walkie-talkie.

"He must drive you crazy at work," she says.

"Yet he's still only a pale imitation of Chaz."

At Jake's suggestion, Annika hired Lex to help her throw a wedding together in thirty-six hours and they've done a great job in a ridiculously short time.

Ahead of us a small white tent sits at the end of a white carpet "aisle" laid over the sand. Jake is standing at the opposite end with the judge and on either side of the carpet folding chairs are filled with guests.

"I'm glad your Mom scaled back her plans," Karis says. "This is so much nicer."

"I'm just relieved she came to her senses at all," I say. "But her timing sucks. Julian and I had plans to go hiking today and I had to cancel."

"Why didn't you invite him? Annika let me invite Jon. It could have been our first double date."

"Julian didn't give me a chance. I guess the 'spur-of-the-moment-wedding' excuse didn't sound legitimate." I sigh. "He thinks I'm as unstable as my mother."

I felt terrible about standing him up again but what could I do? This is my life with Annika, and if Julian can't roll with it, I guess it's not meant to be.

Karis drops the subject and spins in her aqua dress. "At least we all had our fabulous outfits," she says, clearly overcoming her fear of skirts.

"And our jewelry," I add. Henry Winton sent over the necklace I admired and a chunky silver chain for Karis. "Mom wouldn't let Sasha have anything. And she replaced the dress Sasha chose too."

"It's showtime," Lex says, pushing Karis toward a seat in the front row and giving me one of three bouquets of yellow gladioli. He presses the button on his walkie: "Cue the music."

U2's "All I Want Is You" blasts from multiple speakers.

"Cue the snow!" Lex says.

Four silent snow machines on scaffolding high above the crowd begin spewing a light foamy "snow" over the crowd.

"Bridesmaid one!" Lex says.

Ursela comes over in her bronze dress to collect the second bouquet. She passes Olivier, in his little white tuxedo, to Lex.

"Bridesmaid two!" Lex says. He scans the crowd. "I'm missing bridesmaid two. And the groom!"

The judge is now standing alone on a pile of fake snow.

"Jake was there a minute ago," I say.

Ursela points toward the beach house where her father is trying to drag Sasha off the deck by force. Her resistance probably has something to do with her dress, which is electric blue with puffy sleeves and a hoop skirt a mile wide. In addition to the feathered white doves attached to the skirt, there's a belt of silver snowflakes and a fun-fur collar over a high neckline. On her head is a white wig speared with two fake icicles.

Lex clucks disapprovingly. "Very *Bride of Frankenstein*," he says. "I'm surprised at Annika."

I am too but in a good way. It's making a statement that she's a wicked enough stepmother to hit where it hurts.

The fact that Jake is now carrying Sasha down the stairs also makes a statement: He is willing to put his bride before his trouble-making daughter.

Sasha puts up a fight all the way to the beach until Jake finally snaps: "Slap a smile on your face and get down that aisle. I want you to grow up and shut up."

Judging by Sasha's stunned expression, Jake hasn't ever been this angry before. She meekly accepts the bouquet Lex hands her.

With everyone in place, Lex sets Olivier on the white carpet and he scampers up the aisle. Sasha follows, then Ursela and I bring up the rear. When I'm nearly at the front, everyone turns. Lex pulls a silk cord to open the flaps of the tent and reveal Annika standing in her white satin dress and ermine-trimmed coat. Instead of a bouquet, she carries a white muff and under the hood she's wearing shades. It is a bizarre outfit for a beach wedding—or any wedding—but Annika somehow carries it off.

The wedding march begins and she walks up the aisle. Brando, also in a tiny tux, follows, holding the bride's train in his mouth. She must have started teaching him that the day Jake proposed. My dog is brilliant!

When they reach the front, Jake joins Annika and I call Brando to me. As I lift him, he snaps at the birds on Sasha's dress.

★　★　★

"Come on, Verna," Roger says. "Let's merengue!"

I decline politely but now that we have our beautiful friendship, he won't take no for an answer. His feet seem to move in all directions at once and as hard as I try to follow, it's no use. We bump into Jake and Annika and I try to get them to switch partners. Mom shakes her head. Dancing with Roger at her wedding is off-limits.

Instead, she takes me on as her partner and leaves Roger and Jake to chat.

"The merengue is all about small steps," she says. "Take a little step with one foot and slide your other foot in to meet it."

To appease the bride on her special day, I give it a go.

"Step, together, step together," she says, leading me across the dance floor.

Somehow, I manage to follow along. Obviously, the stunt work is improving my overall coordination.

"Very good, Vivien," she says, picking up the pace. "Now forward, together, and back together."

I'm doing the merengue! With Annika! Two years ago, I would have thought it impossible, but we have actually found our rhythm. For the moment at least, we are perfectly in sync.

When the song ends, I surrender Mom to Jake and take a stroll around the tent. It's large enough to hold a dance floor, buffet table, bar, and seating area, and the sides are open to reveal the reflection of the moon on the ocean. The tables feature a simple white cloth, white china, and white candles, but beside each place setting is a splash of color: a claret rose in a simple vase.

Annika canceled almost everything from the original wedding (partly to make up for her spending spree at the Beverly Hills Hotel), but kept the roses because they were designed in honor of her union with Jake. The hybrid is dubbed the "Janika" and at the end of the night, every guest will leave with a bush for the garden.

"Finally, I've caught you alone," Gray says, coming up behind me. "I wanted to tell you how beautiful you look tonight."

A guy with a girlfriend shouldn't be looking at me the way he is right now—even when that girlfriend is wearing the most hideous dress in the world and has a personality to match.

"I also wanted to congratulate you about getting a second season on the show," he continues. "I heard that you're the real star of the show."

"That's not true! The show works because it's an ensemble."

I believe that too. I wouldn't be performing as well if it weren't for the guys giving me a hard time or Sasha trying to upstage me. Or Chaz riding me for that matter. This actor is only one part of the big picture.

Gray is surprised I'm not more flattered. "I was just trying to be nice."

"I know." I point at Sasha, whose hoop skirt is wedged between a tent pole and a speaker. "Go be nice to your girlfriend."

"She's not my girlfriend," he says. "We're just hanging out."

"You hang out a lot in her bedroom."

He shrugs. "Sasha's a laugh but I need someone more polished. Someone who already has a hit show on her hands."

"Sasha's show is a hit."

"But it's not prime time."

I laugh. At least Gray's consistent. "You and Sasha are good together. I wouldn't trade up just yet."

I escape him as soon as I can and cruise the buffet table.

"Is the food just for invited guests?" someone asks.

I turn to see Julian behind me. He looks great in his black suit and powder blue shirt, but I kind of miss the bodysuit and visor.

"Are you crashing my mother's wedding?"

Julian smiles. "I heard there was lobster."

We take our plates to a table on the ocean side of the tent. It's a beautiful view, but Julian turns his chair to face mine. "That's another killer dress," he says.

"Set to stun once again," I say. "I don't want any fatalities tonight."

"Julian!" Sasha calls, hurrying toward us.

"Now *that* is a killer dress," I say.

"It's sure murder to look at."

"Mom is going to let her change so that she doesn't ruin all the photos, but Sasha doesn't know that yet."

Proving that humiliation hasn't dulled her edge, Sasha turns her back on me and asks Julian to dance.

"I can't," he says, taking my hand. "They're playing our song."

★ ★ ★

"Our song is the chicken dance?" I ask, as we flap our imaginary wings.

"Our song is any song that gets me alone with you," he says.

He leans forward.

I lean back. "What are you doing?"

"Trying to kiss you?"

"There's no kissing in the chicken dance," I say. "Chickens don't have lips."

"But I heard you're a very hot kisser."

"Especially with my tusks in."

Julian leans forward again and I raise a hand to stop him. "I don't know about this," I say. "We've got another full season ahead and set romances create tension."

"Tension is just another word for *chemistry*. And audiences love chemistry."

"Audiences love good acting," I counter.

"Good acting comes from good motivation," he says.

He doesn't leave me time for a comeback before kissing me.

Eventually, we part and he asks, "Feeling motivated?"

I smile at him. "Very motivated."

And that's not acting.

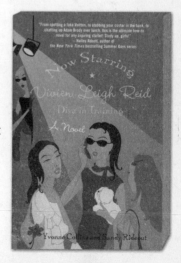